FATAL FORTUNE

A DR PIPPA DURRANT MYSTERY

MIRANDA RIJKS

CONTENTS

1.
2.
3.
4.
5.
6.
7.
8.
9.
10.
11.
12.
13.
14.
15.

16.
17.
18.
19.
20.
21.
22.
23.
24.
25.
26.
27.
28.
29.

31.
32.
33.
34.
35.
36.
37.
38.
39.
40.
41.
42.
43.
44.

Prologue

I look down at my handiwork and smile. The bitch is unrecognisable. If only she had agreed, things would be so different. But it is what it is, and she deserves this ending. I take one final aim right in the centre of her forehead.

Bullseye.

It's surprisingly easy to mash someone's face into pulp with a 5 iron. Who knew!

And now it's time to go. I position her so that she is lying flat on her back, her hands across her chest as if she's atoning for her sins. Then I take off the disposable blood-smeared latex gloves and put them inside a plastic bag. I place the bag in the back pocket of my backpack. Dirties in the back, clean in the front. I remove a fresh pair of blue gloves, slide them over my hands, and carefully take the photograph out of the front pocket. I have kept it flat and clean inside a book. Not any old book, of course, but a book that belonged to her. I position the photograph carefully on her chest so that it leans against her hands. Satisfied with my work, I take one last look around the empty house. It will be a fresh start for everyone.

It's time to leave. I have been meticulous. I walk to the back door, gently removing my balaclava to ensure I don't leave any incriminating hairs, and slip out the way I came in. I remove the white plastic shoe covers and place them in the dirties bag.

No one saw me come in. No one sees me go. No one knows what I have done. No one knows what I have planned.

It's just an ordinary afternoon on an ordinary weekday.

1

Pippa

John Lewis, Horsham

I sense that someone is looking at me.

It is strange how that happens. I wrote an article about it a few years ago. It's not extrasensory perception at all but the firing of brain cells. A primal awareness. I glance up, and the man sitting directly opposite me turns his head away, but he is too slow. His frown is deep, and he pulls at the collar of his white button-down shirt as if it is too small or too hot. I finish my freshly squeezed carrot and orange juice, get up from the table, collect a shopping trolley, and meander into Waitrose. I only need a few bits and pieces, enough to make supper for my brother, Rob.

On the way out, a couple barge past me on the moving walkway, the man's bulging Waitrose plastic bag banging my leg, bottles clinking together. Two young boys scamper behind them, bickering. The taller boy hits his brother with an electronic toy.

'Shut up, you two!' the father yells.

He glances at me and then he stops. I clock the raised inner and outer brows, the raised upper eyelid and the open mouth, the brief telltale expression of surprise. The boys collide with him. Realising he's staring and causing a bottleneck on the walkway, he swivels away, then races forwards, whispering something to his wife. She turns around too and scowls. I don't know what I've done to these uninspiring strangers, so I smile at them. They hurry away, each grabbing a boy's hand, dragging the children forwards.

I may be a psychologist and used to the vagaries of human behaviour, but I am bemused. I look down at myself. Yup, I'm all buttoned up – I'm wearing matching black boots, and my blouse isn't displaying any cleavage. I run my fingers through my hair, which I only coloured last week, and though I say it myself, I think I'm looking good. The auburn highlights take at least five years off my face and make my green-grey eyes look surprisingly vibrant. Downstairs, in the underground car park, I put my shopping bags into the boot of the car and then wheel the trolley back to the front of the store. As I turn, a blue Honda drives past me. Inside are the family with the young boys. Both the man and the woman stare at me. Her eyes are wide, unblinking, as they follow me, and her brows are lowered and her lips stretched flat. I recognise that expression. Fear. What the hell? I've never seen these people before. At least, I'm almost positive I haven't.

Bewildered, I get into my car and angle the rear-view mirror so that I can see my face. It looks exactly as it did when I brushed my teeth this morning. A solid six rising to a seven point five in certain lights and with a little more makeup; worse after a long day such as today, when I'm tired and exhausted from listening to my clients' problems.

I reverse the car and drive out of the car park, but it is rush hour and I have to queue to get out of Horsham. There is stationary traffic going the other way too. I glance over and catch the eye of a delivery driver at the wheel of a van emblazoned with the words *Frieda's Fish*. He frowns and then stares at me. My cheeks are hot. I turn away and keep my gaze firmly on the car in front. How ridiculous that I'm feeling self-conscious for a reason unbeknown to me.

I'm at the Southwater roundabout when my phone rings, sounding through the stereo system.

'Pips, it's Rob. I assume you've seen the news?'

'No, I haven't seen the damned news. I'm in the car on my way home. What's up?'

He hesitates. My brother never hesitates. It makes my heart rate soar.

'Call me when you get home,' he says.

'Why?'

But Rob has already hung up. Damn. I need to concentrate on the road rather than the radio, so I give up channel hopping and tune into ClassicFM in the hope of calming my nerves. But my phone keeps on pinging again and again. Something is going on, but I can't look. I'm on the dual carriageway and there's nowhere to pull over. Instead I drive quickly, and twenty minutes later I am home.

After greeting Mungo, my beloved black Labrador, who acts as if I have been gone for weeks rather than a few hours, I switch my computer on, go on to Google and search for my name. There's nothing under the news section. I exhale with relief. I then click on to the BBC website and flick through the headlines. And I spot it.

Murdered two months after scooping massive win. Leanne Smith celebrated her win of €120 million on the EuroMillions Lottery less than eight weeks ago. On Friday she was found with fatal wounds following what police describe as a frenzied attack. Was this related to her win?

There is a photograph of an ordinary woman with shoulder-length hair, wide-set eyes and a dimple in her left cheek. She looks just like me. I peer closer. Surely she is me.

'What the fuck?' I say it out loud. My hands are shaking as I scroll further down the page.

The stories are short and they all amount to the same. Forty-six-year-old Leanne Smith won the EuroMillions. Her name was released to the media, but there are no photos of her celebrating. And then fifty days later she was found dead in her semi-detached home in Broadbridge Heath, West Sussex. The address is another shock. It's just ten miles from where I live, just two miles from where I was shopping in Horsham. None of the articles say anything about her relatives or give further details about her life. There's just that one photograph, released by the police. The photograph of me.

I try and fail to calm myself, remembering what I say to my clients when they have suffered an immense shock. Breathe. Still your mind. Think of your happy place. But it's so difficult to do, and all I can think is why? Why me? Haven't I been through enough?

My phone rings. I am so startled I let it slip through my fingers, and it narrowly avoids getting a dunk into a mug of cold coffee. The thought makes me laugh, and I realise I am on the edge of hysteria. It's Rob again.

'Where are you?' he asks.

'Home. Who is this Leanne Smith?'

'I don't know, but everyone thinks she's you.'

'Well, of course she's not me! I'm here and she's dead. They must have our photos mixed up.'

'Pack a bag. I'll come over and take you back to my house.' Rob lives in a swish modern house in Hove, only attainable to those on banker's salaries. I live in a modest semi-detached cottage in Storrington, thanks to my divorce. Some things don't change for the better.

'No! Why would I want to do that? I have to go to the police, tell them their dead woman isn't me. Or I'm not her.' I wonder if I'm making sense. 'How did you find out?'

'Saw your picture on the news.'

'But it's not me!'

My brother got the looks in our family, and the brains. He dazzles. On the whole I manage to stop myself from being consumed with sibling jealousy, but sometimes it's hard.

'Someone kindly posted a clip of you filling up your car with petrol. It's going viral.'

'What? I only filled up my car a couple of hours ago. It's not possible; it can't have been me!'

'You're standing next to your VW Golf at the Shell petrol station just off the A24. Are you wearing a navy coat with a teal-coloured scarf around your neck?'

I try not to choke as I look at my coat and scarf, which I dumped onto the chair next to me as soon as I entered the kitchen. 'How is that possible? I know the internet is powerful, but that powerful?'

'It was lucky I happened to be on Twitter at the time,' Rob says. I'm surprised he has time for social media.

'Thank you.' I fall silent for a moment. 'I'm going to go to the police station. Perhaps the one in Crawley.'

'I think you should avoid the police for a little while, just until we've thought things through.'

'Why?' My voice is edged with incredulity.

'We need to find out what's going on. Who knows where this is going to lead! Please, Pips, don't do anything rash. I'll be with you as soon as I can.'

He hangs up on me.

I rub my eyes and take a few deep breaths. Rob never gets stressed. Never. I assume that's what makes him such a successful City trader. What the hell is going on?

2

Ricky

Donna is standing in the living room of their semi in Broadbridge Heath. Her shoulders are shaking so much it is as if they are attached to puppet strings being jerked up and down. If you saw her grey polyester jumper from behind, you would think she was laughing hysterically. In fact, she is weeping. Donna hasn't stopped sobbing since her mother was found butchered in the house Donna grew up in. The doctor gave her some sleeping pills, which she's been taking at night, but she still wakes up after five hours or so, her pillow soaked through with tears.

'You need to calm down, love.' Ricky hugs her again. 'I know it's awful, but think of our babies. They need their mum.'

'And I need mine, but I'll never see her again,' Donna blubs as she pushes Ricky away, her sobs turning into hiccups. The baby starts wailing. Donna doesn't move, so Ricky sighs and picks up their five-month-old girl. He sniffs at her nappy, turns up his nose, and takes her upstairs. Donna's tears don't dry up. Ricky hasn't been to work since the police arrived on their doorstep to announce that Donna's mum, Leanne, had been murdered. He hopes he'll still have a job when he returns. There's only so much compassionate leave the builders will give him – not that he's told them the real reason for his absence. It seemed much more sensible to pretend his own mother had died. Ricky has worked hard to become assistant site manager. Gazza, his boss, is ex-army and hasn't an ounce of compassion. He has fired people for lesser things than taking time off for the sudden death of a parent.

When Leanne won the lottery, they – Leanne, Kevin, Donna and Ricky, that is – were incredulous.

'I don't want anyone to know,' Leanne said. 'We're a private family, and let's keep it that way. The woman at the lottery said I don't have to be in the papers, so I won't.'

'Will we see any of it?' Ricky asked Donna privately when they were cuddled up in bed back at their house.

She shrugged. 'I expect so.' But she wasn't celebrating.

That conversation seems like a lifetime ago.

Seven weeks on, you'd have thought from Donna's reaction to her mum's death that they had been close. Sometimes they were, but mostly they weren't.

The weekend after the win, Leanne and Kevin invited Donna, Ricky and their babies over for Sunday lunch. They were at the kitchen table eating their regular Sunday lunch of roast chicken and mashed potato.

'Your dad and I have decided,' Leanne pronounced, leaning back in her chair and puffing out her ample chest. 'We're both quitting work and we're going to move to Spain. Costa del Sol. We'll have a lovely white Mediterranean house with terracotta tiles and a swimming pool. There'll be enough rooms for you all to come and stay. Your dad is going to buy himself a fancy car. We'll have a housekeeper and a cook. I'm through with housework.'

Donna looked away, busied herself with the children, but not before Ricky noticed the tears smarting her eyes and the little red blotches that bloomed on her cheeks.

'What about Gran?' Donna asked in a small voice.

'What about her?' Kevin said.

'She won't notice I've gone,' Leanne murmured. 'Anyway, you'll visit her from time to time, won't you?'

'Aren't you going to move her out of that piss-stinking care home?' Donna asked. 'She deserves better does Gran.'

'Don't be so overdramatic,' Kevin chastised, taking a large gulp of beer from his lucky tankard.

‘Gran is happy there, love,’ Leanne said. ‘She’d only get confused if we move her.’

‘You could afford to buy the care home,’ Donna muttered, cutting her chicken up into smaller and smaller bits. ‘And you could put in carpet and recruit kind staff and hang those smelly things in all the rooms to get rid of the stink. And you could build en-suite bathrooms for every one of them residents.’

‘Stop being so fanciful.’ Leanne rolled her eyes.

Kevin broke through the heavy silence, speaking with his mouth full, as he was prone to do. ‘We’ll hang on to the house here. You’ll keep an eye on it for us, won’t you? We don’t want to burn all our bridges in case we don’t like it out in Spain.’ He put his giant hand over Leanne’s and grinned at her. In the six years Ricky had known the Smiths, this was the first time he had seen Kevin show an iota of affection towards his wife.

‘We’re going to give you a little something too,’ Leanne said, wiping her mouth with the piece of kitchen paper towel she used as a napkin. ‘Just enough to make life a bit easier for you both, but not too much so that you get spoiled. There’s nothing worse than being spoiled, is there, Kev?’

Donna dropped her fork.

‘We thought ten thousand euros for you, Donna, and ten thousand for each of the babies to put in a savings account, and five thousand for you, Ricky. It’s not like you’re blood family, Ricky love. You understand, don’t you?’

Ricky would have liked to tell Leanne where to stuff it. He didn’t need to see Donna to know that she was bristling, that the red blotches would be suffusing the whole of her face and neck. He kept his eyes on his plate, which was still piled high with food. He had lost his appetite as soon as Leanne started speaking.

There was a crash as Donna shoved her chair backwards and it fell to the ground. The baby wailed.

'You can go to hell, both of you!' Donna screamed. 'You've won a hundred and twenty bloody million euros and you're giving us thirty thousand?' She looked at Ricky beseechingly.

'Thirty-five thousand,' he said quietly.

'Thirty-five thousand euros. Not even pounds. Is that all we're worth to you? Your own family. What's that as a percentage of your win? I'm crap at maths, but it's nothing, isn't it? I didn't expect much, but you could have bought us a new house, put the kids through private school. But no! It's a fucking insult! It won't even pay for the extension!'

'Private school!' Kevin roared with laughter. 'I never thought I'd hear my own daughter say the words *private school*!'

Baby Skye screamed. Ricky leaned over and picked her up. Little Benjie's bottom lip started quivering. With his other hand, Ricky stroked the toddler's blond tufty hair.

'We're going!' Donna said, kicking the chair as it lay on the ground. She stormed out of the kitchen. With his spare hand, Ricky shoved little Benjie's toys into a nappy bag and picked up the child.

'Haven't finished, Dada!' Benjie wailed, grabbing a lump of potato in his chubby hand.

'Sorry, son, but we've got to go.' Ricky didn't look at his in-laws.

Donna was pacing up and down the short driveway when Ricky emerged with the crying infants. 'I want a bloody cigarette.'

'You don't smoke,' Ricky said.

'They're bastards. My own parents are miserly bastards.'

'Get in the car,' Ricky instructed.

She did as she was told.

'We don't need their money anyway,' he said as they drove down the new bypass past the garden centre. 'I've got a good job, and we'll do alright by ourselves. Mike and I'll finish the extension, as we always planned.'

She sniffed. 'Funny how Dad has conveniently fallen back in love with Mum, isn't it?' Donna spat. 'Last month she told me they were going to split up. For the hundredth time.'

Ricky was silent. Whenever he commented on the state of his in-laws' marriage, Donna bit his head off. It was wrong if he criticised them and wrong if he was supportive. He blessed his lucky stars that his parents were long gone and he didn't have to worry about the older generation. Not that Donna's parents were old.

* * *

And now Leanne is dead.

When Ricky returns downstairs, Donna is sitting on the sofa staring at the television, wearing the same filthy grey jumper she's worn every day this week. *The Jeremy Kyle Show* is on, but Donna has the sound switched off. Little Benjie is playing with some toy bricks. He hasn't been to nursery since last week. Ricky wanted to take him, but Donna had hysteria. 'I'm not letting him out of my sight!' she yelled. 'My babies, they're all I've got!'

The doorbell rings.

'Don't go,' Donna mutters.

'I have to, love.' It is Janet Curran, the family liaison officer.

'How's Donna doing?' she whispers to Ricky as she shrugs off her navy coat and hangs it on the hook behind the door, almost as if she lives there.

'Not so good,' he says, grimacing.

'I'm afraid the news I've got isn't going to make things any better.'

She shimmies along the cramped hallway and into the living room before Ricky can grab her and stop her from shattering Donna even further.

'I've got some news,' she says, crouching down into creaking knees in front of Donna.

Donna buries her face in a soggy tissue. 'Have you found him?'

'Yes, we have.' Janet gets up and sits down on the sofa next to Donna.

'Who *is* he, then?' Donna spins around, her face alive for the first time since they heard the news. 'Is he a burglar?'

'No, love. I'm afraid this might come as a bit of a shock.'

Ricky braces himself and wonders if he should swipe the babies away. But Janet is too quick. Perhaps she doesn't realise that little children understand things, even if adults think they don't. Ricky knows all about that.

'It's your dad, love. The police have arrested Kevin, your dad.'

'No!' Donna screams, jumping up from the sofa and making both the babies wail, exactly as Ricky feared. 'You're wrong! You're all wrong. Dad would never do anything like that! Dad would never hurt Mum!'

'Sit down, Donna.' Janet can be quite fierce.

Donna does as she's told. Ricky takes the babies out of the living room and deposits them on the kitchen floor, giving the baby a dummy and little Benjie a lollipop. He hops back into the hallway so he can hear what Janet says.

'I can't tell you much, but I think it's very likely that Kevin will be charged.'

'No!' Donna is mewling, rocking backwards and forwards, snot pouring through her fingers. 'Dad wouldn't know how to do that. He's a good man. He wouldn't hurt Mum. You've got to believe me! He'd never do something like that.'

Donna chokes and Janet thumps her on the back.

Ricky can't watch anymore. He can't listen either. He goes back into the kitchen and puts the kettle on so he can block out Donna's cries.

After a long time, Janet comes into the kitchen. 'I'm going to make Donna a cup of tea and a sandwich. Do you want anything?'

He stares at her. Their world has collapsed and this woman wants to make a sandwich! He watches as she boils the kettle, takes three mugs out of the high cupboard, roots around for the box of PG Tips, pours the hot water, sniffs the out-of-date milk, and stirs in two heaped teaspoons of sugar. Donna doesn't take sugar in her tea, he wants to say, but the words don't come.

Janet returns to the fridge and tuts as she looks at the bare shelves. 'Is there anyone who can do a shop for you?'

'What?' Ricky finds it hard to process her words, or perhaps it's her grating high-pitched voice.

'You haven't got much food in. Have you got enough for the little ones?'

Ricky doesn't answer, so Janet opens the freezer door and shuffles the boxes around in the drawers.

'You've got a pizza for your tea, and there's some fish fingers for Ben. Have you got any more jars for Skye?'

Ricky points to the larder cupboard.

'Will she get the money now?' Ricky asks.

'What?' Janet drops a teabag and it lands on the floor.

'My Donna. Will she get the lottery money now her mum is dead and her dad is going to jail for life?'

'I don't know about that,' Janet says, bending down to pick the teabag off the dirty floor. She shakes it a bit and puts it in a white chipped mug with the wording 'World's Best Mum'.

'Are you surprised Kevin Smith has been charged?' she asks.

Ricky stands up straighter. He can spot a trick question. 'Of course, I am,' he says. 'As Donna said, Kev is a good man. There's been a dreadful mistake.'

After she's made some jam sandwiches and poured the tea and has left Ricky to console Donna yet again, Janet disappears to the loo. Ricky can hear her speaking quietly on her mobile phone. Reporting in, he thinks to himself. He's worried for a moment. Perhaps Janet Curran isn't as thick as he'd thought.

3

Pippa

I fill up the kettle and switch on the small television, turning to News 24. It's the lead story. A man has been brought in for questioning. Although the news reader doesn't spell it out, it's pretty obvious that the man is Leanne Smith's husband. That's no surprise to me; most murders are domestic. I wait for them to show a picture of Leanne Smith, but it's still the same photo. The photo of me. Why haven't they updated it? It doesn't make any sense. Surely her family and friends know that the photo isn't her. She's got a husband; she's probably got children too.

I bite the inside of my cheek until I can taste blood. There is no way that I have a twin that Rob and I are not aware of. Even if she was cold and uncaring and thoroughly unsuited to be a parent, the thought of my prim and proper mother having a child without us knowing is laughable. And I don't believe in doppelgängers. I've seen those photographs in the *Daily Mail* and on Facebook showing lookalikes; there is always some difference. But this woman is me. She has the same hair, at least as it was before I got it coloured last week, the same laughter lines, the same grey-green eyes. It's the person I look at – or at least, try to avoid looking at – every time I glance in the mirror.

After I've flicked through all the news channels and finished my cup of tea, I decide to ignore Rob's advice and call the police.

'Can I take your name and address, please?'

I relay my details, and the call handler double-checks my phone number. She puts me through to the police.

'How can I help you?' The policeman sounds weary.

'The photo you're using that is supposedly of Leanne Smith isn't her. It's me.'

There is silence.

'I'm sorry?' he says eventually.

'The photograph of the murdered lottery woman is me. You've got it wrong.'

'Madam, I doubt my colleagues would have made such a fundamental mistake.' His weariness morphs into pomposity. 'If you would like to leave me your name and address, I will look into this, and someone will get back to you.'

I sigh. I give him my details and hang up. The moment I put the phone down, it starts ringing, and for the next thirty minutes, until I pull the wire out of the wall, it doesn't stop. Everyone I know seems to be ringing me to check that I am okay, to find out why my photograph is in the public domain, to ask whether I have a twin sister. Tragedy is like a magnet: people are drawn to it. I use my mobile phone to order a pizza delivery for later. Despite buying food to make dinner for Rob, I don't feel like cooking now.

And then the doorbell rings. I peer around the closed curtains in the living room. The police. I open the door.

They show me their badges. Detective Sergeant Joe Swain and Sergeant Mia Brevant. If they are surprised to see my face, they don't show it. I lead them into my living room and speak before they sit down.

'As you can see, the photo in the media of Leanne Smith is in fact me. How could you have got that so wrong?'

Mia Brevant takes out a little notebook. She is young; I doubt much over the age of twenty-three. She has dark hair cropped short like a young boy's, but her eyes are lined with charcoal, and her lashes are so long and abundant they must be fake. She glances at me. I think I see an expression of sympathy cross her face before her boss starts with the interrogation.

'Did you know Leanne Smith?'

'No, and before you ask, I don't have a twin sister. That photo is of me, but it's been Photoshopped. I don't have a dress like that. Where did the police get the photo from?'

'It came from Leanne Smith's house.'

'Doesn't she have any family or friends? Anyone who would have told you the photo wasn't her?'

'She has a husband, who you probably know is currently in police custody, and a daughter and son-in-law. They didn't question the photograph. Now we've met you, we will be pursuing this anomaly.'

I shake my head. 'I can't believe you've got it so wrong. Was there just the one photograph in her house? And nothing on social media?'

Detective Sergeant Joe Swain sighs. 'The house was mainly empty. The Smiths were moving to Spain, so most of their belongings are in transit. And it appears that Leanne and Kevin Smith weren't on social media. So yes, it was the only photo we could find at the time. The body was quite severely battered. I would be grateful if you kept this to yourself, but her facial features were beaten beyond recognition.'

'Shit,' I say, feeling a little nauseous. 'Who discovered her?'

'Where were you between 3.30 and 6.30 p.m. on Friday afternoon?'

'What? Why are you asking me that?'

'As we have just discussed, your photo was found on the deceased body. There is obviously some link between you and them. Where were you last Friday afternoon?'

'But I don't know the family!'

'Please answer the question.'

A kernel of panic worms its way up from my stomach, through to my chest. I try to think back, but my mind is blank. Friday. Which clients did I have?

Think.

I stand up. 'I just need to get my diary.'

Joe Swain narrows his eyes at me. I know that look, and it makes me even more uneasy. I hurry into the kitchen, flicking through the diary as I walk back into the living room.

'Friday, 3 p.m., David Fairbright was here. I'm a psychologist. My clients generally come here.'

'And then?' Joe Swain asks.

A lump sticks in my throat. Joan Carpenter was due to see me at 4.30 p.m., but she cancelled due to the flu. My diary is empty from just after 4 p.m. through the rest of the day.

'I-I had a cancellation,' I stutter. 'I finished off some paperwork here, and then I took the dog for a walk, made myself some supper, and had an early night.'

'Do you have any alibis for that period?'

I shake my head slowly. 'No, I didn't see or speak to anyone.'

Joe Swain narrows his eyes at me. 'How inconvenient for you.'

'I have nothing to do with this!' I can't stop my voice from rising a few pitches. Mungo raises his head and looks at me. 'Surely you don't think I would murder a woman! Besides, why would I leave my photo on a person I have killed?'

'I don't know. Why would you?' Joe Swain says, eyebrows raised.

Mia Brevant looks away, her long lashes covering her eyes as if she is embarrassed by the sarcastic, no-nonsense manner of her boss.

'We may need you to come down to the station to make a formal statement and answer some more questions.'

'But what are you going to do about the photo? I can't have my photograph all over the press. I'm a psychologist with a well-established practice. I want to remain anonymous!'

Joe Swain clears his throat. 'I will ask our press officer to get in touch with you, and if, after further enquiries, it is evident that a mistake has been made, we will issue a formal apology.'

'I'm going to get pointed at and be a social pariah because everyone thinks I'm a murdered lottery winner!'

'I'm sorry, ma'am, but there's nothing further we can do at this point. We will keep you updated,' Mia Brevant says.

The police officers stand up. The interview is over.

And then they are gone.

4

Donna

Everything changed the moment Donna's mum won the lottery. We all dream about winning, don't we? We plan our new lives, the escape from the ordinary, the holidays to the Maldives, champagne on tap. But what people don't realise is big money changes everything. Everything.

It was their first night out, just the two of them, since Skye was born. It might even have been since Benjie was born. Donna couldn't remember. She loathed asking her mum to do anything for her, but surprisingly, Leanne offered to babysit.

'Dad's off doing whatever Dad does on a Saturday night,' Leanne said, 'and my friend has bailed out.' Donna had been moaning about how tired she was, how Ricky and she never got a moment for themselves, and at long last, Leanne picked up on the hint.

Benjie was out for the count, a good little sleeper since the day he was born. Skye was moaning and grizzly, and Donna didn't want to leave her.

'Hurry up!' Ricky yelled, stomping up and down the hallway.

By the time they arrived at the tandoori in town, Donna and Ricky couldn't bring themselves to look at each other. Donna put her mobile on the table. She had given Leanne strict instructions to call if she had the slightest worry. Leanne was not a natural grandmother. She turned up her nose when Donna was changing nappies and held the babies away from her as if they were contaminated waste. But when they were clean and cute, then she was all over them. Particularly when other people were around.

Donna and Ricky ordered and were looking around the restaurant like those middle-aged couples who have run out of things to say to each other, when Donna's mobile rang. They both jumped. Donna's heart was in her mouth when she saw it was Leanne calling.

'What is it?' Her voice was wobbly and her heart pumped rapidly.

Ricky paled as he mirrored her expression.

'I've won the lottery!' Leanne whispered.

'For fuck's sake, Mum,' Donna snapped. 'I thought something was the matter with one of the kids.' Blood rushed back into her face.

'I've won the EuroMillions. One hundred and twenty million to be precise.'

'You what?' Donna screeched.

'What is it?' Ricky leaned forwards, catching the sleeve of his only button-down shirt on a bowl of curry.

'She's won the bloody lottery!' Donna panted.

The couple at the adjacent table turned around and stared.

'Keep your voice down,' Leanne said. 'I don't want anyone to know.'

'Not even Dad?'

'Of course I'm going to tell your dad,' she mumbled. But Donna wondered if she would. 'You need to come home.'

'We're going home.' Donna stood up and grabbed her scuffed cream leather Michael Kors bag, the one she had coveted for so long and Ricky had given to her on their wedding day.

'We're eating, Donna,' Ricky said, knife and fork still in his hands.

'This is more important. We've got to go.' She scowled at him.

Ricky sighed and asked the waiter to pack up their food in takeaway containers. Donna shuffled from foot to foot, impatient to get going. *No more crappy tandooris for us,* she thought.

They were in the van on the way home.

'Stop at the off-licence,' she ordered Ricky.

He did as he was told, ran in, and came running back with a bottle of champagne, a massive grin on his face as he swung himself into the van with a swagger, as if he were driving a Ferrari rather than the ancient van.

'The champagne will be all shook up. It'll explode,' Donna said, scowling.

When they got home, Leanne was waiting in the corridor, her pink coat on, her handbag over her shoulder.

'Where are you going?' Donna frowned. 'I thought we would open the champers, celebrate your win.'

'I've got to run,' she said, giving her daughter a quick peck on the cheek. And then she was gone.

'I can't believe she's left,' Donna said. 'She made us leave our food and then buggered off.'

'All the more champagne for us,' Ricky said, grinning as he started laying out the takeaway containers on the kitchen table.

The champagne cork popped out of the bottle exactly as it should, or perhaps not exactly, because it flew straight up to the ceiling with a loud bang and then landed slap, bang in the middle of the container of poppadoms. Ricky and Donna collapsed in hysterics, and Donna's fury with Leanne vanished. It was their best moment, a moment when their future took on a golden hue, when all their worries suddenly dissipated, when they could envisage their dreams becoming a reality. It wasn't until later that Donna realised she and Ricky had never discussed their respective dreams. They just got through each day as it came, hoping his salary would stretch to the end of the month. The extent of their dreams was the little extension out the back that Ricky had recently started building so as to make the kitchen a bit bigger and give the kids a place to play.

* * *

Ten days later, Leanne and Kevin were gone, having flown off to Southern Spain. It's amazing how quickly the money gets transferred when you win the lottery. They come over, check your ticket, help you set up a new bank account, introduce you to your very own personal banking manager, and then the money is all there, ready to be spent.

Donna was shocked when they told her how little they'd be giving Ricky and Donna. It was not as if she had ever expected handouts from her parents, partly because they never had any spare to give and partly because they were bloody awful parents. Some kids get love; some get money. Donna got neither. So she just assumed they'd make up for what they hadn't given her to date. As normal, all she got was a slap in the face. Thirty-five thousand euros between the four of them.

Leanne asked Donna to drive them to the airport, but Donna said she couldn't. In the past she would have given a reason, invented something or other, but Donna couldn't be bothered this time. *Let them go and roast until they're toast in the sun*, she thought.

It was a week or so later. Kerry had come around to Donna's house, and they were giving the little ones their tea. Kerry and Donna went to school together, and then, when Donna was pregnant with Benjie, and Kerry was pregnant with Declan, they found themselves in the same antenatal class. Kerry makes Donna laugh.

'Where are your parents off to?' she asked, taking a sip of milky coffee.

'They're in Spain,' Donna said. How she wished to tell Kerry all about the lottery win, but even though she loathed her parents for not sharing their money, she didn't intend to betray them by telling anyone. It would make her look like a money-grabbing, resentful cow.

'But where are they moving to?'

'Spain,' Donna said, and then it was her turn to frown. 'But how do you know?'

And then the doorbell had rung, and Donna rushed to the front of the house, leaving Kerry to shovel fish fingers into Benjie and Declan.

'Yeah?' Donna had looked at the man quizzically. He had short blond hair and wore a tight-fitting T-shirt that showed off ripples of muscle across his torso.

'I'm Mike,' he said.

'So?' Donna retorted, frowning, looking him up and down and liking what she saw.

'You're Ricky Wiśniewski's wife. Aren't you expecting me?'

Donna shook her head.

'I'm here to help out on the extension.'

'He didn't say anything to me.'

'I work with him on the building site down in Angmering. Promised to help out whenever I've got a bit of spare time. Ricky said he'd be back after work.'

Donna glanced at her watch. 'He's never back before five p.m., so he'll be another twenty minutes or so.'

They looked at each other awkwardly, and Donna felt her cheeks redden.

'Don't worry. I'll wait out here until he's back.'

He turned quickly and strode away. Donna felt embarrassed and confused. She should have invited him in. Why was her heart thumping so hard, and why did her cheeks feel as if they were on fire? She walked back into the kitchen, her right hand stroking her left arm.

'Who was that?' Kerry asked.

'Some friend of Ricky's. A lush friend of Ricky's.'

'So, your parents. Why are they going to Spain?'

Her mind was tugged back as she pushed away thoughts of the lush man whom Ricky had roped in. 'They're on holiday, thinking about moving there.'

'You mean they have moved.'

'What?'

'The removal lorry outside their house this morning – was that taking their stuff to Spain?'

'What fucking removal lorry?'

Kerry looked worried. 'I think I got the right house.'

Donna sank into her chair, her fingers kneading her leggings. Kerry only lived two streets down, and she'd been to Leanne and Kevin's house several times.

'There were four or five men carrying out furniture and boxes, and some officious woman with a clipboard directing them.'

'That's fast.' Donna bit the inside of her mouth and blinked rapidly. It is one thing saying you're going to move to Spain, quite another pulling it off within a fortnight. And it was not like Leanne and Kevin were proactive doers. They still had the same kitchen and bathroom they had when they moved into their house twenty years ago, and they'd only been abroad three times: twice to Lanzarote and once to Costa del Sol. The lottery people must have helped them.

'You look really upset,' Kerry said, her silver nose stud catching the light as she peered at Donna. 'I'm sorry.'

'Not your fault,' she said, sniffing.

* * *

And now Leanne is dead and they think Kevin did it. *It's a joke, a bloody joke*, Donna screams silently.

She is upstairs, curled up on the bed. It's the only place she wants to be – away from the world, trying to sleep to get rid of the horror. Sometimes she sees her mother's bloodied face in her dreams, but mostly she doesn't.

The doorbell rings. The doorbell never stops ringing these days, and now there are journalists camped outside, scores of them, like pesky flies ready to swarm. She hears Ricky's voice and then other voices. It must be the police again. After a while the bedroom door opens. She pretends to be asleep.

'Donna, love, you need to come down. The police are here and they've got some questions for you.'

'Don't want to speak to them,' she says, snuffling.

'You've got no choice. Otherwise, they'll take you to the station.'

'What?' she screeches, shoving the duvet off her. 'Going to arrest me now, are they?'

'Calm down. They just want to talk to you. About the photograph.'

'What photograph?'

'The one in the newspapers and on the telly.'

She falls silent. After a couple of moments, Donna swings her legs out of bed and slides her feet into her furry slippers. Ricky tries to put his arm around her shoulders, but she shrugs him off. She traipses into the living room, rubbing her eyes, which makes them look even more sore.

Detective Sergeant Joe Swain is in the living room with the family liaison officer, Janet Curran. Donna took an instant dislike to Janet when they first met. She reckoned Joe Swain was alright, though: tall, nicely chiselled jaw, dark skin with a hint of stubble.

'Have a seat, Donna,' Janet says.

Donna bites a fingernail that is already bleeding. *It's my bloody house*, she wants to say. But Donna does as she's told. Janet sits next to Donna. Joe Swain paces; he's too big for the room.

'Donna, we've had the results back from the lab. I am sorry to confirm that the murdered woman was indeed your mother, Leanne.'

'No!' Donna howls.

Ricky holds her tight, and they all wait for the waves of grief to stop racking through her body. After a very long minute or so, Donna pushes him away. 'But the photo?' she says through her sobs. 'The photo isn't Mum. Why did you use that photo?'

'There appears to have been a mistake.'

'How can you make a mistake like that?' Ricky yells, and it sets Donna off on another wave of wails.

'It's very unfortunate. The photo was found—'

Donna interrupts him. 'Mum was so clear that she didn't want any publicity over the lottery win. She hates publicity. And when you came up with that photo, then we just went along with it. It looks a bit like her, good enough.'

'Now, now, love,' Janet says, bending down in front of Donna, talking to her as if she is talking to Benjie rather than Donna. Condescending cow. When Donna turns her head away, Janet stands up and wipes down her tweedy skirt.

Donna hopes they will leave, but Joe Swain asks, 'Do you know the woman in the photograph?'

'No,' she whispers. 'But she does look a bit like Mum.'

'The same eyes,' Ricky adds.

'And were there other photos in your parents' house?' He takes a step towards Donna. If he wants to intimidate, it's working.

'Yes,' she says, shaking. 'Photos of Mum and Dad on their wedding day. Photos of me and the babies. Normal stuff.'

'Can I get into the house?' Ricky asks.

'No. It's a serious-crime scene. All I can tell you is that the house was devoid of furniture, with the exception of the kitchen table and two chairs. The photograph in question was found near your mother. We assumed it had been left behind accidentally.'

'Well, you should have checked. Done your job a bit better!' Ricky raises his voice and with his hands on his hips takes a step towards Joe Swain. Donna may have lost her mum and quite possibly her dad, but in that moment her heart swells with love for Ricky.

‘Do you know who might have left that photo at your parents’ house?’ Joe asks.

Ricky and Donna look at each other. It’s the question they can’t answer. When the police said they’d taken a photo of Leanne from the house, it never crossed their minds that the photo could have been of someone other than Leanne. It wasn’t until they saw the picture on the news that they allowed themselves a bit of hope. Perhaps the dead woman wasn’t Leanne after all? Perhaps the police had got it all wrong? When Ricky rang up that Mia Brevant and told her the photo they were using wasn’t of Leanne, the young policewoman had sounded surprised. She said that she had sent Donna an email of Leanne’s photo, but Donna doesn’t recall. She can’t bear to look at any photos of her mum. Not now.

Detective Sergeant Joe Swain repeats the question. ‘Donna, do you know who might have left that photograph at your parents’ house?’

She shakes her head. It’s one of the many things that don’t make sense.

‘You’ve made one almighty big cock-up, haven’t you?’ Ricky shouts at Joe.

‘We’ll be in touch,’ Joe Swain says, narrowing his inky black eyes.

‘Can’t even say sorry!’ Ricky yells when Joe Swain and Janet Curran have left the room. ‘One little word, that’s all it takes!’

When the front door slams shut, Ricky glances at his watch. ‘I’m sorry, Dons. It’s crap.’

Donna sinks into the sofa and listens to Ricky’s footsteps as he sweeps into the kitchen and starts chattering with Benjie.

5

Pippa

'Thank goodness you're here!' I say as I fling my arms around Rob. 'The police have been and they think I had something to do with the murder.'

'What!' Rob pushes me away and stares at me. 'How did the police find you?'

I turn my back on him and walk down the hall towards the kitchen. Mungo rushes forwards, his tail wagging manically.

'I called them.'

'Pippa!' The disappointment is heavy in Rob's voice.

'Trevor rang,' he says.

'What the hell does Trevor want?'

'Reminded me that you're his ex-wife and the mother of his children.'

'Child,' I mutter unnecessarily.

'He doesn't want to be linked to whatever nonsense you've got yourself tied up in.'

I bite the inside of my mouth until I can taste blood. 'I assume you told him to go to hell.'

'I didn't come over to bitch about your ex. Have a look at this. There's a story trending about you.'

Rob hands me his mobile phone. It's the latest iPhone, the screen too large for my liking, but Rob always has to have the newest model whether that's a car, television or phone.

The headline is *Does Murdered Lottery Mum Have Twin Sister?* The associated blurry photograph is of me with my head down as I strode down the aisle in Waitrose a few hours ago.

'My clients,' I mutter. I'll lose all my damn clients. I wonder if I should grab the bull by its horns and ring them all up, or should I wait for them to approach me? I know I should call Peter, my supervisor. This is exactly the sort of conundrum us practitioners are meant to discuss with a colleague, and although I respect Peter and find our monthly chats helpful when debating complex issues surrounding my clients, I know that this will be so far beyond the remit of his experience.

'You need to find out why they've got your photo. And you need to find that out fast. And how do we know that you're not in danger?' Rob says.

I shiver. 'I know. And I'm really scared that they think I'm a suspect. I don't have an alibi for the time of the murder.' I wring my hands.

'This is ridiculous, Pippa. You're not a murderer! You can't even kill a fly.'

'I know that. You know that, but they don't.'

He leans over and gives me a kiss on the cheek.

The doorbell rings and we both jump. Mungo barks.

'I didn't feel like cooking. Sorry. I've ordered a pizza.'

'I'll go to the door,' he says. That's the thing with Rob. One moment he is the most annoying, self-centred man on the planet, who drives me insane; the next he is thoughtful and charming.

'No, it's fine.'

He puts his hand out like a policeman stopping traffic. 'Pips, I don't think you should show your face at the moment. Think about it.'

I sigh. Loudly. And retreat into the kitchen.

Rob returns with the pizza box. He puts it on the table and sits down. He opens the box and helps himself to the slice with the most copious amount of chicken topping.

'It was a massive shock seeing my sister's face on BBC News 24.' Rob speaks with his mouth full. 'Are the police going to issue an apology and put out the correct photograph? It must be awful for the dead woman's family.'

'I don't know.'

'Under no circumstances must they let anyone know your real name.' He pauses for a moment. 'Or where you live.'

'I know, Rob. You don't need to tell me. How am I meant to get or keep clients if my patients think I'm connected to some dodgy dead woman or worse still a suspected murderer?'

We chew in silence for a few moments, and then Rob says, 'Trevor wanted to know if you'd heard from George.'

'No.'

My shoulders sag. We both stare into the distance. George. He was such a beautiful child, with silken black curls and captivating dark-blue eyes. I was convinced that George arrived into the world with many lifetimes of experience behind him. He was quiet, with a pool of wisdom so deep and a maturity we all admired. Although he was three years younger than his sister, he took it upon himself to become her protector. Throughout their childhood he was the model brother, her rock, our perfect child. But perfection is a heavy load to carry, and although we think it is a permanent trait, I now know that it can be shattered in an instant.

When his sister, Flo, disappeared, George discarded all his positive characteristics. Within a year he was unrecognisable. Out went the neatly cropped dark hair; in came the peroxide spikes. Out went the clean-shaven face; in came thick kohl eyeliner and a dark beard. Out went the caring consideration; in came a selfish disregard for everyone around him. Out went the studiousness; in came the free spirit who left home with fifty quid in his pocket to travel the world.

The new George returned home from time to time, but the visits became increasingly sparse, and once Trevor and I split up, the phone calls stopped too. The old George appears to have gone forever. As if I didn't have enough insecurity and grief in my life, I also had to mourn the loss of my perfect firstborn. For all I know, George might be in Australia. The last phone call was five months and thirteen days ago, when, quite surprisingly, he rang to wish me happy birthday. When I asked what he was doing, he replied, 'This and that.' And when I asked where he was living, he replied, 'Here and there.' All he wanted to do was find out about me, how I was, what new clients I had, what articles I had written, where I was going on holiday. My questions to him were bounced back to me with disarming accuracy.

I reckon it's worse for Trevor. George never calls him, and as far as I'm aware, they haven't seen each other in three years. 'Dad betrayed you,' George told me five years ago. 'I'll never forgive him.' I tried to stand up for Trevor; I tried to explain that his father wasn't a bad man. But George was resolute.

As the gay, childless uncle and the self-assigned family mediator, Rob suffers deeply from my family fallout. He viewed our kids as his own. Trevor's shiny new family will never be a substitute.

'George will call you if he sees the story, won't he?'

'Yes, he'll call me,' I say, but deep down I wonder whether if George catches sight of my picture, it might only serve to push him further away.

'So, what are you going to do?' Rob stands up and starts pacing. 'You need a plan of action.'

I sigh. This is Rob all over. Planning. Lists. Action. Achieving. Control.

'Go away, brother. I'm tired. This is my problem and I'll sort it. I appreciate your help, but I'm tired.'

He opens his mouth and then closes it again. 'Okay, Pips,' he says as he walks towards the door. 'But remember you're the only family I've got and I love you.'

'I know, and the feeling is reciprocated.' I blow him a kiss.

When I have heard the front door catch on its lock and I hear the roar of his Porsche fade into the distance, I get up and bolt the front door top and bottom. I grab my laptop and position it next to the pizza box and embark on some research.

It's easy enough to find out where Leanne and Kevin Smith live, thanks to the intense media coverage. And it doesn't take me long to discover they have one daughter, called Donna, who is married to Ricky. Ten minutes later I've found their address too. How dare the police suggest I'm a suspect! I haven't felt such fury, such a need to take action in a long time.

* * *

I awake at 5 a.m. after a surprisingly good, albeit short, night's sleep. It's still dark outside and I have less than ninety minutes before sunrise, so I need to get going. I throw on some old jogging bottoms and my worn navy anorak, then dig around in my wardrobe and find a black woolly hat, which I push down far on to my head, pulling my hair up underneath it. I hate wearing contact lenses, but today I must. I manage to get them in and try to blink away the gritty feeling. My final accoutrement is a thick navy scarf, which I wrap around my neck. I put Donna and Ricky's address into Google Maps on my phone, grab Mungo's lead, and my faithful canine companion follows me out of the house, his tail wagging wildly.

'We're going for a little drive and then a walkies.'

No coaxing is required. Mungo leaps on to the back seat the moment I open the door.

The drive helps me ease the fear and clarify my mind. I need to find out more about Leanne's family, and I need to check that there is no connection between them and me, perhaps via any of my clients. And most urgently, I must establish an alibi for myself. If all else fails, I will get back in touch with my old contacts at the Metropolitan Police. It was a lifetime ago, but when I practiced as a forensic psychologist, I used to work closely alongside a number of senior officers. I'm sure they will vouch for me. I have to clear my name.

Twenty minutes later Mungo and I are parked up on the street parallel to the Wiśniewskis' house. I attach the dog's lead, pull the beanie further down over my forehead, and wrap the scarf around my chin. As I lock the car doors, I hope that I look like a casual dog walker, ready for the cold morning chill.

There's something about the man who furtively jumps over the low garden fence that makes me stop. He glances shiftily from one side of the road to the other but ignores me. And then he races towards a small white van, unlocks the driver's door and jumps inside. I have that sixth sense about him. Ricky Wiśniewski. I'm sure it's him, probably evading the press circus camped outside his front door.

'Sorry, Mungo,' I say as I open the rear door again and chuck a dog biscuit inside. My obedient, led-by-his-stomach Labrador climbs back in. I race to the driver's door and start up the car. I'm going to follow this man. Let's just hope I've got the correct guy.

6

Ricky

Ricky is itching to get out of the house, to get back to work. He finds it stifling in their semi-detached two-up two-down, with the curtains closed and the little ones screeching and Donna either sobbing on the sofa or hiding underneath the duvet in the dark. He made a start on laying the bricks at the back of the house, but Donna had screeched at him to stop, telling him it was disrespectful and the banging was doing her head in.

It has been five days since Leanne died. Ricky has never been off work for that long. Even when he had glandular fever, he battled on until the illness gave up. And now it is just before 6 a.m. and the weak light of dawn is beckoning him. He slips out of bed, tugs on his work gear and gently shakes Donna.

She squeals. 'What's happened?'

'Nothing. I've been called into work,' he lies. 'You'll have to look after the babies by yourself today. If I don't go to work, I'll lose my job and we'll have no money.'

'We're multimillionaires,' Donna says as she shuffles up the bed.

'No, we're not. We've no idea whether you'll inherit the money or even if they'll release it. Right now the only income we have is mine. Love, you're stronger than you think. You'll be fine and I've got to go.'

Donna reaches across the bed and grabs his hand. 'No! Please don't!'

'Dons, it'll be okay. The children need you. And I'll leave my phone on so you can call me anytime.' He takes a deep breath. He knows he should hate leaving her like this, but he doesn't. He's just relieved at the prospect of freedom.

It's been a shock to Donna, to all of them – of course it has – but now life must get back to normal.

'Ask Kerry to come around. I'll text you later.'

The best thing about life on a building site is each day is different. Ricky works for DSD Construction Ltd, a small building firm doing fancy extensions and, when they get lucky, the occasional new house. The current project is creating a leisure wing for a mansion on the Willowhayne Estate, down on the seafront in Angmering. The house is the size of a hotel, all glass and metal. The seagulls will get a great view of all the goings-on inside, Ricky thinks. It has some fancy special glass that repels the salt from the waves that in the winter months surge over the pebble beach, across the strip of grassland and on to the decking of the house.

Ricky wouldn't want to live there. Too windswept, too exposed. He hasn't met the owners. Gazza, the site foreman, reckons they're Londoners who visit on a couple of weekends each year when they're not in the Caribbean. Ricky wonders if they're lottery winners. They are building a gym, a basement cinema room the size of most normal houses, and a space for a massive swimming pool with glass walls that will peel back at the press of a button, along with lavish changing rooms complete with rainwater showers.

As Ricky gets into the van, he wonders whether he and Donna might end up somewhere like that should the money come their way. He starts up the engine and grins as he imagines telling Gazza that he is the new owner of the house.

As he drives out of Horsham, the sun is rising, and he feels the weight of the past few days lifting off his shoulders; it's as if the sun's rays are burning the misery away. Although it's cold, he winds down the windows, tunes the radio to Southern Counties and turns it up loud. He's halfway down the A24 when his phone rings, startling him. The number's withheld, which makes Ricky nervous. He winds up the windows and slows the van down.

‘Is this Richard Wiśniewski?’ The man stumbles over the pronunciation of Ricky’s name, but then most British people do. ‘My name is James Dickson. I’m the solicitor for Kevin Smith. I understand he is your father-in-law.’

‘Yes.’ Ricky feels a quickening in his gut.

‘Mr Smith mentioned that you work on a building site and that first thing in the morning might be an appropriate time to reach you.’

Ricky doesn’t say anything, so the solicitor continues.

‘Mr Smith has asked me to tell you that he has been charged, and in my opinion it is likely that he will be refused bail. We are not sure yet where he will be held, but he would like you to bring his daughter to visit him as soon as he is granted visitation rights.’

The bastard.

‘Mr Wiśniewski? Can you hear me?’

‘Yes, I can hear you.’ Ricky pauses. ‘Tell Mr Smith that he can rot in jail. And if he contacts me or Donna ever again, directly or indirectly, there will be hell to pay.’

He ends the call.

Ricky thumps his fist on the steering wheel and inadvertently veers into the fast lane and quickly back into the slow lane. A jerk in a business suit puts his hand on the horn of his silver Audi and lifts a finger as he screams past. Is Kevin that delusional or that stupid that he thinks he can rely on Ricky? Donna thinks the sun shines out of her daddy’s fat rear end, but Ricky knows better. Kevin never liked him, and the feeling is mutual.

He recalls their first meeting. Ricky had assumed Donna might have briefed her parents – at least told them his name and what he did for a job, especially as she was still living at home. But he was wrong. They’d been dating for about four months and spending most evenings together and every weekend, always at his cramped studio flat near the station in Worthing.

'When are you going to introduce me to your folks?' he'd asked her on more than one occasion.

'Sometime, never,' she'd said, running a finger down his happy line, teasing away the top of his jeans.

'What's the matter with them?'

'Nothing,' she'd said, pulling her hand away abruptly. It had never crossed Ricky's mind that the matter might be him.

The meeting wasn't planned. Ricky had his arm flung over Donna's shoulders as they meandered along Worthing seafront that sunny Saturday afternoon in July. She was finishing off the last of a massive balloon of candyfloss, the sugar creating little wisps of pale-pink hair across her cheeks. Ricky didn't like candyfloss, finding it too sweet, but he couldn't resist pulling Donna towards him and licking his tongue across her face until it found her mouth, and then he sucked her into him like a leech. He pushed her up against the railings, and despite the full daylight and swarming families, he would have taken her there and then. But a voice broke through.

'Donna?'

Donna pushed Ricky away with a strength that stunned him.

'Mum, what are you doing here?' she stuttered, tugging at her hair with her fingers, brushing the tangled strands back into place, wiping her swollen lips with the back of her hand, pulling down her skimpy sundress. By her reaction, you'd have thought Donna was fifteen years old, not twenty-two and all grown up.

'Who's this?' Leanne asked, narrowing her eyes at Ricky.

Ricky glanced from Donna to Leanne and back again.

'This is Ricky. He's my boyfriend.'

'Is he indeed?' The voice was booming despite the roar of the ocean and the screech of children playing and the incessant traffic. Ricky turned to look at the man. Unlike his wife, who was neatly groomed and petite like her daughter,

Kevin was all paunchy stomach and slovenly T-shirt and ridiculous boyish shorts that hung just below his knees.

'How do you do? I'm Ricky Wiśniewski.' Ricky stuck his hand out. Despite being caught off guard, he was determined to make a good impression. He knew even then that he was meeting his future in-laws for the first time.

Kevin ignored the outstretched hand. 'You a foreigner?'

If he'd met this man down in the pub, Ricky might have directed his knuckle to the unfit older man's jaw. Instead he clenched his teeth, pulled back his hand and shoved it in his jeans pocket. 'No, sir. I'm not.'

'Sir? Who the hell says "sir" in this day and age?' Kevin threw his head back and laughed. Spittle arced out of his mouth.

Ricky took a step backwards and stepped on Donna's foot. She yelped. The two women stood looking every which way except at Ricky or Kevin.

Kevin stopped laughing as quickly as he'd started. He put his hands on his hips. 'Come on, Donna. Time to go home now.'

Donna rubbed the flimsy fabric of her dress. She gazed at the pavement. 'No, Dad. I'm with Ricky. We're having a walk along the front.'

'Didn't look much like that to me,' he growled. 'Looked like you were behaving like a slag with this phony foreigner.'

'Excuse me, but I'm not—' Ricky stepped forwards, his fists at the ready.

'Ricky!' Donna screeched.

'You're right,' Ricky muttered under his breath, turning away abruptly. With sagging shoulders he strode away in the direction of the town centre.

'Ricky. Ricky, wait!' Donna came running up behind him and wove her arm through his.

'Are you sure?' he said, knowing full well that things would never be the same again for Donna.

* * *

Kevin is a xenophobe, which made it all the more bizarre that he thought moving to Spain was a good idea. He never forgave Ricky for 'stealing' his daughter, and he never forgave Donna for marrying a foreigner, even if that foreigner spoke better English than he did and the only thing 'foreign' about him was his surname, an inheritance from a father he never met. Relations between the two men improved a little over the years, but only because Ricky bit his tongue time and time again. Ricky was determined to protect the woman he loved from the bully in their lives.

And now that Kevin is behind bars, as far as Ricky is concerned, he can damn well stay there.

He pulls the van up to the tall, imposing, solid gates outside Sun Vista Manor. They are kept permanently shut, but a winking security camera sends information through to Gazza's site office. One of the stipulations of the contract was to ensure someone was permanently in the site office, manning the bank of cameras that survey the perimeter of the property. After three or four seconds, the gates slide open, and Ricky eases the van through. There is an imposing sweeping gravel drive, surrounded by lawn that looks like a bowling green, and strange mirrored-glass structures that Ricky knows are sculptures but seem to him like discarded bits of an aeroplane. Tradesmen and all delivery vehicles have to follow the DSD Construction signs leading them down the side of the property and to a large parking lot especially dug out for the new build. Gazza's van is already there, parked up alongside another white van and a couple of knackered cars. Ricky is glad he is early. There will be fewer questions.

Ricky strides over to the site office, a large Portakabin adjacent to two portable building-site toilets housed in dark-green Tardis-like boxes. Gazza is hunched over his laptop.

'Morning,' Ricky mumbles, grabbing a fluorescent bib and hard hat. He signs himself into the logbook.

Gazza grunts. 'We've got the steels being delivered this morning. Need you to oversee that.'

Ricky nods. 'Is Mike in?'

'Yeah. Kept on asking where you were. Said your mobile was switched off. Why's he so worried about you?'

'He's my mate. Just looking out for me, I suppose. He said he'd help out on our extension at the weekends.'

'It's his last day today.'

Ricky frowns. 'Why?'

'Not allowed to employ casuals anymore. Gotta be full-timers only. Don't ask.' Gazza rolls his eyes. 'Instructions from the top. Guess he can get on with your extension, then!'

'Donna will be happy,' Ricky mutters to himself.

He is walking away when Gazza yells, 'Oi, Ricky! There's a bird at the gates asking for you. Someone called Pippa Durrant.'

Ricky stands stock-still, then does a 360 and strides back to Gazza's desk. He peers at the security camera.

'You know her?' Gazza asks, muting the intercom.

Ricky shakes his head. 'Never seen her before. Tell her she's mistaken.'

Gazza raises his eyebrows. 'Sorry, no one of that name on this building site,' Gazza says, speaking into the intercom. 'There's another build further down the estate. Perhaps you've got the wrong place.'

Ricky is rooted to the spot. He watches the woman hesitate, and then, accepting defeat, she turns and climbs back into her car. He stares as the car disappears out of vision. He can feel tremors working their way down his body right into his toes encased in steel-capped boots. And then he turns and races away from Gazza into the bowels of the building site, swallowing his nausea and trying to banish the what-ifs from his mind.

7

Pippa

I follow the white van out of Horsham and on to the A24, a dual carriageway with harsh bends that don't lend themselves to a fast road. At Findon, he indicates to the right and we meander up over the South Downs on to a beautiful stretch of sweeping road called Long Furlong, with vistas of chalky hills and expansive fields glowing yellow with rapeseed. I let my mind wander.

My first thought is I'm involved in this murder because of a client. It's the obvious conclusion. My clients are troubled, some more than others, but they are all troubled to some degree; otherwise they wouldn't need to see me. Before my own life disintegrated, I was a forensic psychologist, but then I transitioned to counselling psychology. These days, now I've moved away from the clinical work and just have my own private practice, I concentrate on helping people who have Cluster C disorders: the avoidants, the dependents, and the obsessive-compulsives. Many of my clients suffer from anxiety and depression. These more run-of-the-mill problems respond well to psychotherapeutic treatments, CBT and talking therapies.

Last night I did a quick search of my client database. I don't have case files going back more than seven years, but I have been rigorous in keeping names, ages and contact details. It's a common name, Kevin Smith. There was a Kevin Smith who I supported through a particularly horrendous divorce five years ago, but he was only mid-thirties, so the age doesn't fit. Apparently I treated another Kevin Smith, who had schizoid personality disorder. I seem to recall he was sectioned, but it was a long time ago. I'd need to get in touch with some colleagues to see if I can track him down. Data protection and patient confidentiality are so rigorous these days, I'm not hopeful.

I can't fathom why my photograph was left in Leanne Smith's house. There must be a link between me and their family, and I'm hoping Ricky might be able to help me. I'm not ready to intrude upon the grief of their daughter, so her partner will have to do.

I lose his van for a while once we're on the coastal road but manage to spot him meandering through Angmering. And then he's turning into the exclusive Willowhayne Estate, with its multimillion-pound mansions. He slows down in front of some gates, and I spot a sign for a building firm – DSD Construction Ltd. I'm not sure what I was expecting, but I'm a bit disappointed. He's on his way to work. I park up conspicuously alongside a beautifully manicured verge.

'Stay,' I tell Mungo as I hop out of the car and saunter towards the gates. There's an intercom with a flashing eye. I hesitate for a moment. I wasn't planning on confronting him; in fact, I wasn't planning anything at all, and now I'm not sure what to do. But that blinking eye will have seen me, so I press the button.

A gruff voice answers. 'Yup?'

'Is it possible to speak to Ricky Wiśniewski?'

There's a pause. I guess if Ricky is a building labourer, he won't receive visitors at work. I regret asking for him now.

'Who's asking?'

'My name's Philippa Durrant.'

The line goes dead and then it crackles wildly.

'Sorry, no one of that name on this building site. 'There's another build further down the estate. Perhaps you've got the wrong place.'

'But—'

The line is dead.

I walk away. Have I followed the wrong man? No. I'm sure I haven't. He was too furtive, jumping over that fence.

The man at the end of the intercom is lying. I expect he thinks I'm a journalist, a squawking scavenger like the seagulls soaring above my head. It wasn't clever of me, turning up like this.

Back at the car, I speak to Mungo. 'Come on, we're going for a walk along the seafront.' The dog leaps out of the car, his tail going around and around in wild circles as he anticipates a bonus outing.

I stride quickly, keeping him on the lead, as dogs aren't allowed to run free on this exclusive stretch of green verge that stretches above the pebbly beachfront.

'Hurry up, Mungs.' I tug on his lead, barely letting him do his business and certainly not allowing him his regular lengthy sniffing of unfamiliar territory. Normally I enjoy the stroll along here, inhaling large gulps of salty breeze and staring out to sea, counting the wind turbines that seem to sprout up with alarming regularity on the horizon. After ten minutes or so, Mungo stops and looks up at me with his trusting amber eyes. This is just one of many occasions that I sense this dog has a better idea of what is going on in my mind than I do. He looks over his shoulder back the way we came, and moves as if to turn around.

'Shall we go home?' I ask, a beseeching tone to my voice. He trots back easily.

I can't stop thinking about Leanne and her family. There must be a connection between her and me; otherwise why would my photo have been in her home? As I've failed to speak to Donna's husband, I need to try to speak to Donna herself, or at the very least find out more about her. I don't want to intrude on her grief, but at the same time, surely I am owed an explanation.

Quickly I discount trying to turn up at her house. The thought of the media frenzy if they catch sight of me in the vicinity is enough to make me feel nauseous. Instead I decide to contact Donna via the phone or possibly, if I can find her details, social media. I pull up outside a Tesco store near home and switch off the ignition. I turn to look out of my side window, catching the eye of a woman in a khaki Barbour climbing into her SUV. She stops, her linen carrier bag dangling from her arm as if she is frozen. As she stares at me, her mouth opens in a perfect circle, eyes blinking rapidly. I don't wait a moment longer. Reversing quickly out of my parking bay, I get out of there. Damn it. I can't even do a shop, I'm that notorious.

'It's not bloody fair, Mungo!' I yell. The dog barks and I have to coo at him to make him realise that I'm angry with life and not with my beloved pet.

Eventually I walk through the door just after midday. The work answering machine is flashing.

'Hello, Philippa.'

I recognise Carrie Sorrell's voice. She's been coming to me weekly for the past couple of months, presenting with chronic insomnia and mild depression. Her voice is hesitant.

'I'm sorry, but I can't come today. I'll be back in touch when…if I decide to come back. I know you have a twenty-four-hour cancellation policy, but I'm sure under the circumstances…' Her voice peters out and then she speaks very rapidly. 'Anyway, thanks for your support. This is Carrie Sorrell, by the way. Bye.'

The second message is from my 5 p.m. appointment.

'Donald Myland speaking. I was hoping to talk to you directly, but as you're not there, I'll leave a message. I was shocked to see your photo in the papers. I assume it must be your sister who was killed. Sorry about that. But still, you don't expect to see your therapist on the front pages, even if it isn't you. I'll be cancelling for now.' He doesn't say goodbye or sorry, but then I wouldn't expect that from Donald Myland.

I take a deep sigh. I feared this might be the case, but to happen so quickly is shocking. Has the incompetence of the police destroyed my business and my reputation overnight? I bend down to cuddle Mungo, my constant, unjudging canine friend.

'What am I going to do?' I whisper into his fur. When he tries to lick my face, I get up and put on the kettle, fury bubbling up into my chest. How dare someone else's bungling affect my life? I have already had to rebuild it once.

When the phone rings again, just after I have taken a large bite out of a hastily made tuna sandwich from a very stale packet of rye bread and tinned tuna, I assume it is my 2 p.m. appointment cancelling.

'Philippa Durrant.' I try to swallow quietly.

'Ms Durrant, this is Detective Sergeant Joe Swain. I would like to talk to you again. May I visit you later? Or if it's convenient, you could come to the station.'

'What do you want?'

'I have some information I wish to share with you, and I would like to ask further questions.'

'Am I still a suspect?'

'We will discuss that later.'

The man infuriates me, but I refuse to get involved with his power games. I don't want to go into town or anywhere I might be recognised, and I don't wish to make life easy for him. The police's bungling could well have destroyed my professional career.

'You can come here,' I spit. 'Five p.m. is convenient.' I hang up without giving him the chance to confirm whether or not it is convenient for him. I wonder for a moment whether I should give him the benefit of the doubt and insist he uncover my connection with Leanne Smith, but that moment passes quickly. There is no one I can rely on in this world except myself, Rob and Mungo.

I turn on my computer and log on to Facebook. I don't use it. Not after what happened, and besides, I think it would be thoroughly unprofessional of me. Nevertheless I do have a private profile – a fake one, of course, using my middle name and my maiden name. A profile that allows me to be a bit of an online loiterer, seeing but not participating. I search for Donna Wiśniewski. I expect I would have found her even if her surname wasn't unusual. She is a prolific social media user with no password protection or security. Every little detail of her life is documented in pictures, emojis and atrocious spelling. I hope it is some kind of snowflake generation colloquial textspeak but fear it is simply a profound inability to spell.

She used to post several times every day, photos of her children with inane information on what they've eaten, the contents of their nappies and how exhausted she is. I scroll forwards. There are only three recent posts.

Got bi88ist seekret. Wish cud share.

I check the date. It was posted shortly after her mother won the lottery, and I assume she's referring to the win. I open another tab in my browser and do a quick search on 'Leanne Smith EuroMillions Lottery Winner'. All the copy relates to her death. I guess she and her family decided not to go public with the win at the time. Flipping back to Facebook, I see that Donna didn't post anything until yesterday, four days after her mother died.

RIP mum. Luv u.

That post was commented on twenty-four times, mostly by women with spelling as lousy as Donna's.

But it is the last post that causes me to gag. It is a picture of me with the words *Do you know this woman? She's pretending to be mum. Track her down ASAP.*

I look at the date. It was posted this morning at 10.36 a.m. My hand races up to my throat and I stroke my neck. I stare at the words until they swim in front of my eyes, and then I realise. They are written in proper English, no spelling mistakes, no textspeak, no emojis. And the photo of me is not the one that has been in the press. I don't recognise it, but I do know it's me. I'm walking along a pavement with Mungo pulling on his red lead, and I'm wearing the navy anorak I've just flung over the kitchen chair, along with the jogging bottoms I am still wearing.

8

Donna

Donna can't believe Ricky's gone to work. He knows she can't cope, and why should she? She's lost both her parents. Leanne is dead, and Kevin is shoved in the clink. Ricky has always been there for Donna, but now she just doesn't know what's got into him.

Donna is still in bed. Skye starts crying. Donna pulls the pillow over her head to try to block out the baby's wails but then feels the duvet being tugged from her feet, and a hot, sweaty little hand tugs at her hair.

'Mama, gotta get up.'

Sighing loudly, she wipes her eyes, pulls her T-shirt down and climbs out of bed, letting Benjie lead her to his bedroom, where Skye is sitting in her crib having a full-blown tantrum, her face puce and snot pouring from her nose. Donna picks her up, wipes her face with her filthy T-shirt, and bounces her up and down on her hip. Skye is hungry, the poor mite, and her nappy stinks.

Donna's legs feel like logs, but she carries her downstairs, makes her some milk, and tips some cereal into a bowl for Benjie.

'Mama is sad,' Benjie says.

It makes Donna want to cry all over again, but instead she sniffs hard and rips off her last remaining easy-to-bite fingernail. There's no one here to wipe Donna's tears, and she knows she's got to be the grown-up now.

While the children are eating, she retrieves her mobile phone, which Ricky put in the drawer where they shove all their instruction manuals and unpaid bills and other detritus. Donna hasn't dared go online, not since she posted that her mum had died and Ricky went ballistic, screaming at her that it was a private moment, and didn't she have any self-respect, and didn't she understand what damage she was doing to their children with all her oversharing on social media?

Ricky is right, of course, but not for those reasons. Donna hasn't told him the real reason she's gone off social media.

Donna is being threatened.

It started a week after Leanne's lottery win. Donna received a private message from someone she didn't know, a man called Oedipus.

Hello, Donna. You don't know me, but I know all about you. Can we meet up and I'll tell you more?

Weirdo, Donna thought, *probably after some dosh*, and trashed the message. She was used to spam and she was surprisingly diligent about binning it. A couple of days later she got another message.

Donna, don't ignore me. It's important we meet up. How about Costa Coffee in Horsham?

Shit, Donna thought, jumping up from the kitchen table as if she'd received an electric shock. How did this Oedipus know where she lives? Donna showed the message to Kerry, but her friend just shrugged and asked if it was some bloke they used to know at school.

'I didn't know anyone called Oedipus,' Donna said.

Kerry burst out laughing. 'It's not pronounced Oh-idi-puss. It's Oedipus.'

Donna racked her brains for a moment. There were two guys, one they called Weedy – not because he was skinny but because he smoked so much dope, he was always spaced out – and there was another bloke in the same class called Pus because of his virulent acne.

'Do you think the two of them have got together and call themselves Oedipus instead of Weedipus?'

Kerry howled with laughter. 'It's a name from Greek mythology,' she snorted.

Donna pretended she had known that all along.

Later that afternoon Donna sent a message to him. *Who are you?*

But she didn't hear back. And then her mum was murdered and Donna's life disintegrated.

She scrolls through the copious messages left by friends, condolences on the death of Leanne, shock, sympathy. And she notices the people who haven't sent any messages. Lots of them. And just as she's scrolling to the bottom of the list, up pops a text from an unknown number.

You asked who I am. Someone you'll want to know.

Stay away from me, she types.

Don't be scared, Donna. But don't tell Ricky or Kevin about us. If you do, there'll be trouble. Big trouble.

Donna is totally freaked out. It is one thing knowing her name, but knowing Ricky's and her dad's? Who the hell is this? She is desperate to tell Ricky. She wanted to tell him when Oedipus first contacted her, but for some reason she held back and instead she deleted the messages. She wonders again if this Oedipus is after the lottery money. Leanne said that the woman from Camelot had warned about scroungers and hangers-on. Perhaps he is one of them. She decides to tell Ricky when he gets home tonight. He'll know what to do.

The morning drags by. The children are having their lunchtime nap, and Donna is trying to keep her eyes open. Her mobile rings. The number is withheld, but Donna isn't suspicious.

'Yeah?' she answers wearily.

He has a strange voice, as if he is talking through a microphone thousands of miles away. 'Donna, we need to talk.'

She goes very still.

'I know you've been having an affair, and if you don't do what I say, I'll tell Ricky.'

'But I haven't!' she retorts, surprise and indignation mingling together.

'Yes, you have. And I'll prove it to him.'

‘How can you prove something that isn’t true?’ Donna says.

The man laughs, a tinny, mechanical laugh that sends shivers through Donna. ‘Remember, if you say a word about these calls or my messages, I’ll tell Ricky. He won’t stand for having a whore as a wife.’

And then he hangs up, and for several long moments Donna listens to the hammering of her heart, a violent noise over the silence. How can the man know? It was so long ago. Donna was sort of unfaithful. It was ages before the children were born, an inconsequential snog, a one-off when she was pissed in a nightclub, celebrating Carly’s hen do. But perhaps this man knows. She simply can’t bear the thought of losing Ricky. He is all she’s got.

The battery in Donna’s phone is almost dead. She plugs it into the socket in the kitchen next to the kettle. And then Skye starts crying, and Benjie is jumping up and down on his bed, and the afternoon becomes all about the children.

* * *

When Ricky comes home from work, all quiet and sulky, he spots Donna’s phone, and when she isn’t looking, he unplugs it, powers it off, and places it back in the drawer.

9

Pippa

Halfway through my 3 p.m. session, I am, for the first time in my career, seriously debating telling my client that I can't concentrate and offering to return her money, in addition to giving her a free consultation. Felicity Smithers-Wray is proudly telling me how she only checked the locks of her home twice before leaving for our appointment. I force myself to listen, but it is hard. I nod in the right places and ask her leading questions, encouraging her to talk. Normally I choose to cut her off, as she prefers to discuss anything except her obsessive-compulsive disorder. But today I let her talk freely. It allows me time to think about Donna and Leanne and try to work out who posted the message on Donna's Facebook page, because unless Donna, amidst her grief, has taken a crash course in spelling, I'd bet my life on the fact she didn't write the words *Do you know this woman? She's pretending to be mum. Track her down ASAP.*

Felicity is sixty-three years old and, cruelly for an artist of some repute, has severe glaucoma and is losing her sight. I expect that is the only reason she hasn't linked me to Leanne Smith, because she preserves her vision for her painting and doesn't read or watch the television. If my livelihood and principal joy in life was being stolen from me, I would also suffer psychologically. All things considered, Felicity is remarkable.

'What do you think?' she asks me.

I smile at her, hoping she can see me. Then I shift forwards in my armchair. I have two squishy armchairs angled slightly sideways on, designed to put my clients at ease. I take occasional notes on a piece of paper attached to a clipboard on my lap. Next to my client's chair is a low glass side table, on which I position a large box of tissues and a vase of whatever flowers are in season. I am careful to ensure the box of tissues is kept well stocked and that the rubbish bin for used tissues is only partially visible under the table. I am diligent about emptying the bin between clients. No one needs to see the tears of the person who came in before them.

'What do you think?' I throw the question back to Felicity because I have lost track of the conversation.

'I think—'

We are both jolted by the ringing of my practice room doorbell.

'Ignore it,' I say. 'I'm sorry.'

'Please don't be.' Felicity is gracious.

One of the main reasons I bought this house was the fact it has a self-contained study, with a separate little foyer and exterior door, enabling my clients to come straight in rather than through my home. Cold-callers and friends ring the front door, which, as it's the other side of the house, is barely audible from the study. It's only my clients who ring on this door.

The doorbell rings again.

'I am sorry. I don't have another client this afternoon, so I'm not sure who it can be.'

'Go and answer it, my dear.'

'No, I don't want to disturb you.'

But the doorbell rings again, and whoever it is keeps their finger on the buzzer just a little too long. I sigh and stand up. 'I'll be right back.'

'No hurry, dear.'

I shut the door behind me and peer through the peephole on the door. It's DS Joe Swain, standing there looking annoyingly handsome in a dark-navy suit. I open the door a fraction and hiss at him, 'I said five p.m. I have a client right now.'

'Apologies for interrupting, Mrs Durrant.'

'It's "Dr Durrant".' I rarely request that anyone uses my title, but as I have a PhD in psychology, it is technically correct.

'Apologies, but I need to speak to you quite urgently.'

'To arrest me?' I spit.

'No.' He squirms a little, and I feel relief ease through my veins. I glance at my watch. Only ten minutes to go until Felicity's hour is up.

'Take a seat,' I say, pointing at the upright chair positioned next to the door, a makeshift waiting area. 'I'll be as quick as I can.'

'No need, dear.' Felicity makes me jump by placing her hand on my shoulder. 'I've had a good week. You're doing an excellent job with me. This gentleman clearly has urgent needs, so please see to him. I've left the money on your desk and I'll see you next Monday.'

Joe Swain's lips twitch at the sides. I bet he loves being described as having 'urgent needs'. I turn to face Felicity and thank her.

'What is it that's so urgent?' I snap at the policeman. 'I don't appreciate being disturbed when I'm seeing clients.'

He bows his head ever so slightly. 'May I sit?' he asks, hovering above the chair Felicity has just vacated.

I nod. He is a tall man and, standing in my office, he makes the room seem insignificant.

'Some things have come to light that I would like to discuss with you.'

'I assume I am no longer a suspect, then?'

'We have formally charged Kevin Smith with the murder of his wife. His prints were found on what is believed to be the murder weapon. Nevertheless we need to establish how you are connected to Leanne and Kevin Smith. Have you had any further thoughts?'

'I've barely thought about anything else. But no, I don't think I am connected to them or Donna and Ricky Wiśniewski.'

‘How do you know about Donna and Ricky?’ he asks sharply.

‘I don’t, other than through some basic online searching.’ I pause. ‘And I saw the Facebook post that was put on Donna’s page this morning.’

‘That’s one of the reasons I wanted to come and see you.’ Joe Swain leans back into the chair, his long legs stretched out so far in front of him, his brown leather brogues almost touch my shoes. ‘We want to be absolutely sure that you have no connection to the family.’

‘No, I don’t. I’ve checked my patient records.’

‘We’ve spoken to our colleagues in Spain, and the Smiths’ belongings are still in transit. As soon as they arrive, we will get a warrant for them to be searched.’

‘That photo of me on Donna’s Facebook page – I think it was taken this morning.’

‘Really? Where were you?’ He leans forwards.

‘On the seafront at Angmering.’ I decide not to tell him the real reason for my visit. ‘The dog likes it down there.’

Joe Swain frowns, then pulls his phone out of his pocket and types something in. ‘I am not happy with the incendiary comments on Donna’s Facebook feed. There appears to be some finger-pointing towards you.’

‘So not only is my reputation in shreds and my business about to be decimated, but I’m now in mortal danger too! Is that what you’re saying?’ I grip the sides of the chair and wonder if it’ll be me reaching across for a tissue rather than one of my clients.

He tilts his head slightly and speaks gently. ‘We have no reason to believe that you are in danger. But we will, of course, keep tabs on the social media activity, and if we believe there is any credible threat towards you, we will take appropriate action.’

I swallow and nod, looking out of the window. I don’t believe him.

Joe continues. 'We will also make sure that your name is kept out of the press and that you are not subjected to any unnecessary intrusion.'

'I assume you know about my past? The fact that I was a forensic psychologist, that my daughter went missing whilst on her gap year, and that my life crumbled?' I don't wait for his affirmation because I know perfectly well that Joe Swain will have done his homework on me. 'And does your file tell you that I'm pretty fearless these days?' He tilts his head to one side, and I add as an afterthought, 'Because I have nothing to lose.'

'Everyone has something to lose, and I have no intention of testing your fearlessness.' He smiles. His teeth are straight and white. This man is so frustrating with his disarming good looks and superior manner. 'However…'

I guess I should have known there was a *however* or *but* coming.

'The photo of you was not left there accidentally. In fact, it was positioned on the deceased's body.'

'Oh God!' Bile burns the back of my throat. 'And what does Kevin Smith have to say?' I ask as I swallow hard.

'He denies ever having seen your photograph.'

'Why didn't you tell me that before?'

'This is a police investigation, and as I'm sure you understand, we only disseminate information on a need-to-know basis.'

I run my fingers through my hair and look away from Joe Swain. 'I want to meet Kevin Smith. Can you arrange that?'

Joe Swain's eyebrows shoot upwards. He shakes his head. 'Why would that help?'

'I'm a psychologist. I can read people, and I know if they're lying.'

'I'm sorry, Dr Durrant, but that would be contrary to protocol. Kevin Smith is in jail on remand for murder. It isn't something I would recommend.' He stands up. 'I'm sorry to have interrupted your work. Please let me know if you find any connection or feel threatened in any way.'

'I will,' I say politely as I fiddle with the ring on my middle finger. But as I watch the policeman leave, I decide I must get to see Kevin Smith. I just need to work out how to convince the police that it is a good idea.

After feeding Mungo and making myself a cup of tea, I'm drawn back to the computer and can't stop myself from checking Donna's Facebook page again. I understand now why so many people are addicted to social media. There is a stream of comments under my photograph, all saying similar things.

Who is this woman?

Did she know ur mum, Donna?

Wud u like us to track her down?

We'll get her for u hon.

She shud have died instead of ur mum.

Let's get her.

I'm horrified. It's as if I committed the murder.

I pace up and down the kitchen. It is easy for Joe Swain to say that I'm in no danger, but clearly I am. Why was my photo left on Leanne's mutilated dead body? Why is there this ever-increasing invective on Facebook, drumming up hatred towards me? These people don't know me, they don't know anything about me. There is no way that I can let this rest; I need to clear my name and I need to feel safe. I'll call Joe Swain in the morning and tell him that he must facilitate my visit to Kevin Smith. Whatever the consequences.

10

Ricky

Ricky doesn't have many friends. He goes along with the banter on the building site, but he likes to keep his head down and get on with the work. It is his singlemindedness that got him the promotion to assistant site manager, and he intends to carry on until he becomes a site manager himself and then perhaps a director one day. Who knows? If he gets his hands on any of the lottery money, he might even set up his own building firm. There's not much Ricky doesn't know about construction.

Most of the guys leave him alone. He'll contribute a bit to conversations on football, but if they talk about cricket or golf or women, he switches off. Now they've got the children, Ricky hurries back home and never joins the lads for a drink after work. Perhaps they resent his stand-offishness; Ricky doesn't care.

If he's going to have a banter with anyone, it'll be Gazza or Mike. He met Mike on his previous job, and he liked the man's attitude. Similar to him, he gets on with work, no nonsense, head down.

They had stopped for a break one morning – Mike for a cigarette break, Ricky for a cup of tea.

'You look knackered, mate,' Mike remarked.

'It's the babies keeping me and the wife up at night. And at the weekends I'm building an extension. I promised her I'd do it, but I'm so wiped out.'

Mike laughed. 'I know what you mean. It caused the break-up of my marriage. I promised her I'd renovate the house, but then we had a kid, and I just never got around to it. She didn't understand. Busman's holiday, isn't it?' Mike's voice tapered off as he looked away and took a drag of his cigarette.

Ricky grimaced. 'Can't let that happen to us.'

'Learn from my mistakes, mate. Keep them promises.'

The two men sauntered back to the screed floor they'd just laid.

'If you ever need any help – at the weekends, that is – I'd be more than willing,' Mike said. 'I only have my boy every other weekend, and most of the time the ex comes up with a reason to cancel that.'

Ricky wondered how much it would cost him. No one ever offered to help for free. But it was as if Mike could read his mind.

'I don't want payment. Just help me land another job when this one has finished. The only way I can see my son more often is to have regular work.'

* * *

Back on the current site of the mansion on the seafront, Ricky is trying to get a grip on himself after the woman asked for him. He recognised her straight away. The woman from the newspapers, the woman Ricky and Donna pretended was Leanne. How the hell has she found him? And more importantly, what does she know?

'I'm sorry about Donna's mum,' Mike says. 'I tried to phone you to see if there was anything I could do, but your mobile's been switched off.'

'I don't want Gazza or anyone here to know. Told him it was my mum that died.' Ricky kicks at a girder with his steel-capped boot.

'Your secret's safe with me, mate. How's Donna doing?'

'Not great.'

'Do the police have any leads?'

Ricky scowls and snaps, 'Do you mind if we don't talk about it?'

A brief look of discomfort flits across Mike's face before he turns around. Ricky feels bad and remembers that Gazza is booting Mike off the site and Ricky will have lost his builder's mate.

'Sorry that you'll be out of work. Have you got anything else lined up?'

Mike turns back to face Ricky. He shakes his head and runs a filthy hand through his shaved fair hair. 'More time for me to help finish off your extension.'

'But the deal was I got you work, and now I haven't got you work. I can't afford to pay you. I'm sorry.' Ricky squirms, thinking of the son that Mike won't get to see.

'You don't need to pay me,' Mike says, looking at his feet. 'You've been good to me.'

Ricky wonders what Mike means. He hasn't done anything out of the ordinary other than ply the man with beer after he helped peg the bricks at the back of the house and dig out the foundations. And he's only been round Donna and Ricky's house twice.

'Nah, it's kind of you, but I can't have you working for no pay,' Ricky insists.

Mike pauses for a moment. 'Would you give me a decent reference?'

'Of course.'

'That's payment enough.'

As various other workers tumble on to the building site and the heavy machines start up, with their incessant beeping, Ricky and Mike turn away from each other and get on with their day's work.

But Ricky can't concentrate. He sees the woman's face, her lank mousy hair and rimless glasses reflected in the steels, shimmering on the horizon of the sea, and as much as he shakes his head, there she is haunting his mind. Other than the fact Ricky knows the woman in the photo isn't Leanne, he has no idea who she actually is and no idea how to find out. And Ricky hates not knowing. He debates asking the police, but he wants to stay away from them. The last thing he needs is the pigs digging into his past. Maybe they already are. The thought makes him break out into a sweat, large patches seeping under his arms despite the cool day. Ricky had thought coming to work would help him take his mind off things, but it hasn't.

In his coffee break he wanders back to the site office and just hangs around Gazza. He wants some of Gazza's no-nonsense mental fortitude to rub off on him.

'You got any phone calls or ordering you need help with?' Ricky asks, thinking that might keep his brain busier than the physical labouring does.

Gazza looks at him askance but doesn't say anything. He hands a phone to Ricky and a long printout. Ricky sits down at the filthy table, picks up a biro and reads through the list of items that need ordering. After a couple of minutes, Gazza says, 'You can go home if you're not up to it.'

Ricky jerks his head up in surprise. He didn't think Gazza was perceptive.

'I'm fine,' Ricky mutters.

At lunchtime Ricky realises he forgot to bring a sandwich. He curses as he watches Mike take a bite out of a white roll filled with ham and tomatoes.

'Have some of mine.' Mike holds out a second roll.

'Are you sure, mate?' Ricky asks.

Mike nods, and when he has swallowed the last bite, he wipes his lips with the back of his hand and says, 'Who was the broad who came looking for you this morning?'

Ricky is taken aback. A piece of bread gets stuck in his throat and he starts coughing violently.

Mike doesn't let it rest. 'Was it the bitch in the photos?'

Ricky nods.

'Do you know her?'

'No. Haven't got a clue what it's all about. They found her photo in my mother-in-law's house and assumed it was Leanne.'

'Shit,' Mike mutters. 'And she turned up here looking for you?'

'Yup.' Ricky doesn't want to talk about it, to think about Leanne and Kevin, but Mike isn't letting the conversation go.

'Are you going to track her down, find out what she wants?' he probes.

'No.' Ricky takes another large bite of the sandwich. It tastes a bit weird, and he wonders if the ham is off or just very old.

'If one of my relatives had been killed in cold blood, I'd be finding out what the hell that stranger wants and making sure the rest of my family is safe.'

It's like Mike is challenging Ricky, telling him he's not man enough, that he needs to get a grip. Ricky feels like hitting Mike, telling him to mind his own bloody business. He chucks the ball of tinfoil into the skip and stands up.

'Thanks for the sarnie, mate. Going for a piss now.'

Normally Ricky spends as little time as possible in the plastic green Tardis-like box, with its filthy black plastic toilet and stench of stale urine, but he needs some space, some time to think. Mike's words have got to him. Perhaps his friend is right – he should track down the bitch in the photo. If she managed to find him, then he'll be able to find her. It's the least he can do for Leanne. And then it strikes him. Perhaps the woman in the photo, the woman who came looking for him, was having an affair with Kevin. Could that be the connection?

By the time Ricky comes out of the Portaloo, he has a new sense of urgency. He'll clock off work early; Gazza won't mind. And he'll track down that woman.

11

Pippa

I have a good practice, with a large roster of private clients, and some months I even have a waiting list. I don't like to see more than seven clients a day. It's hard work concentrating on every word they're saying, picking up on nuances, giving them my full attention. Despite all my training and experience, it takes an emotional toll. At the end of every day I write up my notes on each client, and that takes time. If there are any issues, I write referral letters and touch base with my colleagues and advisor. And then occasionally I have an article or two to write.

Because I earn decent money, my settlement from Trevor was lousy. Divorce is tough, and mine was particularly difficult. The only thing of significance I took away from the tatters of our marriage was Mungo. I had to fight tooth and nail for my beloved dog.

I'm up at seven, let Mungo out, and switch on the laptop as I eat my muesli. Today my diary is even fuller than normal, but I've had four cancellations come in via email. I sigh. It's putting me off my breakfast. There are other emails from clients. I offer an email support package. It's not my favoured form of support, but if someone needs me in between sessions, I would rather it was by email than being bombarded by telephone calls. That used to happen, and it drove Trevor to distraction.

I have had to be strict about cancellations in the past, and unless there are exceptional circumstances, such as genuine ill health or other emergencies, I charge the full fee for patients who forget to, or don't, turn up. I've only ever had one patient point-blank refuse to pay, and decided it wasn't worth going down the debt-collection route. But today it's different. I know exactly why these patients have decided I'm not the therapist for them. If I saw my psychologist's picture plastered across the newspapers, I would also choose to go elsewhere.

This association with Leanne Smith is killing my business. Literally. Overnight. All the years I worked hard to get an excellent reputation, to build up my client list, to become the go-to expert psychologist in Sussex would be for nothing, and I feel utterly helpless. I can't afford not to work. There's the mortgage on the cottage, my comfortable lifestyle, and the large pot that I put on one side for my children, to be used as a down payment on a property for George whenever he decides he wants to settle down, and the money I need to pay the private investigator whom I keep on a monthly retainer in my search for our daughter, Flo, even though I promised Trevor that I stopped employing him three years ago. Not only do I need the money, I need to maintain my reputation. I enjoy being a somebody, a professional, towards the top of the psychologists' tree, called upon for my expert opinion. But most of all I get a deep satisfaction from helping people, making them feel better, supporting them as they unleash their potential and feel fulfilled in their lives. I simply can't imagine never working. If I'm being honest, helping others has helped me redirect my focus away from my own problems. Call me a hypocrite, but I've no desire to wallow in my own grief.

I need to know why my photo was on Leanne Smith's dead body. And I need the media and police to admit they were wrong in allowing my photograph to go to the press. This is a deeply painful conclusion, as yet again my story will be made public, and that is exactly what I have tried to avoid. But most of all, I don't want to have to look over my shoulder in case I'm being watched or about to get beaten to death like Leanne Smith.

And then, *ping*, I get a text from Brent.

He is one of my waifs and strays from my previous life, one of three whom I've kept up contact with. Brent, Joelene and Donny. Back then I did pro bono work for a children's home. Joelene had been in and out of foster care and had seen the inside of a young offenders' institution three times by the age of fifteen. Donny was the only one who kept on the right side of the law, largely because he was so damaged he rarely spoke. He will always be a painfully shy introvert, but these days he has a long-term girlfriend and a good job doing something I don't understand in IT. Joelene has struggled the most of the three; not surprising, as she suffered a childhood of abuse, physical and emotional. She's recently come out of prison for dealing, and despite all the programmes and support, I dread the day when someone from the world of officialdom rings me to say that she's been found dead from an overdose. I'm not her psychologist and haven't been for years, but I am her friend and the only constant in her life.

Brent is the most complicated of the three, but I have a soft spot for him. When he was a young adolescent, there was something angelic about those big blue eyes and tufty hair, so at odds with his behaviour. These days he does alright. After a few years of drifting, he got his act together and went to college. With a qualification in mechanics under his belt, he works in a garage. I keep on hoping he'll settle down, but when I ask if there's anyone special in his life, he does a fine job of changing the subject. I was happy to cut Brent loose years ago, but he was insistent that we keep meeting, so we convene in local coffee shops and have catch-up chats. It's never a therapeutic session. Sometimes I reckon my now grown-up three know more about me than I do about them.

Can we meet up today?

It's unusual for Brent to instigate our get-togethers. Normally I'm the one who contacts him, sending him cards on his birthday, giving him a call to find out how he is. I wonder what's happened to make him reach out to me. He's a proud young man, and despite all the hardship in his life, he never asks for anything. I assume he's seen the photo of me in the media and wants to find out what's going on. With unexpected large chunks of free time in my day, I text him back.

Costa Coffee in Horsham at lunchtime or a drink after work?

He replies immediately. *Tnx. Costa at 1pm.*

And then I regret choosing to meet in a public place. Will I get stared at? Will I be recognised? I debate suggesting he comes to my house but eventually decide against it. Then I make the mistake of checking Facebook. The list of awful things people are saying about me has grown longer, and to my dismay, I notice that Donna herself has commented.

Did she kill ur mum, D?

We'll get her for you. Luv u Dons.

Hope she dies a horrid death 2.

Did you know this woman is a therapist? She's always preying on other people's problems.

Anyone no were she lives??

Bitch.

This cow isn't my mum. RIP mum. I luv u.

I gasp. The abuse has ramped up a gear, and now someone has identified me as a psychologist. And that person doesn't have atrocious spelling or use textspeak like the rest of Donna's friends. It must be the same individual who posted previously. I click on the name: Cindy C. The account was only established on Facebook a month ago, and all the privacy settings are on private, so I can't access any information. A fake account.

The landline rings. It's Joe Swain.

'Just calling to check that everything is alright.' I am surprised by his tone of concern.

‘I’m not happy about all these vitriolic Facebook comments, and I think whoever this Cindy C is, is highly suspicious. Have there been further developments?’ I ask.

‘We are aware of the Facebook comments and will be investigating further. I just wanted to check in with you.’

‘Oh,’ I say. Is this normal? I wouldn’t know. My dealings with the police have been from the other side. It makes me feel very uneasy.

I sit for a while staring out of the window, looking at my simple patch of lawn that is more moss than grass and my bedraggled flower beds, leaves heavy with water from the night’s downpour. When I moved in, I had plans to create a cottage garden full of hollyhocks and delphinium with climbing roses up the back of the cottage and a wisteria gracing the front. But life and work have got in the way, and I haven’t had the money to employ a gardener. My mind wanders to Joe Swain. Has he got a wife who prepares a meal for him at the end of his long days, and a garden that brings him beauty and tranquillity? And why does he seem concerned about me? Is it just because he is a caring man, or does he know something, something that might put me in danger? He is attractive, with a strong jaw and teeth that sparkle against his ebony skin. And then I catch myself. Ridiculous. I am being ridiculous.

I stand up and turn to the dog. ‘Come on, Mungo. Let’s go for a walk.’

* * *

Brent is already there, large rough hands cradling a cup of black tea. He has dark rings under his eyes despite the tanned face. There is something skittish about him as his trainer-clad foot jumps up and down under the table and his eyes scan the room. When he sees me, he raises a hand, and tea slurps over the side of the cup. He scowls, nostrils widening. I haven’t seen him like this in years. The rage he displayed as a boy seems disconcertingly close to the surface.

I buy a cappuccino and an egg mayonnaise sandwich for myself and a chocolate brownie for Brent. He's always had a sweet tooth.

'What's up?' I ask as I place the tray carefully on the table and shrug off my coat.

'Been a bad week. What's with your photo in the papers?'

I roll my eyes, trying to make light of it. I didn't catch anyone staring at me as I hurried from the car park to Costa Coffee. 'Mistaken identity. Tell me what's going on with you.'

'I've found my mum.'

'Oh,' I say. 'I didn't know you were still looking.'

'Never gave up,' he mumbles. 'She doesn't want to know me.'

I lean forwards, placing my palms face up on the table. 'I'm so sorry, Brent.'

'You warned me about this years ago. Dunno why, but I always thought you'd be wrong. That she'd welcome me with open arms.' His laugh is brittle.

'What happened?' I sit back and take a sip of coffee.

'Nothing much. I found her. She told me to go to hell. And that's that.'

'Do you want to tell me more?'

Brent shakes his head. 'Just thought you'd like to know you were right.'

'This is an occasion on which I really wish I'd been proven wrong,' I say gently.

'Yeah, well, it is what it is. What's the connection between you and the murdered lottery woman?'

'None. Or at least I haven't found any connection.'

Brent breaks his chocolate brownie in half and stuffs too large a portion into his mouth. 'What do the police say?'

Crumbs hang at the edge of his lips. I look away.

‘Nothing. They don’t know anything, or if they do, they haven’t told me.’

‘Most exciting thing that’s happened in ages, seeing your photo on the front page like that.’ He smirks.

‘Excitement I could do without. How’s work?’

‘Fine. I’ve met someone.’

‘Oh yes?’ I sit up straighter. Brent has never talked about his love life before. ‘What’s she like?’

‘Lovely. Fragile. Kind.’ He looks towards the window, his gaze softening.

‘I’m so pleased for you,’ I say. ‘Is it serious?’

‘I don’t know. We’re not living together. Not yet anyway.’

‘I hope I’ll be able to buy a hat sometime soon.’

‘Don’t believe in marriage.’

It’s not surprising Brent doesn’t believe in marriage. He hasn’t had any positive role models for the institution of marriage. Considering what he has been through, it never ceases to amaze me that he can hold down a job, that he is articulate, even charming when he chooses to be so.

‘I’m delighted you’ve found someone special,’ I say, smiling.

He rummages in his jeans pocket and removes his phone. It’s vibrating in his hand. He glances at the screen and then stands up, taking a swig of his tea before wiping his mouth with the back of his hand. ‘I’ve got to go.’

‘Oh,’ I say, thinking that I’ve only just got here.

‘See you soon,’ Brent garbles before striding away.

I eat my sandwich, but it tastes of cardboard and I struggle to finish it. Brent was definitely acting strangely. Whilst he’s never been loquacious, today he was unusually uptight. We normally chat about this and that and always set a date for our next get-together. The rejection by his birth mother must have hit him particularly hard.

12

Donna

It's Peekaboo Singalong at the local church hall, Benjie's favourite outing of the week. Kerry hammers on the door at 9.50 a.m.

'Hurry up, Donna. We'll be late.'

Donna yawns as she opens the door. She's wearing her pink tracksuit. Baby Skye is asleep, her head rocking on Donna's shoulder. Benjie has turned up the telly to full volume, watching some animation that is full of screeching animals and high-pitched voices.

'Why aren't you dressed?' Kerry scowls.

'I'm not coming.'

'Oh yes you are!' Kerry tugs little Declan up the step and into Donna's crowded hallway. 'You haven't been in ages, and it's not fair to the kids.'

'Don't tell me what's fair and what isn't!' Donna snaps, turning her back on Kerry.

'It'll do you good. All of you,' Kerry says more gently. 'I'll look after you.' She pats Donna on the shoulder.

Donna wipes the tears from her eyes with the back of her hand.

Kerry moves past Donna and walks into the living room. 'Come on, Benjie! We're off to Peekaboo's.'

'Yes!' squeals Benjie as he rushes out of the room and into the hall, where he jumps up to reach his bright-blue anorak. 'Mumma put coat on!' he says, looking at Donna with big beseeching eyes.

Kerry takes Skye from Donna and with her free hand pops up the collapsible pram stuffed underneath the pile of coats.

'Go and get some proper clothes on. I'll get the kiddies ready,' Kerry urges her friend.

Ten minutes later they are strolling down Station Road. Donna realises it's the first time she's been out – properly out doing something normal – since her mum was killed. It makes her eyes well up, and her throat feels scratchy. Benjie dances along in front of them.

When they get to the red-brick church, with its tall, austere tower, the green side door is closed.

'We're late,' Donna mutters.

'Doesn't matter.'

Kerry parks Skye's pram to the side. She holds the door open for Donna, but Benjie rushes through.

'Wait for Mum,' Donna instructs, but he ignores her and gallops down the dark, vinyl-floored corridor.

'Wait for us!' Donna says more urgently, picking up the sleeping Skye more carelessly than she should, hurrying after Benjie. She can hear all the mothers singing 'The Wheels on the Bus', accompanied by the cute high-pitched voices of the toddlers. There is one low voice. It's rare for a dad to come along to Peekaboo.

The hinges on the door squeak as Kerry pushes it open and Benjie rushes through. Donna hesitates. How will they react to her?

'*The Wheels on the bus go round and round, round and...*'

The voices peter out mid-song. Donna stares at her grubby pale-pink trainers. She can feel eyes on her face. A silence settles on the room.

'Carry on!' Kerry whispers loudly, all cheery, as if everything is normal. But it isn't normal.

Donna looks up and catches the expression of pity on the instructor's face, and she hears whispers that become louder than the singing, and she just has to get out of there. Fast. Donna turns around and stumbles, almost dropping Skye, who wakes up with a start and immediately wails.

'Wait!' Kerry shouts, but Donna isn't going to wait for anyone.

'Mumma!' she hears Benjie screech. 'Mumma!'

Donna flees down the corridor. She grabs the pram with one hand, keeping the baby clutched to her chest with the other. She can hear Benjie crying, but then female voices rise until she can't discern her son's cries anymore. Kerry will look after Benjie. She just needs to get away. Now.

When she is halfway down the street, she pauses and places Skye back into the pram. Tears fall from her cheeks on to the baby's face. Startled by the wetness, Skye stops crying and stares at her mother with a look of bemusement, an expression Donna has never seen in a baby before.

'I'm sorry,' Donna whispers to her baby, stroking the little girl's head, winding her finger around the spattering of curls. 'I don't know if I can be a mummy when I haven't got mine anymore.'

She turns away from the infant and pushes the pram forwards, barely seeing the pavement through her tears, forcing herself to keep moving, keep moving until she is outside number 41 and can collapse inside the privacy of her home.

'Donna?'

Donna squeals. She hadn't noticed the man leaning against the side of the house.

'What are you doing here?' she yelps, wiping her wet face furiously with the sleeve of her cardigan.

'Didn't Ricky tell you?' he asks, frowning.

'Tell me what?'

'That I'm carrying on with the extension whilst he's at work.'

'Why aren't you at work?' Donna sniffs.

'I've been laid off. Here, pass me the pram,' Mike insists as Donna struggles to get the key in the door. 'Have you been crying?'

‘Yeah. Took the little ones to Peekaboo, and they all stared at me.’

Mike sighs. ‘Not surprising. You’ll be the source of their gossip for a few days, and then something else will happen and they’ll forget all about you. You need to ignore idiots like them.’

‘You’re right, I suppose.’ Donna pushes the door open with her backside. Mike follows her in, and when she lifts Skye from the pram, he collapses it and places it neatly in the corner.

‘Would you like a cuppa?’ Mike asks.

It isn’t until they’re both in the kitchen that Donna realises how odd it is that Mike, this almost stranger, is making her a cup of tea in her own kitchen, whilst at the same time she feels at ease with him, even more relaxed than she has been with Ricky over the past few days. She places Skye in her bouncing chair and then sits down at the kitchen table.

‘Where do you keep your cups?’ Mike asks.

She points to the top cupboard above the kettle. He makes two cups and passes her one, but he doesn’t sit down.

‘I’ll be out the back getting on with the extension. I know what it’s like losing someone you’re close to, so give me a shout if you’re feeling down. No point in suffering all alone.’

Mike strides away.

‘Has Ricky been laid off too?’ Donna speaks to Mike’s retreating back.

He pauses. ‘No. Only me.’

‘Did Ricky say we’d pay you? Because we haven’t got any money, and we may never get it.’

Mike turns around. ‘No. I’m doing it because he’s my mate. Mates don’t need paying.’

‘Oh,’ Donna says, and feels the tears welling up all over again. It’s been a while since someone has been really nice to her and Ricky, doing something just because.

13

Ricky

Ricky accepts Gazza's offer of leaving work early, but as he's sitting in the van, he realises the last place he wants to go is home. That woman – the one whose photo they used, the one who turned up at the gates this morning. Who is she? On a whim he calls DS Joe Swain.

'Just the person I want to talk to,' the police officer says when Ricky introduces himself.

'Why?'

'You failed to tell us about your colourful past,' Joe Swain states.

'It's not relevant and a long time ago.'

'I think I should be the judge of that, don't you?'

Ricky considers hanging up on the policeman, but it's as if the officer can read his mind.

'Don't do a runner on me. Why don't you pop over to the police station and we can have a chat? I'm assuming you'd like to keep your wife out of this.'

Ricky shivers. He needs to keep everyone out of it – Donna, Gazza. Especially Gazza. Ricky's worked hard to get his job and even harder to keep it. He supposes he shouldn't be surprised the police have looked into his background, but with Kevin behind bars, he had hoped he would get away with it. After a long pause he agrees.

'Come to Crawley and ask for me when you arrive,' Joe Swain instructs.

The journey north is nothing like the one he took south only a few hours ago. The past weighs heavily on Ricky, the silly mistakes he made in his youth. He's a different person now, and it's bloody unfair that anyone would assume otherwise. If he was a lurid, neon poster paint at seventeen, he's a subdued, sophisticated Dulux today, a family man with strong values. He drives slowly, as if he's trying to prolong the trip to Crawley, where his life might veer off in an altogether different direction.

* * *

Joe Swain seems bigger, an even greater presence than Ricky recalled, now he's in his own environment. The interview room is small and it stinks of stale sweat. Ricky turns his nose up in disgust and wonders whether the policeman has no sense of smell or if he's become immune to it.

'Your father-in-law reckons we should do a bit of investigating into you.'

'Kevin is a murderer and a bastard.'

'He was right that we should investigate you though, wasn't he?'

Ricky slams his fist on the wooden table. 'Is this a formal interview?'

'Would you like it to be?'

Ricky wants to scream, but he knows the games the coppers play, so he looks around the room, takes a deep breath and digs his fingers into his thigh, kneading his muscles through the dense fabric of his jeans.

'I rang you. I came here voluntarily.'

'So you did.' Joe Swain tilts his head to one side. 'What is it you want to tell me?'

'That Kevin Smith's a bullying bastard who couldn't give a toss about his wife or daughter and just wants to get his hands on the money.'

'You've got a criminal record, haven't you, Ricky? I'm wondering why you didn't tell us.'

'It was a long time ago. I'm a different person now.' Ricky glares.

'Aggravated vehicle taking involving an accident causing death is an offence that will never be expunged from your records.'

Ricky bunches his fingers into fists and rubs them into his eyes. 'I know,' he says quietly. 'There isn't a day that goes by when I don't think about it. When I don't regret it.'

'Ah, a man with a conscience.' Joe Swain lets the words hang heavily in the fetid air.

Ricky knows he will be cynical. Everyone is cynical when you've committed a crime like that.

'I served my time. I repented. I'm a different person,' Ricky mutters, and then he leans forwards, elbows on the table. 'I'm here to discuss Leanne and her murder.'

'Indeed you are,' Joe Swain says, straightening up a folder in front of him. 'Could you tell me where you were on the Friday sixteenth of March?'

Ricky lets out a groan. 'I've already told you this. You took my statement, so why do we have to go through it all over again? Besides, you've got Kevin in custody.'

'Quite possibly not for much longer. Can you please just answer my question? Where were you on the sixteenth of March?'

'What do you mean, not for much longer? You're not letting him go, are you?'

Ricky can't stop himself from standing up. How the hell can they let him go? Surely a murderer wouldn't get bail.

'Sit down, Ricky,' Joe Swain says gently.

Ricky does as he's instructed.

'Kevin Smith is very likely to be released on bail. Kindly tell me where you were on the sixteenth of March.'

Ricky can't think straight. How can they let the bastard out? He murdered Leanne! Who knows what he'll do next? Might he go after Donna?

Joe Swain clears his throat, and Ricky notices he's staring at him.

‘As I already told you, I was at work, on the building site down on the seafront at Angmering. I assume you’ve spoken to my boss.’

‘Yes, we have. And after work, where did you go?’

‘I went straight home, as I always do.’

‘Can anyone other than Donna vouch for what time you got home?’

Ricky shakes his head. He can’t remember if he saw anyone. He can’t really remember much about that day. It’s as if the shock of Leanne’s murder has erased all memories of the mundane.

‘I think I saw my mate Mike. I haven’t done anything wrong. It’s Kevin who’s the bastard. Anyway, I thought this wasn’t an official conversation. Are you tricking me?’

‘No, I just want to be sure you’re not withholding any further information that might be relevant to our investigation.’

‘Well, I’m not.’ Ricky is feeling belligerent now. ‘I assume you know Kevin is a wife beater?’

‘Is he indeed?’ Joe Swain raises his eyebrows. ‘And what proof do you have of that?’

‘She was trying to leave him. Leanne wanted to get out of that marriage. With the money she won, she was going away to start a new life. She’d been to see a solicitor to start divorce proceedings.’

‘In Spain?’ Joe Swain leans forwards.

‘Yeah. She wanted to move to Spain. She saw a solicitor here about the divorce.’

‘Did Kevin know that Leanne was instigating divorce proceedings against him?’

‘I don’t know,’ Ricky says, shrugging his shoulders.

‘Did Donna confide in you about her parents’ impending divorce?’

‘No. She doesn’t know. Leanne told me. We were close. I said I’d help her.’

‘And why would you do that?’

‘She’s Donna’s mum, my mother-in-law. She didn’t deserve to be treated like that bastard treated her.’

‘And can Donna corroborate the fact that Kevin Smith abused his wife?’

Ricky is still for a moment. He doesn’t want the police stirring things up with Donna. She’s got enough on her plate as it is.

‘She had bruises,’ Ricky whispers.

‘Did you see these bruises?’

Ricky nods. ‘Am I free to go now?’

Joe Swain hesitates. ‘Would you be willing to testify to that fact?’

‘I don’t want any more trouble for my family than we’ve got. Donna loves her mum, and in her own way she loves that bastard who calls himself her dad.’

‘So you answer is…?’

Joe Swain’s eyes are piercing, and Ricky has to look away. He doesn’t reply. The silence is long and uncomfortable.

Joe Swain breaks it. ‘Exactly how close were you with your mother-in-law?’

Ricky cannot contain the surge of fury. He slams his fist on the table, stands up and shoves his chair backwards so that it topples to the ground.

‘How dare you?’ he screams. ‘How dare you?’ He strides to the door. ‘I came to you willingly and you treat me with total contempt. Next time I’ll have a solicitor with me, so you can stop those filthy thoughts. Let me out!’

Joe Swain shrugs, languidly stands up and opens the door, holding it for Ricky. The men stride in silence, Ricky’s trainers and Joe Swain’s brogues silent as they walk along the carpeted corridor to an external exit. Joe Swain swipes the pass he wears around his neck in front of the electronic panel, and the door clicks open. Ricky gets out of there as fast as he can.

It isn't until he's about to turn the key in his ignition that he remembers the reason for contacting Joe Swain in the first place. The woman in the photograph. The woman who is shadowing him.

'Fuck,' he says, and slams his hand against the steering wheel. *I'll just have to find her myself,* he decides as he drives home too fast, thinking about his Donna and their babies and how he wants to scoop them all up and keep them safe.

Forever.

14

Pippa

Rob calls.

'How are you doing?'

'Other than the fact this tawdry murder is decimating my business and reputation, and I wonder if I'm next in line to be killed, just fine,' I spit.

'I'm sorry.'

'What's up?'

'Would you like to come for supper tonight?'

Under normal circumstances I would leap at the invitation. Rob is the best host, but today I am feeling lethargic and don't feel like being jolly. Besides, the car is nearly out of petrol and I can't be bothered to drive all the way to Hove.

'I'm really tired, Rob. Can I come another time?'

'Um, no. I need you to come tonight.'

'Why?'

'It's important, Pippa. Please.'

I let out a frustrated groan. 'Have you found something out about Leanne Smith?'

'No. Anyway, see you later.'

That was a weird conversation, even for my brother. I run my fingers through my hair and then lean down to give Mungo a hug. He responds by licking my arms. Normally I pull away, but today I let him.

* * *

It's almost half past seven by the time I arrive at Rob's glossy new-build mini-mansion in Hove. The windows are large and framed with anthracite grey set in bright-white walls. Stark and modern, boxy, with sharp, clean lines, it is surrounded by grass so green it looks fake. It isn't. Rob pays for a gardener to tend it to perfection. With such a modern exterior, one would expect the interior to be minimalist, with plenty of chrome and contemporary designer furniture. In fact, it is filled with eclectic antiques that Rob collected during his years of travel to India and South America before he decided being a City banker was a good idea after all.

'Sorry I'm late.'

I give him a kiss on the cheek before hurrying into the house, holding a bottle of red wine aloft. It won't be up to scratch for my wine snob of a brother, but he can pass it on to someone else. I can hear male voices in the kitchen. I wonder if he wants to introduce me to a new lover. I stride through the spacious hall, past the metal-and-glass staircase and along the corridor, pulled in by the scent of fine food.

'Pippa,' Rob says urgently.

But it's too late. I'm in the kitchen, and standing there is George.

My son, George.

I burst into tears.

'That's a fine way of greeting me, Mum,' he says, reaching forwards to pull me into a hug.

I have dreamed of this moment for so long. My son returning, us having a normal mother-son relationship devoid of bitterness or failed expectations.

'Oh,' I say, wiping my eyes. 'Sorry, love. These are happy tears. I wasn't expecting you, and what with everything that's happened this week…'

'That's why George is here,' Rob says. He pulls out a chair and indicates for me to sit down at the kitchen table. 'George was worried about you, and he tipped up here yesterday.'

I want to ask why George didn't choose to come to my house, why he decided to take sanctuary at his uncle's. I want to ask where he's living, what he's doing, but I don't, because I've gone down that route before and it pushed him away.

He looks well does my son. His dark hair is cut short, and unlike the last time I saw him, he is clean shaven, with a light tan. The travelling hippie appears to have been replaced by a conventionally dressed young man, fitting the image I had aspired for him. I blink several times to ensure I'm not hallucinating.

'I saw your photo in the papers,' George says, taking a sip from a tankard of beer. 'I've taken a couple of days off work, wanted to check you're all okay.'

'You're working?'

George rolls his eyes. 'Yes. Uncle Rob helped me get a job at the bank in Geneva.'

I can't process this. Rob has been in touch with George, been helping George, and never said a word to me. And my son is in Geneva, working in a normal job. All this time I have been worrying about him needlessly.

I turn towards Rob. 'How could you—?'

George interrupts me. 'I swore Uncle Rob to secrecy. I'm sorry, Mum, but I needed to clear my head and sort myself out without you and your psychoanalysing. I expect you're angry, but it had to be like that.'

Rob puts a hand on my shoulder. I shrug him away and stand up.

'Can you excuse me for a moment?'

I rush out of the room and dart into the downstairs loo, which is lined in a navy wallpaper depicting branches and golden squirrels. On the wall there is a new exquisite botanical drawing in burnished coppers and gold. I don't bother to switch the light on but sit down and let the tears flow. I can't quite work out if they're tears of betrayal, frustration or relief. I think of Flo and how George was so angry with me after his sister disappeared. Flo was in Cape Town, South Africa, on her gap year. She had a place at

Durham University to study sociology. She was young for her year, so she decided to take a year out, and she signed up with one of those community development programs helping kids in townships. The programme was brilliant and she fell in love with Cape Town and the children, so much so that when the eight weeks were up, she begged us for permission to stay on for another month. Trevor didn't hesitate. I did, but eventually I agreed. Flo stayed on, but she never came home. George blames us for terrible parenting. 'It's all your fault,' he yelled. And then when Trevor left, George swore he would never speak to his father again. I understand my son's anger. Really I do, but it doesn't make it any easier to bear.

After a minute or so, I blow my nose, splash my face with cold water, and pat it dry with a pretty hand-embroidered hand towel. I take a deep breath, come out of the room and walk straight into Rob.

He grabs my hand. 'Don't be angry, Pippa. I did what George wanted to protect you and to rein him back in. It was the right decision.'

'I'm not angry. I'm relieved. Do you think I've got my son back?'

'Come on, dinner's ready.'

Rob has done his normal: bought-in food. Not ready-made meals from M&S or Waitrose, but food prepared by a catering company. It's the sort of extravagant behaviour my brother, who earns too much, thinks is normal. I can't help grinning at the sumptuous platter of salmon decorated with finely sliced pieces of cucumber to resemble fish scales and surrounded by carved pieces of lemon.

'What is life like in Switzerland?'

'I enjoy it. The job's a job but better than I thought it was going to be. I swore I'd never work in an office, but I actually enjoy using my brain.'

George is hiding something. He should know better than to hide things from me.

'Have you heard from Brent recently?' George asks, neatly changing the subject away from himself.

'Yes. I think he's struggling. If you're here for any length of time, you should contact him.'

'I won't have time this trip, but I'll get hold of him when I'm next over.'

Theirs was the strangest friendship and one that I have regretted instigating numerous times. My code of ethics is very clear. Do not mix clients and family. But I did. Brent and George are the same age. When they were fifteen, Brent had been rejected by yet another foster family. I thought that if I gave him a taste of functional family life, it might help him. It was the summer holidays. Trevor was in America on business, and Flo had gone missing a few months earlier, so it was just George and me. He wanted to go camping, but his best friend was abroad, somewhere hot, with his parents. The thought of going camping, just George and me, held little attraction for either of us, so I invited Brent.

There could not have been two different boys. One with no experience of a secure family life; the other whose life was abundant with love, security and money, albeit tinged with grief. One who worked conscientiously at school; the other who rarely attended. I'd be lying if I said it didn't cross my mind that Brent might be a bad influence on George, but I felt it was my duty to give Brent a chance.

To my surprise, the boys hit it off immediately. They bonded over a love of fishing, of all things. The campsite was on the banks of the River Test, and a local angling shop offered starter courses. I signed the boys up. Brent showed a natural aptitude for angling and patience far greater than George's. At the end of the week, Brent became sullen and withdrawn. He broke George's rod. George tried to cover for him, saying it was an accident, but I knew exactly what was going on. Brent wanted to stay with us.

I promised him that he could join us for a week every summer holiday. I kept that promise for a couple of years, but then when Trevor left, Brent said he understood. Both the boys were eighteen by then, too old to be going on holiday with us anyway. When George went off the rails, I blamed Brent. At the time I was angry, but now I know it was largely my fault. I should have set better boundaries.

* * *

We don't make much of a dent into the salmon, but in typical Rob style there are two desserts to choose from: a rhubarb crumble with clotted cream and an exotic fruit salad.

'I'm surprised you aren't obese,' I tease Rob. There's little chance of that, as my brother takes his fitness so seriously, employing a personal trainer who arrives at 5.30 a.m. twice a week to put Rob through his paces in his private gym, built into the cellar.

'I've taken up cross-country skiing,' George says.

I glance up with surprise and have to pinch myself to remember that this is my son. 'Does Dad know you're here?'

As soon as I say the words, I know I shouldn't have. The atmosphere darkens instantly. George's face clouds over. 'No. I don't want to see Dad.' He changes the subject immediately. 'Why was your photo in the papers? Who is the dead woman?'

'I don't know. The police are still investigating.'

15

Donna

'I'm here to take Benjie to playgroup,' Kerry says. Declan is all wrapped up in a fluorescent yellow jacket and is bouncing up and down. Donna nods, relieved that Kerry doesn't suggest that she and Skye come too. She zips Benjie's jacket up and hands him BaaBaa, his bedraggled, greying little lamb toy with its bald patches, furless where Benjie rubs it between his index finger and thumb as he drifts off to sleep.

'You won't lose BaaBaa, will you?' Donna whispers to Benjie as she kisses the top of his head.

'I'll keep a special eye on both of them,' Kerry says, holding out her hand to Benjie.

Donna gives Kerry a tight smile. She stands in the doorway and watches them as Kerry walks slowly down the street, Benjie holding her left hand and Declan holding her right hand. She thinks the uncharitable thought that she's glad Benjie is on Kerry's left, furthest away from the road and idiot drivers, and hopes he'll walk on the inside of the pavement on the way home too. She feels bad for a moment that she might be wishing harm on Declan instead and wonders if that makes her a very bad person. A bad person, bad people – the thought brings to mind Donald Trump, and she wonders what it would be like to go to America and, if they eventually get Leanne's lottery money, whether they might go to New York or even Los Angeles on a family holiday.

Donna has only ever visited two places outside of England: the Isle of Wight, which doesn't really count because it's still the UK even though you have to take a ferry to get there, and Magaluf, where Ricky took her for their honeymoon. She didn't enjoy it much, with all the loud noise and drunks and naked bodies, although she pretended she did. The more she thinks about America, the more she thinks it could be a real possibility. A chance for them to make new, happy memories; a place that is foreign but where they still speak English.

Whilst Skye is happily gurgling on a cushion in front of the television, Donna goes in search of her phone. She is sure she left it in the kitchen, but she can't find it. Instead she takes Ricky's iPad, which is in the drawer of his pine bedside table underneath a packet of condoms, some strips of pills and a packet of tissues. She can't remember the last time she and Ricky had sex, and it worries her. Those magazine articles all say that no sex signals the end of a marriage. She cannot lose Ricky now, not after everything that's happened. Perhaps she should make an effort.

Donna takes the iPad downstairs into the living room, goes on to Google and types in 'America package holiday'. She loses track of time as she browses through all the amazing places they could visit. Going on a Greyhound bus would be fun. She telephones a holiday company.

'I'm interested in a holiday to Florida,' Donna says. And before she knows it, she's booked her and Ricky and the two babies on a holiday, putting the deposit of over five hundred pounds on her credit card, because of course they don't have that sort of money. Not yet, anyway. Yawning, she notices that Skye has fallen asleep. Donna stretches out on the sofa and lets her eyes close.

She wakes with a start. Skye is crying, little hiccup sobs. Confused as to why she is on the sofa when it's daylight outside, Donna sits up and for a moment feels at peace, grateful she has her lovely little family. And then she remembers. Her mum is dead, murdered. Her dad is in jail, accused of killing her mum. Donna's life has disintegrated. She can't help it – she bursts into tears. Pulling herself off the sofa, she leans down to pick up Skye, who is so shocked that her mum is crying that she stops. But that only lasts a moment and then the baby's sobs become screams.

It isn't until Donna hears the knocking on the back door and then a voice calls out, 'Is everything okay?' that she realises they're not alone.

She's confused. It's only been an hour since Kerry went off to playgroup; they won't be back until lunchtime. Didn't she lock the doors? With Skye over her shoulder, she walks barefoot into the kitchen, her heart pounding. But it's only Ricky's friend Mike. She'd totally forgotten that he had told her he'd be back working on the extension this morning.

'Yeah, I'm okay. Sorry. Just having a moment.' Donna wishes she had put on some make-up and that she wasn't wearing her scummy old pink tracksuit.

He stands there, hands in his jean pockets, a tight black short-sleeved T-shirt skimming his rippled torso despite the cold, damp day. Donna feels awkward.

'Would you like a cuppa?' she suggests.

'Only if it's no bother,' Mike says with a grin. His cheeky smile makes Donna wipe away her tears. 'Shall I hold her whilst you make the tea?' Mike asks, tickling Skye under her chin. The baby stops crying and blinks at Mike.

Donna hesitates. The only man to have ever held Skye is Ricky. Even Kevin never asked to hold the babies. But he's nice is Mike, so she hands Skye over, and the little girl puts her clammy hands around Mike's neck whilst he wriggles her up and down.

'You're a natural!' Donna says.

'I've got one of my own,' Mike murmurs, jiggling the baby as he walks around the kitchen. It makes Donna feel more relaxed knowing that Mike is a dad.

'How old are yours?' she asks as she pops the teabags into two chipped mugs.

'Just the one. He's seven. His mum and I aren't together anymore, so I don't see him as much as I'd like.'

'I'm sorry,' Donna says, putting the mugs on the kitchen table.

Mike hands Skye back to Donna, and then he pulls out a chair, sitting at Ricky's place, facing the back door and the window.

'It'll be lovely, this room, when we've built the extension. Your kitchen will be twice the size. Plenty of room for your kiddies to play, and you'll be able to keep an eye on them when they're out in the garden.'

'That's the plan,' Donna says, and then remembers that Mike is helping free of charge. 'It's really kind of you to do this.'

'Your old man is helping me get another job. It's the least I can do.' He takes a sip of tea, and Donna wonders how he can drink it when it's so hot.

They're quiet for a moment and then Mike says, 'Tell me about your mum.'

She gulps.

'That's if it won't upset you too much. From my experience the best thing is to talk about the stuff that's painful. If you keep it all bottled up, it only makes things worse.'

Donna nods. She knows he's right, but it's still a bit weird talking about her mum to this stranger.

'Have you had the funeral yet?'

'No, it'll be a while yet before they release her body. That's what Janet says, anyway.'

'Who's Janet?'

'Our family liaison officer. She's a right cow.'

'Your mum sounds like she was a lovely person.'

Donna wonders where he heard that from. Leanne has been called many things, but lovely isn't one of them. She wonders what Ricky has told Mike. 'Yeah, she was alright. She was Mum and all, so I loved her. I think I'll always miss her.' Donna's throat tightens.

'Do you have any siblings?'

'No. I'm an only. What about you?'

'I've got a sister,' he says.

'That's nice.'

'What was it like growing up? Did you have a nice childhood?'

'Yeah, I suppose so. Mum and Dad used to argue, but he never laid a finger on me.'

'Did your dad hit your mum?' Mike asks sharply.

'No, no!' Donna is embarrassed. She didn't mean to say it like that. 'I know they think my dad killed my mum, but he would never do anything like that. Never. He wouldn't hurt a fly.'

'Why do they think your dad did it?'

'Don't know. DNA and fingerprints, I think. Janet says Dad beat up Mum with a golf club. Dad doesn't even play golf, and now he's locked up in prison. It's not fair.' Donna sniffs.

'Have they set a date for the trial?' Mike has nearly finished his tea.

'No. Janet said it could take months, a year even. They need to collect more evidence.'

'So the police are not sure your dad did it?'

Donna shakes her head. 'They are sure; it's just they're wrong.'

Mike puts his empty mug in the sink. 'Better get on.' He smiles. He's got nicer teeth than Ricky's, Donna thinks.

* * *

Ricky comes home early. Donna is happy to hear his key turn in the lock, and she bounces out into the hall to greet him.

'I've had a great idea,' she says, flinging her arms around his neck and giving him a kiss on his cheek. She doesn't notice that Ricky's jaw is tight and his eyes are narrowed. Ricky doesn't notice that Donna appears almost happy.

‘Come and have a look.’ Donna lets go of his neck and pads bare feet into the living room. She picks up Ricky’s iPad and puts in his security code.

‘How do you know my PIN?’ he asks sharply.

‘It’s 1209 – twelfth of September, my birthday. Always has been.’ She frowns. It never crossed her mind that Ricky might have stuff on his iPad that he might not want her to see. ‘Anyway, do you want to see what I’ve found?’

Ricky grunts. He wonders if it is something to do with that Pippa Durrant bitch. But no. Donna shows him pages of holidays, to America of all places.

‘I’ve booked us a holiday to Florida. We’re going in July! We’ll have the money by then, won’t we?’

It’s the final straw.

‘We’re not going to fucking America!’ he yells.

Donna’s jaw drops. She was sure Ricky would be receptive to the idea.

‘Why?’ she asks.

‘I’m never going to that shithole of a country and neither are you. Besides, we’ve got no money and your mum is dead and your dad is in prison. Not exactly a good time to be thinking about a holiday, is it?’

Tears well up in Donna’s eyes and she shrinks away. ‘I’ve always wanted to go to America,’ she says quietly. Donna glances up at the window that looks out at the backyard. Mike is there, staring at them, but when he catches her eye, he drops the shovel he is holding and turns around.

‘Shit!’ Ricky says, realising Mike must have heard their argument. ‘I’m sorry, love. I know it’s a bad time, but we can’t go to America. You’ll have to get a refund. We’ll go to Cornwall or the Isle of Wight.’

‘But why?’ The tears are back in Donna’s eyes.

Ricky shakes his head. Now is not the time to admit to Donna that he has a criminal record and that he’s not allowed into the United States of America. Donna turns away from her husband and stares at Mike’s back, which is rippling with muscles as he hauls the bricks around. Ricky grabs Donna and pulls her towards him as if he is going to give her a kiss, but she wriggles free and disappears upstairs.

16

Pippa

When I get home, my business answering machine is flashing. I debate whether to listen to the message, knowing it is likely to be another cancellation. But as it's Friday night and I don't practise at the weekend, curiosity gets the better of me.

He speaks hesitantly, with a broad south-eastern accent, pronouncing words that begin with *th* as if they begin with *f*.

'Have you got anyfink free in the next couple of days?' he asks. 'I assume you don't work over the weekend, but if I could have an emergency appointment, I'd be grateful. I'm not in a great place. Can you send me a text message?'

I write down his name, Richard Jones, along with his mobile number.

I don't see clients at the weekend, but as my list has decreased by about ninety per cent this week, I decide to pursue it.

The next morning the doorbell rings on the dot of 10.30 a.m. I have set up the room and have a new client form ready on a clipboard, alongside a glass of water and a box of tissues on the low table next to my patient's chair. I plaster my face with my warm, confident new-client smile and open the door.

'Welcome,' I say, and step to one side to let him in. My hand falls from the door handle, and my heart starts thumping fast. I can't be sure, as I only glimpsed him from a distance, but this man looks just like Ricky Wiśniewski. It's something about his gait, the way he holds himself rigidly, the unsmiling eyes.

He paces into the room, then turns towards me, his arms crossed. 'Do you know who I am?'

I nod. 'I think so. And I think you should leave.'

'No. You need to tell me what the hell is going on!'

I wish I had my mobile phone in my hand; I wish I could call DS Joe Swain right now. I curse my professionalism for leaving my phone switched off on the kitchen table. I can hear the blood pumping in my ears; my breath is shallow and fast. I swallow and try to compose myself. He mustn't know what I am feeling. I smile and take a slow, deep breath to regain control.

'Please sit down.' I gesture to the chair. When he is seated, I sit too, my knees tightly together, my fingers gripping the arm of my chair. 'Are you here to see me in a professional capacity, or has this got something to do with your mother-in-law?'

'Ha, so you do know who I am! Let's be clear, it's me that's going to be asking the questions.' He leans forwards menacingly. 'What do you want with me and my family?'

'Nothing,' I say. 'I don't want anything—'

'Then what were you doing following me to work?'

I let out an audible exhale. 'I'm sorry, that was wrong of me.' I don't intend to tell him that I was a suspect too at that point, and that I was simply looking out for myself. 'Why did you let the police use a photograph of someone who wasn't your mother-in-law?'

He smiles, and it creeps me out. His front tooth is chipped and he has a dark bruise on his index fingernail. There is something inherently unpleasant about this man. Perhaps it's his cold pale-blue eyes, which are too small and positioned a little too closely together. I try to reassure myself that the murderer is behind bars and this man sitting in front of me is more of a victim than me. I try to remind myself that I know about people, I know how they tick, I can read micro-expressions, I know when people are lying. But the more I think that, the more unsettled I feel.

'It was a police cock-up. Nothing to do with us, so what do you want with following me? We're a private family, we are. Leanne didn't want the world to know about her lottery win, and now everyone knows all about her.'

'What was their marriage like, Leanne and Kevin's?'

He leans forwards so much, he is almost out of his seat. I can't help but shrink backwards into my chair. Stupid, really, as I know I should be mirroring his movements to regain control of the conversation.

'That is none of your business. I have told the police everything they need to know. That man is a bastard, a wife beater and a murderer.'

'So why was the photograph of me found at your in-laws' house?' My fingers are digging deeply into the arm of the chair, and my knuckles are white.

'That's what I bloody well want to know from you!' Ricky yells as he stands up and takes a step towards me. 'If you can't answer me, woman, butt out of our lives. You're nothing to us.'

He kicks the side table, and water slurps out of the glass I have left there for him. He takes a further pace towards me, and I am convinced he's about to grab me by the throat. I remember what I said to DS Joe Swain only a couple of days ago – that I am fearless. It was a lie. One can only know fear when one stares into the eyes of death. And right now that is what I am convinced I'm doing.

'Mungo!' I gasp, but my faithful dog is shut in the kitchen behind two closed doors.

Ricky laughs again. 'Mungo?'

'My dog. And he bites.' Mungo has never bitten anyone, and I hope Ricky doesn't catch sight of my soppy black Labrador.

Just as he takes a further step towards me and I am positive that he is going to reach out and throttle me, he steps back and strides out of the room, letting the door slam behind him. I sit for long minutes, listening to the blood pound through my head, waiting for my breathing to slow down, for the fear to slowly dissipate. And then I get up, walk to the kitchen and sit down on the floor next to Mungo's bed. I wrap my arms around his neck and bury my face into his soft fur.

I don't know what to do. I want to call Joe Swain and tell him that Ricky Wiśniewski is threatening me, but if I do that, I will have to admit that I followed him first. I am sure Joe Swain thinks I'm an innocent party in all of this, but if I tell him about my erratic behaviour, then his attitude towards me could change. If the press gets wind of that, then my reputation and career will certainly be over.

17

Donna

Ricky gave Donna the silent treatment after their argument last night. She tried to reach across to him in bed, run her hands down his body, but he had pushed her away and turned over. Donna stared at his bare back and tried to stop the tears from flowing. Her sobs came as little shudders, which Ricky cannot have failed to feel, but he ignored her, pretended to be asleep.

When Donna wakes up, Ricky's side of the bed is empty. She runs her hand across the bottom sheet, but it is cold. Glancing at the alarm clock, she is surprised that it's already 8.10 a.m. Ricky must have got the children up. He may have been in a foul mood last night, but he's a star is her Ricky. She stretches and gets out of bed, padding downstairs. Ricky has made breakfast for the children. Skye is sucking on a bottle of milk, and Benjie is shovelling Coco Pops into his mouth, as good as gold.

'Morning,' Donna says quietly.

Ricky looks up and grunts. Benjie ignores his mum, and Skye babbles something incomprehensible.

'I thought we could do something all together today,' Donna says in a tone much more cheery than she feels. 'Go to the park or the soft play centre.'

'Sorry, I can't.' Ricky takes a bite out of a piece of toast and chews it loudly.

'Why? It's Saturday.'

'I've got an appointment, and this afternoon I expect you'll want me to work on the extension.'

Donna is stumped. Ricky is normally so loving and patient, and since when does he have an appointment that he doesn't tell her about? So much has changed in the past few weeks. Donna can't take it. The tears come again and she retreats upstairs, stumbling on the stairs and throwing herself back into bed, tugging the duvet over her head.

She must have fallen asleep again, because she is woken brutally. Ricky is shaking her. 'You need to get up, Donna. I'm going out.'

'Okay.'

She listens to Ricky's heavy footsteps going back downstairs. The television is on loud, silly little high-pitched voices interspersed by simple jingles. Donna wants to know where Ricky is going, so she swings her legs out of bed and rushes downstairs. Ricky is in the hallway, putting on his jacket.

'Where are you going?'

'Out.'

'Aren't you going to tell me?'

'Just got to do a few errands. Nothing for you to worry about.' Ricky crosses his arms.

'But,' Donna says, and then stops talking. She knows she's needy at the moment, and she knows that Ricky hates weak, clingy women. Ricky often tells her that the fact she stood up to her father made her even more attractive to him.

'I'll be back later and we can do something together. Okay?' Ricky's eyes narrow and a little nerve pulsates in his jaw. Donna takes a step backwards, but Ricky doesn't notice. He's out the front door, slamming it shut behind him. Donna collapses on to the bottom step of the stairs. The carpet is dark red, inherited from the previous owners. It's filthy with stains from spilled drinks and crumbs that haven't been vacuumed up in weeks.

Once again the tears flow. *I've got no one*, Donna thinks to herself. Not even a loving husband. What have I done wrong?

The knocking at the back door is gentle at first but then becomes a little louder. Donna gets up and peers around the kitchen door. Damn. It's Mike. But it's too late. He's seen her looking bedraggled with raw, red eyes, snot coming from her nose, and a T-shirt that shows her large drooping tits. She backs away, but Mike opens the door and walks into the kitchen.

'Come here,' he says, opening his arms. 'Come here and give me a hug. I've never seen anyone who needs one more.'

And Donna does. She walks into his arms despite the fact she's only wearing a thin, short T-shirt with a picture of Snoopy on the front and no underwear. He wraps his strong, wiry forearms around her shoulders. He's taller than her Ricky and rests his chin on the top of her head. It feels weird but somehow right. After a few long moments, her eyes dry and embarrassment settles over her. When her nipples harden, she pulls away and crosses her arms over her chest.

'I'm sorry,' she mumbles, looking everywhere except at Mike.

'Don't be,' he says, smiling. 'It's what friends are for.'

'Mumma!' Benjie shouts over the top of the animated voices.

'Thanks. Gotta go.' Donna turns and scoots out of the kitchen, leaving Mike to make his own way out of the back door.

* * *

It's late afternoon and dark, and still Ricky hasn't come home. Donna has rung his mobile a couple of times, but it goes straight to voicemail. Mike left about 3.30 p.m., knocking on the window and giving her a wave. She blushed as she waved back. It's times like this when she's all alone that she misses Leanne the most. *Everyone needs a mum to talk to*, Donna thinks, and she blinks hard to stop the wave of grief from taking hold. Donna knows it's not good to plonk the kids in front of the TV all the time, but needs must. She tried some colouring with Benjie earlier and they played trains, but now she needs some me time. She goes in search of Ricky's iPad. If America is out, then perhaps they can go somewhere else. France maybe; Kerry had a fun holiday in France last year.

Ricky's iPad isn't in his bedside drawer but half hidden under the bed. It's only because she stubs her big toe on the side of it that she finds the device. She puts in the code, 1209, but the little box just wiggles from side to side. She tries again. *Passcode not recognised.* Donna sits down on the side of the bed and stays very still. Ricky has changed the passcode so she can't get in it. She puts her hand around her neck and strokes it up and down to try to ease away the tightness.

'Oh God, I'm losing Ricky,' she mutters to herself. 'I'll have nobody.'

After a few moments she runs around the house in a blind panic, pulling out drawers, throwing open wardrobes, searching, searching for her mobile phone. 'Where the hell did I leave it?' she yells. She curses to herself, and then finally she opens the drawer in the kitchen where they keep all the instruction manuals and where she normally keeps her phone, and there it is, at the bottom of the pile. With shaking fingers, she turns it on, relieved that there's twelve per cent battery left.

It's a relief to be back on Facebook, scrolling through her messages, remembering that she actually does have some friends, even if they never meet up in person or pick up the phone. She loses herself in a silly animal video, even letting out a simpering giggle as she watches a cat being chased by a mouse. And then her phone pings with an incoming text.

You've been a naughty girl. Better watch out; otherwise I'll tell Ricky. Oedipus x

She clicks on the attached photo and yelps when she sees what it is. It's a bit blurry, but there's no doubt who the couple are. It's a photograph of her and Mike embracing, his arms around her, her T-shirt riding right up so that the bottom of her buttocks are visible, her breasts compressed against his chest. From the angle the photo is taken, it looks like they are snogging.

'No!' she wails. How is it possible that someone got a photo of them? Who was walking past this morning? Was it Kerry? Surely her best friend wouldn't do something like that.

Donna's first instinct is to ring Mike, get him to contact this Oedipus on her behalf, but then she realises she doesn't even know Mike's last name, let alone where he lives or his mobile number. It's totally futile. There is absolutely nothing she can do.

18

Pippa

I spent the rest of Saturday trying to build up profiles of the Smith family. It was easy enough to find out about Donna because she's all over social media. Ricky, her husband, was a bit harder to track, but I noted down everything I could remember from our unpleasant meeting: his words, the micro-expressions that I could recall, the lies I thought he told, his body language.

It was nigh impossible pulling together profiles for Leanne and Kevin Smith because neither of them were on Facebook or LinkedIn or any other social media sites. Neither were company directors or attended parish council meetings or gave money to charitable causes or applied for planning permission. Or if they did, I couldn't find evidence. Of course, their commonplace names didn't help matters, but by the end of the afternoon I reckoned I had exhausted my online secondary research.

* * *

After a fragmented night interspersed by nightmares, I'm woken by Mungo nudging me with his nose, one paw on the bed. He's not allowed to do this and being a typical eager-to-please Labrador, rarely misbehaves. I sit bolt upright in bed.

'What is it, Mungo?'

When I glance at the alarm clock, I know exactly what the problem is. It's 9.50 a.m., nearly three hours later than the time I normally wake up. The poor dog must be starving and desperate to go outside. That's what happens when I stay up too late, can't get to sleep, and take a sleeping pill at 4 a.m.

After feeding Mungo and letting him out into my small garden, I put the kettle on and switch on my mobile phone. There's a message from Brent asking whether I would like to go for a walk with him and Anna, his new girlfriend. They'll be passing through Storrington around 11.30 a.m. for a walk on the South Downs. I smile. Mungo will love that, and I am delighted that I'll get the opportunity to meet the significant other in Brent's life. Although I met his foster parents over the years, he has never reached out to me on a social level. I've tried, telling him stories about my own life, laughing about Mungo's antics, about the distance I have with George, but Brent doesn't share easily. I text back:

Yes, would love to. Will you come to mine, or shall I meet you somewhere?

We'll come to you. What's your address?

I have forgotten that Brent has never been to this house. How things have changed now I have my private practice working from home. Back in the days when I volunteered for the children's home, security was paramount, and I would never share my personal details, but these days the type of patient I treat tends to be educated, middle class, socially normal. No threat to me.

As I come out of the shower, my landline rings. Hair dripping wet and clasping a towel around me, I dash to answer.

'Hi, Mum, it's me.'

My heart leaps.

'Have you seen the papers this morning?'

'No.'

'Maybe don't look. Anyway, I'm flying back to Geneva tonight. Would you like to have lunch? It'll have to be an early one, as I need to get to Gatwick.'

'Yes, George. I'd love to.'

We agree to meet at a lovely country pub that serves hearty Sunday roasts, and when I put the phone down, I do a little jig around my bedroom. I don't care what the newspapers say about me! I've got my son back, and that's all that matters.

I know it's silly being unable to decide what to wear to meet my grown-up son, that it's vain to spend too long carefully applying make-up to my middle-aged face, but that's what I do. George has been distant to me for so long that I am desperate to make this right. To restore our relationship to one of ease, where I am not overbearing or threatening or needy but relaxed and happy and normal. As I double-check myself in the mirror, tucking in my plain white shirt and adjusting the simple silver necklace with the solitaire diamond that Trevor gave me for our tenth wedding anniversary, I let out a sigh. Normality hasn't featured for many years, or at least, not the normality I had envisaged for our family.

I am about to race out of the door, collecting Mungo's lead, when I remember that I was meant to be going walking with Brent and Anna. Damn. I find Brent's number and call him, but it goes straight to voicemail. I leave a quick message apologising that I'm going to have to cancel because George has come home, asking if we could rearrange for another weekend and wishing them a lovely walk. And then I lock the doors and open the car boot for Mungo to jump in, and off we go.

The Duck and Pheasant Inn is a quaint Sussex pub located in the heart of the countryside down roads overhung with tree branches and, at this time of year, banks of primroses. We used to go there often when we were a family of four. The kids would clamour up and down the complex wooden play equipment, and Trevor and I languished over long lunches, a few pints of beer for him and a small glass of white wine for me. I haven't been for years, and the inn has changed. It's gentrified now, with hanging baskets and a blackboard listing the daily specials written in fancy calligraphy. Inside, the walls are painted in a pale-blue grey, and the beams that were once blackened and a little oppressive have been sandblasted to their natural oak colour. The staff wear starched grey linen aprons.

The car park is almost empty; not surprising, as it's only just noon.

'Can I help you?' The young waitress has frizzy blonde hair piled on top of her head and a slash of pale-pink lipstick on an otherwise make-up-free face. I glance around but can't see George, so I ask for a table for two near the windows that look out on to open fields.

As I follow her to the table, I catch the eye of an older man, paunchy with a closely shaven auburn beard – the maître d' perhaps – who stares at me before glancing down at a table to his left on which there is a stack of newspapers. My heart sinks. Surely they haven't printed my photo again.

I debate asking the waitress to bring me one of the newspapers but decide that what I don't know can't hurt me, and today it must be all about George. So I keep my eyes firmly on the menu, wondering whether George will choose what used to be his favourite meal: roast beef and Yorkshire pudding.

'Hello, Mum.' George bends down and gives me a kiss on the cheek. He's holding a plastic bag stuffed full of newspapers, but it isn't the bag that captures my attention, it is the young woman hovering behind him.

'This is Marie.'

'Hello.' She extends her hand, but I can do nothing except stare at her enormous belly, then up at her face and back to her vast bump.

'You're pregnant,' I mutter, and then remembering that I promised to be normal towards George, I get up, plaster a smile on my face and say, 'Lovely to meet you.'

George drags a third chair to the table, and once Marie sits down and her pregnant stomach is largely hidden from view, I can't take my eyes off her face. Is it the aquiline nose that is elegant but a little too big for her face, or the grey almond-shaped eyes, or the tumbling dark curls? I can't work it out, but what I know for sure is that this young woman looks disconcertingly like Flo, and it pierces my heart. Perhaps I shouldn't be surprised that George has fallen in love with a woman who looks uncannily like his sister, or at least how I imagine she would look in her mid-twenties, but nevertheless I am flustered. I can't get my words out and my cheeks feel as if they're burning.

George sits down next to Marie, flinging his arm across the back of her shoulders.

'You're going to be a grandmother, Mum,' he chirps.

'So I gather.' I pause. 'Congratulations to you both.'

I want to ask whether they're getting married, how long they have been together, whether the baby was planned or a shock, and say that, goodness, I didn't think anyone had children under the age of thirty these days. But instead I just sit there and grin at them inanely.

'I promised Marie that our child won't have psycho genes and that you're nothing to do with this dead lottery winner, but it's difficult not to believe what the papers say.'

He pulls out a pile of newspapers from the carrier bag and passes them across the table. The Sunday papers are turned to the pages with articles about me. Small mercies, I'm no longer front-page news, but the headlines on the articles are still chilling:

The Mystery of Murdered Lottery Winner Leanne Smith and Reclusive Psychologist Philippa Durrant

Is Shrink Philippa Durrant a Fraud?

Get Out of Our Lives, Says Family of Dead Lottery Winner

I grab on to the edge of the table as a wave of nausea grips my insides.

'Are you alright, Madame Durrant?' Marie's eyes are wide as she leans across the table towards me.

'Yes. Sorry, it's just a shock.'

'I thought you said the police were going to sort this out, keep your name out of the press.' George scowls.

'I thought that too.'

'You'll need a good lawyer.' George leans backwards and tips his chair on to its rear legs. When he was a kid, it used to terrify me how he balanced so far back. I was always waiting for the chair to slip to the ground and for George to break a bone or two, but fortunately it never happened.

'I know a couple of people who might be able to help.'

All I can think about is how George has morphed into his father, in control and sensible. It seems inconceivable that he went through a happy-go-lucky hippie phase so very recently.

'Have some water.' Marie moves a glass towards me. She has a charming French accent.

We talk, or at least George does, with a few words interjected by Marie, and I suppose I listen, but nothing sinks in. All I can think about is Leanne Smith, Ricky, and how something that happened to a family totally unconnected to me is, within the space of just a few days, destroying my life. This moment, the one where I reconnect with George, was a moment I had dreamed about for so long, and it is being ruined.

They decline coffee or pudding. George looks at his watch. 'We've got to go; otherwise we'll miss our flight.'

'Eet was a pleasure to meet you, Madame Durrant.' Marie smiles at me as George helps her stand up.

'When did you say the baby is due?' I ask as George shoves the newspapers back into the carrier bag.

'I didn't,' he says tightly. 'You didn't ask.'

'I am sorry. I'm so sorry,' I say, putting my face in my hands. 'I am very distracted at the moment.'

'We'd noticed.' George rolls his eyes. 'See you, Mother.'

I lean forwards to kiss him, but he takes a step backwards and I balance precariously in thin air. Marie puts a hand out to steady me.

'Take care,' I say with surprising vehemence. 'Take care. Both of you.'

Marie turns and gives me a weak smile and a little wave. George doesn't turn but puts his hand on Marie's back and propels her away from me. As I watch them leave, I feel a deep terror. A terror that I might never see George again. I can't work out if it is because I am afraid for him, or just afraid that I have totally failed in our big reunion, and this time I won't be getting a second chance, and I may never meet my grandchild.

19

Donna

When Donna wakes up, her face is wet with tears and Ricky is cradling her in his arms, stroking her forehead, saying shush as if she is a baby. Her first thought is, *Why am I crying?* Then she remembers the dream. Both Leanne and Kevin were lying prone on their living room floor, bullet holes in their foreheads, blood pooling across the carpet. She – Donna – was holding a gun. Her second thought is one of relief. Ricky is home, and not only is he home, her caring, loving husband has returned.

'Had a bad dream,' she says, sniffing, although the dream isn't so far off reality.

'I know. You were calling out.'

Donna wipes her eyes and tries to settle her pounding heart. The air smells fetid; it's Ricky's breath, the stench of stale beer. Donna lights up her alarm clock. It's 4.56 a.m.

'Go back to sleep,' Ricky says, groaning as he turns over, his back towards her.

'I've got to get up in an hour.'

'Why?' His voice is languid, as if it is oiled and the muscles in his mouth are so relaxed he can't form proper sounds.

'Visiting time at the prison. I'm taking the kiddies.'

Ricky sits bolt upright and it startles Donna.

'No, you're bloody not!'

'Yes, I am. Janet's fetching us and driving us there. You don't have to come if you don't want to.'

'I forbid it!' Ricky spits.

Donna frowns in the darkness. She can't recall Ricky ever forbidding anything in the past. 'He's my dad and I want to see him. He's got no one else.'

'Absolutely not. And why didn't you discuss this with me?' Ricky switches on his bedside table lamp. It blinds Donna. She buries her face in the pillow.

'You weren't here yesterday afternoon when Janet Curran called. She said I can visit Dad three times a week for an hour a time, but as the prison's so far away, I won't be able to go that often. If you'd been here—'

Ricky slams his fist on the bed just inches from Donna's head. 'Kevin is a murderer. Have you forgotten that he murdered your mum? You are not going, and that's the end of that.'

He swings his legs out of bed and stomps out of the room. A couple of minutes later, Donna hears the loo flushing. She hopes it won't wake the babies.

'He didn't murder Mum,' Donna says, sobbing silently into her pillow. 'Dad would never do anything like that.' The dream comes back to Donna, and she sees both her parents dead on the floor; she sees the gun in her right hand, and it makes her wonder: was she responsible for any of what has happened?

* * *

When Donna wakes up, the sun is pouring through the gap in the bedroom curtains, and she can hear voices downstairs. She tries to make out who they are, and when she realises it's Janet Curran talking to Ricky, she jumps out of bed and pulls a sweatshirt over her T-shirt and tugs on the pair of jeans crumpled on the floor.

I'm going to miss visiting hours, she thinks. *Hurry. Hurry*. She finds her handbag, but just as she is rushing downstairs, the front door slams and all she can hear is Benjie's high-pitched voice in the kitchen.

'Has she gone?'

Ricky looks up. He's feeding Skye. 'Yup. I told her you're not going.'

'But I am!' Donna races to the front door, opens it and peers both ways down the street, but she can't see Janet and she can't see any car driving away. Leaving the door open, she runs back to the kitchen. 'Where is she?'

'Calm down, Donna.' Ricky puts Skye's spoon down on her tray, and the baby grabs it and throws it to the floor, splattering the already-sticky lino with pureed apple. 'I explained to Janet that it isn't appropriate for you to visit Kevin. That you don't want to see him.'

'But it's not true. I do!' Donna slumps down on the chair next to Benjie. 'He's my dad,' she whispers.

'Cheer up, Mama,' Benjie says, peering at her and sliding his empty bowl of Coco Pops towards her.

It's all too much for Donna. She jumps up and runs out of the house, not thinking about where she is going or what she is doing, but just knowing she needs to escape before she explodes. Tears blur her vision. And then she slams straight into someone.

'Whoa! Are you alright?' Mike holds Donna by her shoulders and peers down into her face. 'Obviously not,' he says, his brow creased with concern.

'Just need to get away,' she says, sniffing. 'Sorry.'

'Would you like to go and get a coffee?'

'Um, yes. No. I don't know.'

'Come on.' He grasps her arm and steers her towards town. 'I think you need a friend.'

Donna runs her fingers through her bedhead hair. She knows she looks terrible, and how she wishes that Mike wasn't seeing her like this: make-up free, red-eyed, scruffy clothes and once again no bra.

There's a little greasy spoon café around the back of the station that Donna has passed numerous times but never been inside. It's normally frequented by workmen, and she's surprised it's even open on a Sunday morning. Mike steers her in.

'Tea or coffee?' he asks, pulling out a chair for her at a little table near the back.

'Tea, please. White, no sugar.'

Mike nods. Donna looks around and wonders if they've got a toilet, where she can go and put some make-up on, assuming she's got any in her bag. But she can't see any signs. Besides, Mike is quick, returning with two cups of tea and a couple of doughnuts. They're the only people in the café other than the ball-shaped waitress lounging behind the counter, who appears to be more interested in reading *The Sun* than listening in to their conversation.

'Do you want to tell me what's going on?' Mike leans forwards as if to put his hand over Donna's, but to her disappointment he pulls it away at the last moment.

'Other than my mum's been murdered, my dad's in prison, and my husband is…' She pauses. She cannot be disloyal to Ricky. Ricky has always been there for her – up until now, at least – and besides, this man is a friend of Ricky's. Who knows what he might tell him?

'Ricky is…?' Mike probes.

'Nothing. I'm just pissed with him because he doesn't want me to visit Dad.'

Mike chews the inside of his mouth and takes a sip of boiling-hot tea. 'Kind of makes sense. He's just trying to protect you.'

Donna nods. 'We've all been under a lot of stress. And I miss them terribly.' She swallows hard. 'We used to go to their house every Sunday for lunch. Mum does roast chicken.' She looks at the large blackboard on the wall listing all the items on the menu and reads through them slowly: eggs; eggs and bacon; eggs, bacon and tomatoes; eggs, bacon, tomatoes and toast; eggs, bacon, tomatoes, toast and beans. 'Mum *did* roast chicken,' she corrects herself.

‘I wish I could make things better for you, Donna,’ Mike says.

‘Aw, that’s really sweet.’

Donna isn’t sure what’s going on here, but she knows she shouldn’t be thinking the thoughts she is. She wishes Mike would pull her into his arms again. She looks at those lips; they’re thin with a distinct Cupid’s bow, unusual for a man, and she imagines his tongue, and then—

‘What do you think?’

Donna shakes her head. She didn’t hear what Mike has just said, but she knows she has to get out of the café as quickly as possible before she does something very, very bad, which will destroy the only family she has left.

‘Are you helping Ricky today?’ she asks.

‘What?’ Mike screws up his eyes. Donna realises her question is a non sequitur, but she needs to get away from this conversation and go home. Fast.

‘Are you helping on the extension today?’

‘I was going to, but I thought that you and me could—’

‘Sorry, gotta go. Thanks for the tea and the doughnut.’ She considers picking up her uneaten doughnut and taking it home for Benjie, but then she’d have to explain to Ricky where she got it from, so she just stands up, gives Mike a little wave, and runs out of the café, not stopping until, totally out of breath, she collapses on the doorstep.

20

Pippa

There are a few books that have changed my life. The first was a little pamphlet given to me by my grandmother when I was eleven or twelve years old. It was an unattractive orangey brown with a bold title: *Understand Personality Through the Science of Graphology*. It lay in a drawer for a few years, and I must have stumbled across it at the age of sixteen or seventeen when I was going through a period of introspection, troubled by a lack of boyfriends and the bitching of girlfriends. Perhaps if it hadn't had the word *science* in the title, I might have read it earlier. In those days psychology wasn't a subject that could be taken at A level, so I waited until I got to university to read history and promptly changed courses to psychology.

Over the years I studied everything that could turn me into an expert people reader, accumulated qualifications, and immersed myself in every new technique that was developed. I used that knowledge when I was a forensic psychologist. Today it's not so relevant to my professional practice, but I carry on learning for me. It gives me the confidence to pursue my chosen profession.

I may be able to help others, but I find it almost impossible to help myself. After leaving The Duck and Pheasant Inn, I return home and sink into an apathy I haven't experienced for a long time. I debate calling Rob, but I'm angry with him for lying to me about my son. I pour myself a large gin, lie down on the sofa and turn on the television. When I wake up, Mungo is snoring on the floor at my feet. Outside, the light is beginning to fade, and I have a raging headache. The phone rings, and with my head pounding, I can't be bothered to answer it. But when it rings again immediately after stopping, I sigh and stagger across the room to find it.

'Yes?'

'Madame Durrant, this is Marie.'

'Is everything alright?'

'*Non.*' She is crying, little hiccups that she can't seem to control.

'What's happened?'

'George' – she pronounces his name with a soft *j* sound – 'George is in ze hospital. And I…Ouch!'

'What is it?'

'Baby ez coming.'

It sounds as if she has dropped the phone. I can hear muffled voices, noises; I can't make out what they are saying.

'Marie!' I yell. 'Pick up the phone! Where are you?'

'Hello?' She has a lilting Scottish accent.

'Who is this?'

'I'm a nurse at East Surrey Hospital, in Redhill. Who am I talking to?'

'Pippa Durrant. I'm George Durrant's mother, and Marie is…' I realise I don't even know her surname. 'Marie is having my son's baby. My grandchild.' I can't believe that I am saying those words.

'Marie is safe. She's having some Braxton Hicks, and we're just checking to see if the baby is on the way, but we doubt it.'

'And George? What about George?'

'He's currently in the operating theatre. We'll have more information soon.'

'What's happened?' I shriek.

'I believe there was a car accident. They've been brought in by ambulance, and Marie is being transferred to the maternity ward.'

'Is he going to be okay?' I whisper as tremors course through my body. I cannot lose George. I cannot!

'My understanding is that the injuries aren't life threatening, but I'm afraid I don't have any more information at the moment.'

'I'm coming!' I say. 'I'll be there as soon as I can.'

* * *

I drive like a lunatic, weaving in and out of cars, speeding through amber lights, and then, as I am racing up the A24, flashing my lights at any car in my way, hand liberally slamming the horn, I hear a siren. A police car is on my tail, shining its light at me, the siren piercing my already-sore head.

'Fuck!' I yell as I indicate to the left and pull over on to the hard shoulder. I stay in the car, shaking, the seat feeling hot and slippery under my legs. I wonder if they'll breathalyse me. Am I over the limit? I only had one gin earlier, didn't I? I can't remember now. Does my pounding headache suggest I'm drunk?

As the policeman walks up to my window, I open it.

'Please get out of the car.'

I do as I'm told. I feel truculent, like an angry child.

'Could you explain why you were driving well over the speed limit at over eighty-four miles an hour?'

'Yes. My son is in hospital in the operating theatre, having had a car accident, and his fiancée is giving birth to my grandchild. I've got to go!' I open my hands out.

He nods. No doubt he's heard all sorts of excuses for erratic driving. I wait for him to comment that I should know better; that if my son had a car accident, shouldn't I be showing extra vigilance? But he doesn't.

'Please show me your driving licence.'

I lean back into the car, grab my bag and fumble around in my wallet, eventually producing my licence. I assume he recognises the name, because he does a double take, peering at me with narrowed eyes and then glancing back at the card.

'Wait here.'

I put my hand in front of my mouth and discreetly blow out through my mouth, trying to smell my own breath. I can't tell if I reek of alcohol. I find an old packet of half-eaten mints in my bag, quickly unwrap one and chew it hard. I pray he isn't going to breathalyse me.

The policeman returns to his car, and I watch him in my rear-view mirror. I can see that he is on the phone to someone; he's gesticulating. And then he gets out of the car again and walks, a little more slowly this time, towards me. He's young enough to be my son, a nice-looking boy with a square jaw and tight milk-chocolate-coloured curls.

'If you would like to lock up your car, we will leave it here, and I will drive you to the hospital.'

'Really?' I am flabbergasted. He puts a sign on the windscreen of my car that says 'Police Aware', and then I follow him back to his vehicle.

'Get in,' he says, gesturing at the front passenger seat. I wonder for a moment whether this is a catch and I am under arrest. The police don't normally do this, do they? He pulls away from the lay-by, driving at a steady speed but always within the speed limit.

'DS Joe Swain will meet you at the hospital,' he says. His nose twitches.

'Oh,' I reply.

'Can you find out anything about the car accident my son was in?' I ask.

He shakes his head and doesn't say another word until we arrive.

It takes too long to get there. In the thirty minutes or so of the drive, my mind has played all the what-if tricks in the book. What if George is dead? How could I lose two children? Am I really the world's worst mother? What if he is severely disabled; will Marie stick by him? Could I adapt the house to meet the needs of someone in a wheelchair? And is the baby okay? Should I ring Trevor, or have the police already contacted him? Will George be livid with me if I reel in the father he doesn't want to see? I do exactly what I tell my clients never to do: envisage all the worst-case scenarios and play out in my head how I will react if I'm faced with them. By the time we pull up in front of the hospital, I am exhausted and close to having palpitations.

Joe Swain opens my car door. It is a relief to see a familiar face.

'Thank you. I'm so glad you're here,' I murmur.

He gives me a tight hint of a smile. And then I wonder, why is he here? What has George's accident got to do with DS Swain's murder case? I stand still, and people mill around me: people hurrying into the hospital; a woman dressed in a blue-and-white hospital gown puffing hard on a cigarette outside the entrance; a man in a suit shouting into his mobile phone; a young woman wearing psychedelic harem trousers with dreadlocked blonde hair sobbing quietly.

Joe Swain must realise that I'm not following him, because he stops and turns around and walks back towards me.

'Is George okay?' I whisper.

'I don't know, but I think he will be. Come with me.' He holds out his hand but quickly retracts it, putting it into the pocket of his dark-grey trousers. We walk along a short corridor devoid of people, which seems to be an administrative area of the hospital rather than clinical, and then he opens the door to a room with the sign '1.02'. It's a small room with two wooden chairs and a low wooden table. I can barely breathe, and I shiver under the blast of cold air conditioning.

'Please sit down, Pippa.'

He hands me a plastic cup filled with water; I don't notice where he produced it from. As he sits down, he inhales and says, 'We think George's car was run off the road deliberately.'

'What?' I say, gasping.

'There was an eyewitness, and it appears that this was a deliberate attempt to cause harm. My colleagues are interviewing the witness.'

'How did you know that George is my son?'

Joe Swain gives a quick smirk. 'We do have a bit of joined-up thinking here.'

I nod. 'Why would anyone want to drive George off the road? He doesn't even live in this country.'

Joe Swain's dark, bushy eyebrows rise.

'He's living in Geneva. I only just found that out this weekend.' He tilts his head to the left but doesn't say anything, so I stumble on. 'I've been estranged from George for a while, and he came back this weekend. So I have got something to thank the Smiths for. He saw my photo on the news.' I take a sip of water and almost choke. 'This hasn't got anything to do with them, has it?'

Joe Swain sighs and leans back in the chair. 'We don't think so, but we need to explore every angle. If he's living abroad, it does explain why your son was driving a hire car.'

'They were on their way to the airport. Going home. The reunion didn't go so well.'

'I'm sorry to hear that.'

He looks genuinely sorry, and I wonder if he has children of his own.

'Please, I need to see George.'

'Of course.' He stands up. 'How are you coping with the media interest?'

'I'm not, and you need to make it all go away. It's a nightmare and ruining my business.'

He nods but doesn't say anything. I follow him back into the corridor and then get confused as we walk along a maze of corridors before climbing up a flight of stairs. There is a reception desk with several nurses behind it: a couple on computers, one on the phone, another leafing through a binder. A nurse with short bright-red spiky hair dressed in a dark-blue uniform looks up at us. Joe Swain holds out his police badge.

'George Durrant. Is he still in the operating theatre or in ICU?'

The nurse types something into the computer. 'Still in theatre.'

I try to contain a sob. 'Who will let me know how he is?'

She looks at me, an expression of sympathy passing over her worn face. 'The waiting area is over there. Have a coffee, and one of us will come and find you as soon as your son is out of theatre.'

'And Marie? Where's the maternity ward?'

The nurse looks confused.

'Don't worry.' Joe Swain flutters a hand towards the nurse. 'We'll go to the maternity ward now and see how Marie is doing. Nurse, please, can you call me if you have any news?' He passes her a business card.

The maternity ward is at the opposite end of the hospital. Security is tight, and a nurse looks at us askance as we stand at the entrance door. DS Swain shows his police identity card.

'We're here to find out about Marie.' He turns to me. 'What's her surname?'

'I don't know.' I shrug my shoulders. 'She's Swiss, French-speaking Swiss.'

'Ah yes, the young lady who came in after the car accident. She's doing well. Braxton Hicks have slowed right down, and other than a few cuts and bruises, she's fine.'

'And the baby?'

'Baby's heartbeat is strong and regular. There's no reason to worry.'

I let out a loud sigh of relief, already caring about this girl I've barely met and the grandchild I didn't know I was going to have until a few hours ago.

'Would you like to see her?'

I nod. We follow the nurse down a corridor, where I try to block out the screams of mothers in labour and the shrill wailing of babies. Joe Swain grimaces as he looks back at me to check I'm following.

'Here she is!' The nurse swings open a door, and Marie is lying on a bed in a small single room. She is ghostly pale; her eyes are red and sore.

She bursts into tears when she sees me, and I rush to the bed to hug this woman with whom I feel an immediate bond.

When we have both composed ourselves, Joe Swain clears his voice.

'If I may, I'd like to ask you some questions.' He takes out a little notebook and pen from his jacket pocket.

Marie nods, placing her hands protectively over her vast stomach.

'Do you remember what the vehicle looked like that pushed you off the road?'

'It was white. *Un fourgon blanc.*'

Joe Swain frowns.

'A small white van,' I say. In other circumstances I would be proud of my linguistic skills. And then I recall what I have just said and repeat it again. 'A small white van.'

'Did you get any of the number plate?' DS Swain peers at Marie.

She shakes her head.

'This is consistent with what the witness saw. A small white van. Unfortunately we don't have a number plate, but we will scour the cameras from the locality.'

I can feel myself quivering now; my teeth start chattering.

'Are you alright?' Joe Swain frowns with concern.

'Ricky Wiśniewski. Ricky drives a small white van,' I say.

Joe Swain pauses, then stands up.

'Excuse me,' he says before leaving the room.

21

Ricky

Ricky is livid. He wanted to go out, have a session down at the gym, and then chill in front of the football on the telly with a beer or two. Once the game had finished, he was planning on going out the back, mixing a bit of concrete, and carrying on with the bricklaying. Perhaps Mike would join him. But Donna has stormed out, and now he's been left to look after the children.

He supposes he was a bit harsh with her, coming across as angry when she'd said she wanted to visit her dad in prison. But he knows Kevin. The bastard will try to twist things and will convince Donna that he is the injured party, the innocent victim in a potentially massive miscarriage of justice. He'll twist things so that Donna will provide an alibi for her dad, not realising she is being played. Kevin always plays Donna.

For the first few years, he assumed Leanne was like Donna and thought the sun shone out of Kevin's flabby backside. Ricky learned not to say too much and never criticise Kevin in front of Donna or Leanne. It wasn't difficult for him to keep his thoughts to himself; he'd been doing that as a matter of self-preservation for most of his life.

He liked Leanne. She looked out for Ricky, asking for his opinion, deferring to him on pretty much every topic. 'Ricky knows best,' she said to Donna time and time again, even when Ricky knew he didn't know best. In the early days of his relationship with Donna, he thought of Leanne as the mother he didn't have. But that changed about eighteen months ago.

Ricky had a toothache. The pain was horrendous: bone crunching, throbbing and sometimes searing up the side of his face. He'd never felt anything like it. Donna wasn't that sympathetic.

'Don't be a wuss,' she'd mocked. 'You don't know pain if you haven't experienced childbirth.'

That evening she was on the phone to Leanne, telling her mum how Ricky couldn't get a dentist's appointment for another three days. When she finished the call, she stroked the side of Ricky's face and said, 'Mum's got some ointment she says will help the pain. Do you want to go round and get it?'

'I've drunk too much,' Ricky said, holding up the fourth bottle of beer he'd consumed to try to numb the pain. 'I'll go in the morning.'

But Ricky woke later than normal and didn't have time to nip around to Leanne and Kevin's before work. The building site he was on was only in Southwater, just a couple of miles down the road from Broadbridge Heath, where his in-laws lived. He decided to go at lunchtime, and at least that way he'd avoid seeing Kevin, who worked in a warehouse at Gatwick Airport.

The pain hurt too much for him to eat his sandwich, so he got in the van and drove to Leanne's house. He knocked on the front door, but there was no answer. The electronic doorbell that played 'When the Saints Go Marching in' had died months earlier, and Kevin hadn't got around to replacing it. Ricky strode to the side of the house, opened the little gate by the rubbish bins, and walked through into the rear garden, which had a door that led into the kitchen.

Whether it was a shadow or a sound he couldn't be sure, but something made him look up at the bedroom window above the kitchen. And then he saw her. Leanne was standing in profile, naked, rubbing her wet hair with a towel so her tits jiggled backwards and forwards. Ricky felt himself blush, and for a second he looked away, but his eyes were drawn back to her. She was in good shape, her bust smaller than Donna's, her waist nipping in, and she had a neat dark-brown bush. Ricky was horrified that he fancied his mother-in-law. He shook his head and crept backwards towards the side of the house, his eyes firmly fixed on the upstairs window.

Just as he was about to open the gate, he saw a man lean towards Leanne and bend down to give her a kiss. She let the towel drop to the floor and lifted her head upwards to kiss him, holding on to his tie to stop him from coming up for air. When eventually the man pulled away, Ricky saw his white shirt and tie, a suit jacket flung over his shoulder. A businessman. Kevin could never be described as a businessman. And then both Leanne and the man disappeared from view.

Ricky stood next to the bins, holding his breath, praying he wouldn't be spotted. He waited until he heard the front door close. Then he waited as he heard the sound of a car engine start up and fade into the distance. And only then did he return to the front door and knock.

'Hello, love,' Leanne said. She was wearing a dressing gown made from a floral, chintzy fabric that clung to her curves. Her nipples were erect. 'How's the toothache?'

'Um. Okay.' Ricky stumbled over his words and felt his cheeks get hot and flushed.

'Sorry I'm in a dressing gown. Just had a shower because I came back from a Zumba class all hot and sweaty!' Leanne laughed. 'Come on in.' She held the door open.

Ricky slid past her, holding in his stomach so as not to get too close.

'Where's my normal kiss, then?' Leanne asked, turning her cheek towards Ricky.

He couldn't help it. He hesitated, and then it was as if a switch had turned on inside Leanne's head.

She crossed her arms across her chest and stared at Ricky. 'How long have you been here?'

'Long enough.' Ricky hung his head.

'It's not what you think.' Leanne blinked hard.

Ricky had no idea what came over him, but he grabbed hold of Leanne's shoulders and pulled her towards him before covering her mouth with his own. He wanted to have this woman now. All thoughts about Donna and the fact Leanne was his mother-in-law flew straight out of his head. The pain in his jaw vanished. He just needed this woman.

Leanne struggled and pushed Ricky away.

'What are you doing?' she said breathlessly.

'Fuck. I'm sorry.' Ricky couldn't believe it. What the hell had he done? He turned towards the wall and buried his face in his hands. 'Fuck,' he said again quietly.

After a long moment, he said, 'Don't tell Donna. It'd break her heart. I've never been unfaithful to her. Never. I love your daughter.'

Leanne sighed and put her hand on his shoulder, forcing him to turn around to look at her. 'I won't say a word if you don't tell anyone about Abdul.'

'Fuck,' Ricky said even more quietly this time. It was bad enough Leanne having an affair, but with an Arab? Kevin would kill her, kill both of them. 'Do you love him?'

'Who? Abdul or Kevin?'

'Both?'

'Neither,' Leanne said, sighing. 'There's not much to love about Kevin. And Abdul.' She exhaled. 'He's a sweet man and an amazing lover, but he'll never leave his wife. It's an affair, Ricky. That's all it is. Once a week, twice if we're lucky. Let's not rock the boat.' She put a hand on Ricky's arm. It sent a shiver through him. 'Let's not rock the boat,' she said again. 'Neither of us.'

Ricky left quickly, his head in a whirl.

That night he made love to Donna, exploding inside her with a ferocity unlike anything he'd ever felt before.

'Bloody hell,' Donna said, panting afterwards. 'Did Mum give you the right medicine?'

Ricky shifted away from Donna when he realised that Leanne hadn't given him any medicine. But he was pretty sure that that was the night Skye was conceived, the night when he was imagining he was making love to his mother-in-law.

* * *

Now that Leanne is dead, he's glad she had a secret life that Kevin knew nothing about. Although Ricky supposes that Kevin found out eventually. Or did he know all along? The police must have tracked down Abdul and the other lovers who came before and after, and told Kevin all about her infidelity. But Ricky made Leanne a promise, and he intends to keep that promise until the day he dies. He just hopes the police don't tell Donna that her mother was unfaithful. Ricky doesn't want Donna's memories of Leanne to be tainted, but most of all, he's worried that if Donna thinks it was alright for her mum to sleep around, then she might think it's okay for her to do it too. And it is absolutely not okay.

By the time Donna returns, Ricky has decided that it might be best if she does visit Kevin; that if he takes her and sits alongside her throughout, he'll be able to control the conversation, and if he thinks Kevin is about to divulge something he shouldn't, then he will be able to pull Donna away. That has to be the better option. If he says no, then there's the possibility Donna might visit Kevin behind his back, when he's at work. And Ricky can't risk that happening.

22

Pippa

'Who is Ricky Wiśniewski?' Marie turns to me with big eyes.

I hesitate before telling her. 'He's the son-in-law of the murdered lottery winner.'

I am sickened at the thought Ricky might have knowingly caused my son harm. Could it really be him? But how would he even know who George is, let alone where to find him? And the fact that George was driving a hire car. The more I think about it, the more ridiculous it seems. I feel bad about mentioning his name. Have I just worried Marie unnecessarily, and have I sent Joe Swain in pursuit of an innocent man? I stand up.

'I'm just going to have a word with the policeman. I'm sure it can't have been Ricky. I'll be back in a moment.'

But I can't find Joe. I walk along the corridor towards the main nurses' desk, trying to ignore the noises, glancing in an open ward, where mothers lie exhausted but content with their newborn babies swaddled, lying in clear Perspex cots, startled from the trauma of their births, bemused by the bright, loud new world they have been thrust into. There is no one at the desk, so I return to Marie's room. She's on her phone, speaking rapidly in French. She smiles at me.

'My parents. They are at Genève airport. They will be here late tonight.'

'I'm so glad.' It means I can leave her and concentrate on my boy. 'Will you be alright if I go back to find out about George?'

Her eyes glisten. 'Yes. Please call me as soon as you know anything.'

I pass her my mobile phone so she can put her number in it. I want to ask her if I can put my hand on her stomach, but I hold back and instead surprise myself by depositing a brief kiss on her forehead.

I am at the door when she says in a low voice, ‘Am I safe? This Ricky, is he coming after George and me?’

I shake my head. ‘No. I think it’s a coincidence. There are thousands of small white vans on the road. I can’t see why Ricky would want to cause you or me any harm. After all, it was just a coincidence that my photo was found with his mother-in-law.’

The trouble is I’m not sure. I’m being threatened on Facebook, my photo was found on Leanne’s body, and now my son and his girlfriend have been involved in a car accident that may not be an accident at all. I don’t believe in coincidences.

* * *

‘Mrs Durrant. I am Dr Rhandeshi. I operated on your son.’

He doesn’t look much older than George and is strikingly good-looking, with coffee-coloured skin and sparkling green eyes. He is wearing a white coat over an open-necked pale-blue shirt and beige chinos.

‘George is in ICU,’ he says, holding my gaze. ‘The operation went well, and he is expected to make a good recovery. He has several broken ribs and a punctured lung, which we needed to operate on, and his right femur was quite badly broken, so we inserted a titanium plate, which will hold it together. Recovery will be fairly slow, but we expect him to be walking soon, and there shouldn’t be any long-term effects.’

I want to hug this young man, to thank him for stitching my boy back together again. I can’t get any words out to express my relief.

The spiky-haired nurse rubs my forearm. 'Come and get a cup of tea.'

'Thank you,' I murmur to both of them, and follow the nurse into a waiting room lined with blue plastic chairs and a television blasting out a family-friendly quiz show. She hands me a steaming cup, way too milky for my liking.

'Your son will be in ICU for several hours, and then we'll get him settled into a bed on the ward. Why don't you come back to see him tomorrow?'

'Can't I see him now?' I urge.

She gives me a sympathetic smile. 'Visitors aren't allowed in ICU, and by the time he's settled here, it'll be long after visiting hours. You go home, have a good night's sleep, and come back tomorrow.'

'You will call if anything changes?'

'Of course,' she reassures me.

I walk slowly towards the exit, past people hurrying in the opposite direction – an elderly man with the pallor of paper being wheeled on a trolley by two orderlies; a harried mother trying to stop her toddler from screaming – past corridors lined with posters and notices, and then out into the entrance lobby. It isn't until the cold, fresh air brushes my face that I realise I don't have any way of getting home. My car is parked up on a lay-by twenty miles away. I'm rifling in my wallet to see if I even have enough cash for a taxi when a hand grasps my shoulder. I jump.

'Dr Durrant, would you like a lift?'

I hesitate. I'm not sure that I trust Joe Swain.

'I'm going your way and can drop you off at your car.'

But I'm too tired to argue, and I know I've only got about ten pounds in my wallet, insufficient to pay cash for a taxi. 'Thank you,' I say and then immediately regret accepting the offer.

As we're walking towards the car park, he throws me a surprisingly warm smile and says, 'Call me Joe.'

I am expecting a lift in a marked squad car similar to the one that brought me to the hospital, but Joe Swain drives a dark-grey Audi with no markings to suggest he is a police officer.

'Was it Ricky's van?' I ask as we edge out of the hospital car park.

'I don't know. We're investigating. Why did you think it might be Ricky's van?'

I take a deep breath and decide I need to tell him about Ricky's visit to me and how I followed him to his workplace. As I'm speaking, I watch Joe's face, his strong profile. He doesn't show any emotion, his eyes blinking slowly as he navigates the traffic.

'The thing is,' I say, desperately hoping that my background, qualifications and experience might mitigate my actions, 'I'm quite knowledgeable in deception detection, micro-expressions, handwriting analysis and the like. That's why I want to meet Kevin Smith, and that's why I know without a shadow of a doubt that Ricky was lying to me.'

Joe shakes his head almost imperceptibly, and then he is silent for several long moments. 'I am aware of that. We did a few background checks on you, and I understand you were a forensic psychologist working with repeat offenders. Very highly respected by my colleagues in both the Met and Sussex police by all accounts.'

'That's good to hear. I gave it up quite a few years ago. Latterly, I haven't had any contact or workings with the police.'

'Would you like to?' he asks.

'Yes, yes, I would,' I say, startling myself. Eight years ago, I swore I would never work with the police and put myself in danger ever again. But eight years is a long time, and things change. 'But I don't suppose I can be involved in this case? Because I am…you know, involved.'

'Strictly speaking, no, but off the record, I think you might be able to help me.' He chews the side of his mouth, and then as we are idling at a set of traffic lights, he turns to look at me, his fingers drumming on the steering wheel. 'Do you fancy a bite to eat? It's late, but we still might find somewhere.'

This is surprising. Whether it's the relief that George is alright, or the fact that Joe isn't angry with me for following Ricky, or that I genuinely think I can help in this case and perhaps look after myself in the process, I say yes. I glance again at Joe and realise that he is a disarmingly attractive man.

Somewhere between Crawley and Horsham, Joe turns off the dual carriageway and takes a narrow, winding road deep into woodland. The beams from his headlights bounce off low-hanging branches, and the car rattles over potholes. After a few minutes he pulls up into the parking lot of an attractive-looking pub.

'I haven't been here in a while, but they used to serve good food. Traditional English fare – is that alright with you?'

As I hop out of the car, I check my mobile phone. There is a signal, and I haven't received any messages. I suppose that is good news. I know I should tell Trevor about George's accident and operation, and I hesitate for a moment, wondering if I should do it now. But as Trevor doesn't even know George is in the country, and as I know my son will not want to see his father, I decide it won't make any difference if I call him tonight or in the morning.

As we stand at the bar, Joe asks, 'What would you like to drink?'

'A tomato juice, please.'

'Is the abstinence because you're with a policeman?' he jests.

I squirm. 'No. I really don't feel like alcohol.' I order fish and chips, while Joe goes for a steak. He selects a table at the side of the room and we sit down.

'Tell me about your work,' he says.

'I'm FACS trained.'

Joe frowns.

'It stands for "facial action coding system". It's an anatomical system that describes every observable facial movement. It was developed by Ekman and Friesen, and it basically lets you describe each facial-muscle movement through a set of action units.'

'Ah, you're talking about micro-expressions.'

'Exactly. Do you learn that at police college?'

Joe shakes his head. 'We should do, but no, we don't. That's why we need experts such as yourself.'

'The latest developments have been by Dr Freitas-Magalhães, a Portuguese professor of psychology. He has created the most advanced system for reading human faces using 4K and 3D computerised technologies.'

'I understand the basics of micro-expressions, but how, for instance, can you be so sure that Ricky was lying to you?'

'I don't think he was lying, but I do think he was withholding information. He definitely had something to hide. It was a mixture between linguistics, body language and micro-expressions. For instance he said, "I have told the police everything they need to know." That's an expanded contraction. In other, more innocuous sentences he said "I've" and "didn't", which is a more normal manner of speech. And then rather than using Kevin's name, he said "That man", which is typical distancing language. His micro-expressions demonstrated momentary signs of disgust. But it's obviously much easier for me to be accurate in my analyses when I'm reading a transcript of an interview and watching the individual on video. I wasn't expecting Ricky's visit, and I was scared, so my assessment wouldn't have been as accurate as I would have liked.'

'Wow, that's impressive.' Joe stares out of the window for a couple of moments and then leans forwards towards me. 'We could do that with Kevin Smith.'

‘Really?’ I can’t help grinning. How exciting that I might be able to put my skills to proper, valuable use at the same time as helping solve a crime.

‘Let me see if I can pull it off. It’ll require a bit of wrangling behind the scenes.’

23

Donna

Donna's head is like a casserole of boiling ingredients that shouldn't be mixed together. She's furious with Ricky for not letting her visit her dad, but she's also a little bit fearful of him. She's falling for Mike, and that terrifies her too. And she's missing her mum so badly it is like someone has chiselled out her heart and left an empty hole in the centre of her chest, leaving just a bit around the edges to encompass her love for the kids and Ricky.

When Donna gets home from her impetuous rendezvous with Mike, Ricky hands her Skye and strides out of the room. He doesn't even ask her where she went. In some ways that's a relief, as she doesn't have to lie. On the other hand, it's so unlike Ricky.

'I'm going out,' he states coldly as he walks past the open living room door with his blue-and-white sports bag flung over his shoulder.

'Will you be back for lunch?' Donna asks.

'No.'

'I could do roast chicken like Mum did.' She can't stop the whining tone in her voice.

Ricky turns around. 'Oh, Dons, I know you're hurting, but I've got things I have to do. You'll be alright. I'll be back later.' He gives her a quick peck on the cheek and then he's out of the front door. Donna hears him start up the van, with its distinctive cough and stutter, and then he's gone.

It's the worst day of the week for her to be alone. She can't call up any of her friends, because they're with their families. And it's the day she misses her parents the most, because Sundays were invariably spent at their house. Ricky knows that, which makes it all the more unfair that he's disappeared off and left her alone with the kids. Again.

Donna doesn't know how she gets through the day, but somehow she does. She hopes and prays Ricky will come back soon, but by mid-afternoon, when he hasn't appeared, her hopes land on Mike. How her day would be better if Mike was there to comfort her. And then it's bath time, and still Ricky hasn't come home, and Mike hasn't been in touch either.

Benjie loves splashing in the bath, whereas Skye just screams, so Donna gives Benjie a bath first, letting him play with his little plastic boats and blow bubbles with the soap. She lifts Benjie out, rubs him down with the yellow towel with a hood that makes him look like a duck, pulls on his Thomas the Tank Engine pyjamas, breathes in his delicious fresh skin, and tells him to go and read a book. She knows he won't, that he'll put the telly on, but she hasn't got the energy to object.

She's just lowered Skye into the bath when the front doorbell rings. Donna expects it is one of the horrible journalists, so she ignores it; besides, she needs to concentrate on Skye.

'Mama, someone at the door,' Benjie shouts up the stairs as he bounces up and down.

'Yeah,' Donna grunts.

But Benjie thinks it might be Declan coming over to play or one of his other little friends, so he races to the door. He's not tall enough to reach the handle.

'Come back!' Donna yells, but Benjie ignores her.

He can see a pair of eyes peeping through the letterbox. This is fun.

'Hello, Benjie!' There's a voice with the eyes. It must be someone who knows him.

'Hello,' he says, curling his fingers under his chin in his cute little toddler-ish way.

'Can you ask your mum to let us in?'

Benjie turns around and runs back to the foot of the stairs. 'Mum. Door. Lady.'

Donna sighs. 'Ask who it is.'

Benjie hops back down the corridor and stands at the front door, looking up under his long dark eyelashes. 'Who it is?' he asks parrot-like.

'Tell your mum it's Janet Curran. We need to talk to her urgently.'

Benjie can't say her name properly. It sounds like 'Jam and Come On', but Donna understands her son's quirky pronunciations. She whisks Skye out of the bath, swaddles her in a pink towel and, with a little tremor of fear coursing through her torso, walks slowly down the stairs.

'Stand back,' she instructs Benjie as Donna holds the scratched wooden door open just enough for her to peek around the side.

'Hello, Donna,' Janet Curran says. 'Can we come in, please?'

Reluctantly Donna opens the door, and in comes Janet, followed by Mia Brevant, the young policewoman who visited before, and DS Joe Swain. Janet leads the way into the living room. Donna wishes she had tidied up. The children's toys are scattered across the floor, and Janet has to lift toys and dirty plates off the sofa and chairs to make space for them all to sit down.

'What's happened?' Her voice quivers.

'We need to ask you and Ricky some questions.'

'Ricky's not here.'

'Do you know where he is?' Joe Swain asks.

'No.' She shakes her head. 'He's been gone since this morning.'

The police officers glance at each other, and Donna's gut clenches.

'What do you want with Ricky?'

'We need him to answer some questions,' Mia says.

'We'd like to ask you some questions too,' Joe Swain says.

'I haven't done anything.' Donna clutches Skye so tightly, the baby begins to whimper.

'Why don't I take the kiddies whilst you have a chat with my colleagues?' Janet suggests.

Donna thinks that's a terrible idea, but she just stares at the stained carpet and doesn't say anything.

'Would you like me to read you a story?' Janet crouches down in front of Benjie.

He nods and sticks his thumb in his mouth. Janet stands up and holds her arms out to Donna. Donna hopes that Skye will scream so Janet will have to hand back the baby. But Skye doesn't. She is so tired after her bath, she just rests her head against Janet's shoulder and nods off to sleep. With the baby firmly clutched against her bosom, Janet extends her left hand to Benjie, who takes it and follows her out of the living room without a backwards glance.

Donna puts her hand over her mouth to stifle a sob as it crosses her mind that Janet might be taking her babies away from her forever. There is a girl Kerry knows whose children were taken away by social workers. It's been fourteen months, and they're still in care and no one seems to know why. Donna tries to reassure herself that her situation is totally different. She doesn't do drugs or drink excessively and she's a good mother – most of the time anyway. And who would be so cruel as to take away her children just when she's lost her own mother?

'And…?' Joe Swain's eyes are locked on to Donna's face.

'I'm sorry,' she mumbles. 'Can you repeat the question?'

'Where have you been today?'

Donna can feel herself blushing. She thinks of Mike and how he came on to her and how she so nearly betrayed Ricky.

'I was here,' she says, looking at her trainers.

'Can anyone corroborate that?' he asks.

'What?'

'Is there anyone who can confirm that you've been here all day?' Mia explains softly.

'Yes. Ricky.' *Except when I was with Mike*, she thinks, crossing the fingers of her right hand and shoving her hands under her thighs.

'You just told us that Ricky is out, so how can he be your alibi?' Joe Swain snaps.

Alibi, alibi, Donna thinks, recalling all those television programmes they've watched, programmes like *Happy Valley*. *That must mean they think I'm guilty of something.*

And then Donna recognises the familiar cough of Ricky's van and she freezes. Is Ricky about to walk into the lion's den? Should she rush out and tell him to drive away as quickly as he can, or can she draw on some magical powers of telepathic thinking to stop him from blurting out something he shouldn't? As she wavers, she hears the van's door slam, followed by the metallic clicking noise of Ricky's key in the lock of the front door.

Dithering. She always dithers, leaning on Ricky or Leanne or Kerry to make decisions, and now it could be too late. Her fingers twist the thin gold chain with the letter *D* on it that Ricky gave her for her last birthday. She can taste the bitterness of fear, smell something acrid in the stale living room air, and she wishes she could sink into the chair and vanish. But it's too late for that.

Ricky is inside the cramped living room, scowling at Mia Brevant and Joe Swain.

'What are you doing here?' he asks.

24

Pippa

Trevor is incandescent with rage when I ring him in the morning. By the time I got home after the late supper with Joe Swain, I was exhausted and didn't feel like pacifying my ex-husband or, worse still, having to speak to the new, younger Mrs Durrant. Leaving my phone on, I went to bed and slept surprisingly well.

I call the hospital at 8 a.m., which is a bad time, as it's in the middle of the shift change – so the nurse tells me – but after I apologise to her, she relents and says George is doing fine, is back on the ward, and has had a reasonable night's sleep. She can't give me any news on Marie, but I'm not so worried about her, especially as her parents will be looking after her. My next call is to Trevor, who, judging by the background noise, must already be at work.

'How dare you not call me immediately you found out?' he yells. 'George is my son too.'

I try to pacify him but just end up snapping and telling him it's his fault that George wants nothing to do with him. If he'd been a better father and hadn't walked out on me during the hardest time of our lives, he might have a relationship with our son today. Unsurprisingly, and not for the first time, Trevor hangs up on me. I wonder if I should ring the hospital and warn them that Trevor might turn up, and tell them to send him packing if he does, but then I think how petty that sounds, and perhaps Trevor might get the reconciliation with George he's so desperate for. Despite our considerable differences, I don't want to deprive him of that possibility.

A few minutes later Joe calls me.

'Thanks for a lovely evening. How are you set for later today?'

‘As my client list has been pretty much wiped out thanks to my newfound notoriety, I have plenty of time on my hands.’

‘Good news. We’re going to interview Kevin Smith.’

‘That was quick!’

‘I was able to pull a few strings. Can you get up to London? I’m getting him transferred to Wandsworth Police Station. Kevin Smith has a bail hearing.’

* * *

My first job of the day is to contact the local dog walker. Harriet has a thriving business, driving around the local villages, collecting dogs left behind by their owners, and walking them on the South Downs. Unfortunately, it’s nearly 9 a.m. and she’s not answering her phone. I don’t know who to ask, and I hate the thought of leaving Mungo alone all day. Ten minutes later I try her again, but it still goes to voicemail. I leave her a message, begging her to collect Mungo for a walk later on today. ‘I’ll leave the front door key underneath the blue flowerpot next to the bins around the side of the house,’ I say.

It’s hard not to be maudlin thinking about my old life, the days when I would have had five or six people eager to look after the dog: friends, even Rob before he moved down to Hove, my cleaning lady. How small my new life is, with just a handful of friends and neighbours, with whom I only pass the time of day. Sometimes I wonder whether anyone would notice if I collapsed or was seriously ill. Before last week, my clients might have banged on the door, but now, as I’ve lost most of them, my life is so empty. Perhaps I will end up like one of those sad old ladies whose rotting bodies are discovered after weeks or months because they have no one in their lives to actually miss them.

I decide to take the train, because a car in London will only be an expensive noose. The last time I drove up to town, it took me two and a half hours and cost a fortune in parking. I intend to go to Redhill first and see George, and then will continue up to London for my meeting with Joe.

I hug Mungo, double-check he has plenty of water, and then, feeling sorry for my dog, I give him a large chewy. Leaving the car at Pulborough station, I run to get a ticket and race on to the platform, only to hear the announcement that the train is delayed. No surprise there. Out of breath, I collapse on to one of the uncomfortable white wrought-iron benches next to the platform.

'Pippa?'

I jump.

'Sorry to startle you.'

'What are you doing here?' I ask Brent as I stand up to greet him.

'I'm collecting a car for a customer. It's a 7 Series BMW that needs a service,' he says, wiping his hands on his jeans.

I've gone for months without seeing Brent, and I don't recall ever having run into him by chance. I narrow my eyes at him, wondering why he's lying. That fleeting sneer before his face settles into a smile is a sure giveaway, combined with too much information. Why is he lying to me? Perhaps he's lost his job and that is why he has been reaching out to me. It wouldn't surprise me that this proud man would try to cover up the humiliation of being let go.

I know better than to rile him by exposing my suspicion, so I change the subject. 'I'm sorry about yesterday, having to cancel. Did you have a good walk?'

'Yes. How was it with George?'

'It was lovely and then it wasn't. He and his girlfriend were involved in a car accident yesterday.'

My words are cut off by a train announcement. 'The 9.51 to Bognor Regis, calling at Amberley, Arundel, Ford,

Barnham and Bognor Regis, will shortly arrive on platform two.'

'Gotta go! I'm on the wrong platform.' Brent races away, and then the train pulls in on the opposite platform, and I can't see if Brent made it on time. I hope so. I send him a text.

If you'd like to meet up again soon, let me know. My diary is empty!

* * *

As I approach George's bed, I can see he already has visitors. I feel a surge of jealousy. As I get closer, I realise Marie is sitting next to his bed, her hand over his. George has the complexion of parchment, and the healthy vibrancy I so relished yesterday has vanished.

I hesitate at the end of the bed. I wonder now whether my need to see him is in fact much greater than his need to see me.

'Hello, darling,' I murmur.

George looks at me, his face expressionless.

Marie stands up with some difficulty, her stomach appearing even larger than yesterday. 'Mrs Durrant, these are my parents.'

My first impression is that they are suave, moneyed, cosmopolitan and would fit in just fine with Trevor and his friends. I glance down at my dowdy, safe navy trousers, taupe bobble jumper and navy anorak slung over my arm. Marie's mother is wearing what looks distinctly like a Chanel suit and little kitten heels, and her hair is styled into a perfect caramel-coloured bob. Her father – wearing a blazer with gold buttons, a dark tie, cream trousers with an ironed crease down the front, and reddish, soft suede moccasins – shakes my hand with a strong grip. They are both good-looking.

'We are sorry to meet you under these circumstances,' he says in flawless English. 'George has become like a son to us.'

I try to hide my dismay. Just because I can read other people's expressions doesn't mean I can control my own. It seems that George is closer not only to Rob, but this couple too.

'How are you, love?' I direct the question to George.

'Alright,' he mutters.

I glance at Marie, who is peering at George, her pretty face contorted with concern.

'*Es-tu sûre que tout va bien, ma chérie? As-tu besoin de plus d'analgésiques, mon amour?*'

He shakes his head.

Perhaps I shouldn't be surprised that she and George communicate in French – after all, they are living in Geneva – but as far as I was aware, George never progressed beyond GCSE level in French. How little I actually know about my son.

When a nurse comes to take George's blood pressure, she does a double take upon noticing me. In the drama of the past twenty-four hours, I have forgotten about my unwelcome notoriety.

'I've got to go to London for a meeting. Shall I pop in later on my way home?' I suggest.

'Don't bother,' George says in a rasping voice. 'I need to sleep. Marie's here.'

I feel like a spare limb, superfluous in my son's life. Discarded all over again.

'Dad wants to come and see you.' I let the words slip out without thinking.

George gets agitated, his face flushes, and a machine starts bleeping. 'No.' He almost chokes on the word. 'Don't want to see him.'

'Shush,' Marie says, stroking his forehead, dropping little kisses on the back of his hand.

Doing my job, I think harshly.

I stand up. I am lost for words. What does one say to one's semi-estranged son, who seems more relaxed with strangers than he does with his mother? I may be able to advise my clients in such a scenario, but there is no way I can apply the advice to myself.

'I'll see you tomorrow,' I say eventually, but George has his head turned away from me, and when I angle myself to look at him, I see his eyes are closed.

Marie's parents stand up, and his father extends his hand. 'It was a pleasure to meet you.'

'I'll call you later,' I say to Marie.

She nods but stays at George's side.

I walk away slowly. I was a wife. I was a mother. I was a psychologist with a thriving practice. But now I feel like a snail with a crushed shell, and I wonder who I am.

25

Ricky

'We'd like to ask you a few questions,' DS Joe Swain says.

'Can't you lot just leave us alone and concentrate on getting the evidence to convict my bastard father-in-law?'

Donna gasps.

'We can either talk informally here or formally down at the police station. It's your choice.'

Ricky shrugs. There aren't enough chairs, so he leans back against the wall, with his head resting on the large, framed photograph of the four of them. Leanne organised a photo shoot for Ricky, Donna and the kids shortly after Skye was born. They were doing a special offer at the shopping centre, twenty-five per cent off for immediate sign-ups. Donna doesn't like the picture. She thinks she looks fat, with her oversized boobs and folds of flabby midriff and dull hair that was, and still is, crying out for some highlights, but Ricky insists on leaving the picture up on the wall. 'I like to look at my family,' he's said proudly on several occasions.

'Fire away, then.'

Ricky speaks nonchalantly, but there's something in his expression that suggests to Donna his relaxed demeanour is a pretence.

'Can you tell us where you've been today?'

'Today?' Ricky frowns. 'What's happened today?'

'Please just answer the question.'

Ricky's hands clench and unclench at his sides, and then he sticks his thumbs in his front jeans pockets. 'I was here with the kids this morning, then I went to the gym, and then I went for a drive.'

Donna pales. She doesn't like the sound of that. Ricky doesn't just go for a drive. For starters, the van is on its last legs, and she knows he doesn't like to take it too far in case it breaks down, like it did a couple of months ago on his way to the coast.

'Which gym do you go to?' Mia Brevant asks.

'The leisure centre at Broadbridge Heath.'

'Are you a member?'

'Yes. And you can check up on me if you want, because they scan my membership card when I go there, and there's a bloody app on my phone. Do you want to see it?' Ricky's tone is sarcastic and stinging.

'And after your session at the gym, where did you go?'

'Just a drive, here and there.' He pauses to glance at Donna, then turns his attention back to Joe Swain. 'We had an argument, Donna and me, and I needed to sort out my head.'

'This drive.' Joe pauses and peers at his large silver watch. 'Did it last five hours?'

'No. I stopped for a cuppa.'

'Where?'

Ricky starts to get agitated. His foot is tapping on the floor, and he scratches his head and then his left forearm.

He turns to Donna. 'Shouldn't you be looking after the children, love?'

'Janet is with them,' she says.

'Please don't tell me that a stranger is putting our little ones to bed. You need to go!' He gesticulates towards the door.

The police officers glance at each other. Donna doesn't know what to do. If Ricky wants her out of the room, it's because he's got something to hide. Her shoulders sink at the realisation that he's having an affair. Why else would he be gone for so long? Her throat chokes up and she coughs.

'If you would rather have this conversation in private, then we can go to the station,' Joe Swain says, cutting through the thunderous atmosphere.

Ricky looks as if he is about to burst a blood vessel. 'I was going to come back and work on the extension after the gym.' He waves his hand towards the back of the house. 'But the mate who's helping me didn't show up and, as it's been pissing down rain most of the day, there didn't seem any point. So as I said, I went for a drive. What the hell's this got to do with Leanne's murder anyway?'

'We didn't say it did.'

Donna glances up, her eyes wide. Ricky scowls again.

'A white van similar to yours was in a road traffic incident earlier this afternoon, and we have reason to believe you might have been involved.'

'Well, I wasn't.'

Mia Brevant interjects. 'If you could tell us where you were, then we can check cameras and eliminate you from our enquiries.'

Ricky stands up straight and puts his hands on his hips, his chin pressed forwards as if he's ready to fight. 'What makes you think it was me? There are thousands of white vans out there just like mine.'

'The people in the other car were run off the road,' Mia says.

'If you're so sure it was me, then arrest me. Did you get my number plate?'

Joe Swain uncrosses his legs and leans forwards. 'No, we only got a partial number plate, which is why we want to eliminate you from our enquiries. Why won't you tell us where you were?'

Ricky closes his eyes and sighs. 'I don't know exactly. I went to London.'

'London?' Donna exclaims. She feels an almighty relief. Surely Ricky doesn't have a lover in London. It's too far away. But then she realises the error of her thinking. Perhaps he took his mistress to London for the day. She wonders who she is, what she looks like. Thin, blonde and pretty with no children, she assumes. And then Donna decides.

'I'll go and check up on the children now.'

She stands up. It's better she doesn't hear whatever it is Ricky has to say. She knows all too well that once you hear something, you can never unhear it.

'Donna!' Mia calls after her, but Donna is already racing up the stairs. She needs to hold her children. Urgently.

'Will you tell us where you were now your wife is out of the room?'

Ricky walks over to the chair that Donna just vacated and sits down, perching on the edge of the seat. 'I went to London to see Kevin Smith, but they sent me packing because I hadn't pre-booked.'

'Where were you at fifteen hundred hours and thirty-seven minutes this afternoon?'

Ricky hesitates.

Mia says, 'Twenty-five to four this afternoon,' as if she's a translator.

'Somewhere on the A3, I presume, driving southwards,' Ricky says sulkily.

'Were you alone?'

Ricky nods.

'And why didn't you want your wife to know you were visiting her father?'

'I just don't.' Ricky crosses his arms and legs.

'Were you involved in a collision with a silver Kia driven by George Durrant?'

Ricky recoils his neck and squints at the police officer. 'Durrant, did you say?'

Joe Swain nods. Mia Brevant scribbles something on her notepad.

'So this *is* something to do with Leanne's murder,' Ricky says, snorting.

'I assume the name is familiar to you.' Swain leans forwards.

Ricky sits back. 'Yeah. The woman in the photograph. Philippa Durrant. Who's George, then?'

Joe Swain narrows his eyes at Ricky, then slowly lifts himself out of the chair. 'What did you intend to say to Kevin Smith?'

'To butt out of our lives. To have it out with him man to man. To tell him to keep away from my Donna, who still thinks the sun shines out of her daddy's backside despite him being a murderer.'

Joe nods. 'We will be following up on the information you have given us, and I have no doubt that our next conversation will be down at the station.'

Joe Swain turns towards the door. Mia Brevant follows her boss's lead, stands up, pats down her dark trousers, and glances back at Ricky, who is now slumped in the chair as if all the bones in his body have come loose.

'Incidentally, there won't be any need for you to visit Kevin Smith in prison. He's up for his remand hearing, and we have every expectation that he will be released on bail. It's extremely likely that he will be home this week.'

26

Pippa

Joe sent me a message asking me to meet him in a coffee shop called Cacao Beans just off Wandsworth High Street. It's one of those New Age trendy places serving weird and wonderful types of coffee in bamboo mugs and offering an extensive vegan menu. Joe's choice of venue surprises me. I had him down as a middle-of-the-road, no-pretension type of guy.

He is already there when I arrive, dressed in a button-down pale-blue shirt and navy tie. He's typing something into his iPad. When he sees me, his face lights up, and my heart does a little jump. As I settle into the chair opposite him, he puts his iPad away and clasps his hands in front of him.

'Kevin's up for a bail hearing. We're pressing for him to be kept on remand, but I think he'll be granted bail.'

I scrunch up my forehead. 'Why am I meeting him now? Wouldn't it be easier once he's out on bail?'

Joe shakes his head. 'No. Unless we find new evidence, it won't be easy to get you in front of him. Today is likely to be our last chance before trial.'

'I'm surprised you think he'll be granted bail,' I muse. 'He's charged with murder.'

'As you probably know, in the UK there's a presumption of innocence, even if we think he's as guilty as hell. His defence lawyer will undoubtedly argue that it was a domestic crime of passion and that there's no significant risk that Kevin Smith will harm anyone else whilst out on bail. He's got a clean record. Done for speeding a couple of times, but that's it.'

'But you think it's more than a domestic crime…' I let my words trail off.

'Yes.' Joe stirs his double espresso with a wooden stick. 'Your photo on Leanne's mutilated face doesn't fit. Not unless you and Kevin have some connection.'

I stifle my gasp. Naively, I thought Joe wanted my help, that Joe likes me, that we have some kind of special connection. But now I wonder whether I'm being used. Whether he wants to put me and Kevin in front of each other to gauge our reactions. Both of our reactions to each other. I try not to show my dismay. I lift my Americano to my lips, but my hand is shaking, so I put it down again.

Joe notices and frowns. 'Are you okay?'

'Yes. Fine. Just overwrought with everything that's happened. Worried about George. And I didn't sleep much last night. I get a bit hypoglycaemic from time to time.'

Joe jumps up and then leans on the table close to me. 'I'll get you a piece of cake. The carrot cake is especially good.'

'No, it's fine,' I urge, but Joe has already leaped away and is on the other side of the coffee shop, pointing at a massive cake cut into giant slices, taking out his wallet, chatting to the blue-haired girl at the till.

I don't know why I said that. I'm not hypoglycaemic, and the last thing I feel like is a piece of cake. But it gives me a moment to think and breathe. I remind myself I have nothing to worry about. I haven't done anything wrong.

'Here you go.' He puts the plate in front of me and settles back into his chair. 'So, when we meet Kevin, I suggest that I ask the questions and you observe. Is that alright?'

I nod, trying to swallow a piece of cake. I am surprised how delicious it is, being free from gluten, dairy and sugar, but even so, I don't feel like eating.

'I'll just watch,' I agree in between mouthfuls. 'Can we organise a transcript of the conversation, or better still a video, so I can analyse it afterwards?'

‘Yes. All interviews are recorded, but not all will be able to be used in evidence.’

‘Can I butt in with a question? Sometimes specific questions can elicit certain responses that can ultimately result in a confession. Questions phrased in a particular way will certainly elicit physical responses that can contribute to clusters and micro-expressions.’

Joe sucks in his cheeks. ‘I would hope that with over thirty years’ policing experience under my belt, I am fairly competent at cross-examining a suspect.’

‘Sorry.’ I backtrack fast, bringing my hands up to my face in a futile attempt to hide the redness in my cheeks. ‘I didn’t mean to question your skills; it’s just I have done some training with VeritusQ2U in the States and—’

‘VeritusQ2U?’ Joe interrupts. ‘Who are they?’

‘It’s a company that specialises in uncovering deception. They offer training on critical interviewing, behavioural analysis and deception detection. The guys who run it are all former US intelligence officers.’

Joe’s eyebrows have nearly hit his hairline. ‘Why did you do that?’

‘It was part of my PhD thesis. I was studying how psychopaths lie.’

‘Do you still work with psychopaths?’

I squirm. ‘No. I finished my PhD a year before Flo disappeared, and since…I haven’t felt like picking it up again.’

It’s Joe’s turn to look uncomfortable. He glances at his watch. ‘Goodness, we need to go.’

I’m relieved to have an excuse not to finish the cake. Fortunately Joe doesn’t suggest we take it in a doggy bag. I think of Mungo and hope that Harriet has picked up my message and that my beloved hound isn’t stuck indoors all day.

* * *

Wandsworth Police Station is a modern, solid, square building, rooted in the ground with brick footings. The exterior of the upper floors is constructed with glass and what looks like slate but is coloured concrete. I expect to see a counter and people milling around, but it's nothing like that. It's more like a functional office block merged with a hospital.

'The front counter was closed last year,' Joe explains. 'Don't get me started on police cuts.'

After going through the mandatory airport-style security machines, I follow Joe and another police officer to the basement. I am beginning to feel a fluttering of nerves. I don't belong here. What if Kevin decides to come after me when he's released? Mungo will likely roll over and lick him, and there's no one else who will come to my rescue. Why did I ever think this was a good idea? I thought I was fearless, but now I'm not feeling the slightest bit brave. I hang back, letting the physical distance increase between Joe and myself. I am just trying to formulate the words to get out of this interview when Joe turns around and extends his hand, beckoning me forwards.

'Hey, don't worry. You'll be safe.'

My smile is tight. I think of Flo and George and the business I worked so hard to build up and, digging my fingernails into the palms of my hands, I follow Joe into the room.

It's a small room with white walls and no windows. There are two cameras positioned in the corners of the ceiling. Kevin Smith is seated on the other side of the table, and there is a middle-aged man with plump lips and round steel-rimmed glasses in a dark-grey suit and gaudy yellow-and-green tie seated next to him. There are two brown wooden chairs waiting for us.

Kevin is exactly what I expected him to be but at the same time not. Jowly, with a red, veined and bulbous nose and a vast stomach, both suggestive of an affinity for copious quantities of beer, he has lank, thinning greying hair that he has attempted to comb over his bald patch. His hazel eyes are small and recede into his plump face. But although he is overweight, with the look of an ageing lager lout, he also appears deflated, as if any vitality has been extracted from him. From first impressions, this is a man who has lost everything. But one thing I am totally sure of: I have never met this man before.

I am aware of Joe's eyes flitting back and forth between Kevin and me. I know he is assessing whether we recognise each other. And whilst I certainly don't recognise him, Kevin immediately knows who I am.

'What's she doing here?' He attempts to stand up whilst pointing his index finger at me.

'Sit down, Mr Smith.' The man next to him puts a hand on Kevin's arm and tries to get him to sit. A nugget of fear clenches my sternum. But then he sits, as if he is resigned to accept any punches that might be coming his way.

'James Dickson, Kevin Smith's solicitor.' He leans across the table and extends his hand to me. It is clammy and unpleasant. Under the table I wipe my palm on my trousers.

Joe switches on some equipment and announces the date and time and asks each of us to say our names.

'Do you recognise this lady?' Joe asks Kevin, pointing at me.

'Yes.'

'How do you know her?'

'I don't know her,' he says sulkily. 'She's the woman in the papers, in the photograph. The photo you said you found on Leanne.' He swallows audibly and his left eye twitches.

I know the interview will be recorded and I will have plenty of time to watch it back, analyse his actions and study his words, but even so, I am hyper-vigilant, concentrating on those first five seconds after Joe has asked his question, forcing my brain to look and listen at the same time.

'When was the first time you saw Dr Durrant?'

'Saw her photo when you showed it to me. Now is the first time I've met her.'

'Have you ever visited a psychologist?'

An expression of disgust crosses Kevin's face. 'There's nothing wrong with my head.'

I have to restrain myself from correcting him about the work of a psychologist.

'Did any member of your close family visit a psychologist?'

Kevin looks up at the ceiling, then scowls, answering in a sarcastic tone. 'No, of course not.'

Joe leans forwards. 'Kevin, what do you know about the murder of Leanne, your wife?'

Kevin's bottom lip quivers. It's as if his body is folding in on itself, and I wonder if he is going to burst into tears. Briefly, he shuts his eyes. 'Nothing. Nothing other than what you lot told me.'

'What involvement did you have in the murder of Leanne Smith?'

'None!' Kevin shouts, leaning forwards, placing his forearms on the table. 'We've been through this time and time again!' His face is puce, and there are tears gathering in the lower lids of his eyes.

'How do you explain that we found your DNA all over the crime scene and that your fingerprints and only your fingerprints were found on the golf club used to kill your wife?'

'I lived there. It was – is – my home. I don't know about DNA and fingerprint stuff, but surely if someone lives there, their prints and all will be found there. I didn't do it. I already told you that again and again.'

'And the golf club?' Joe says.

‘It was mine. I already told you that. I bought them new ’cos I thought I’d take up golf when we’re in Spain.’

‘What handicap do you play off?’

‘What?’ Kevin frowns. ‘What’s that, then?’

‘So you don’t actually play golf?’

‘I just told you. I’m going to take it up when we go to Spain. But now—’

After sitting still when the questions were asked and sitting still during all his responses, Kevin sinks into his chair like a paper bag emptied of its contents.

‘What sentence do you think your wife’s killer should receive?’

‘Life. Life behind bars. And if capital punishment were legal in this country, then he should be executed.’

‘Do you know who killed Leanne Smith?’

‘No.’ Kevin’s voice cracks into a sob.

‘Did you know your wife had a series of affairs, the longest being with a man called Abdul Bahar?’

‘No!’ Kevin slams the palm of his hand on the table. ‘No! Leanne would never do that. She loves me. Don’t lie to me.’

‘When did you confront your wife about her affairs?’

‘You’re lying! I didn’t. I couldn’t because I didn’t know! It’s not true!’ He breaks down into sobs, loud heaving gulps that sound pathetic coming from such a large man.

I shift uncomfortably in my seat.

‘If Leanne had an affair, then it’s probably him that done it! He was jealous of the new life me and Leanne were going to have in Spain!’

‘Abdul Bahar was on a business trip in Singapore on the day of your wife’s murder. But he did tell us that your wife was instigating divorce proceedings against you, and Ricky, your son-in-law, also confirmed your wife was divorcing you. We have spoken to her solicitor, who corroborated he met with Leanne on two occasions to discuss ending your marriage. When did you find out that Leanne was seeking a divorce?’

Kevin clutches his throat. He goes bright red in the face, and I wonder if he is going to have a heart attack. 'You're wrong! Leanne would never do that! She's my wife and she loves me! Me and her, we were going to have a new life in Spain with the lottery money! You're wrong!' And then Kevin bursts into blubbering tears, his shoulders shaking.

I find it hard to watch. There is no doubt in my mind that Kevin Smith's reaction is genuine.

He had no idea that his wife was about to leave him.

James Dickson peers at Kevin with a look of concern. 'Would you like to take a break?'

Joe speaks before Kevin can answer. 'I think we're done here. Although, Dr Durrant, from your professional viewpoint, is there any final question you would like to put to Mr Smith?'

I flounder for a moment. Joe told me that I couldn't ask any questions, that I couldn't butt in, and now he's throwing the floor open to me at the time when Kevin Smith is broken and likely to be truthful. I dig deep to try to recall what a good final question could be, a question that might uncover otherwise hidden lies. After chewing the side of my mouth for a moment, and waiting for Kevin Smith to control his emotions, I remember the catch-all question and lean forwards.

'What hasn't Detective Sergeant Swain asked you that you think he should know about?'

Kevin Smith shakes his flabby face and wipes the snot from his nose with the back of his hand. 'Nothing,' he whispers.

I look away and chew my bottom lip. I will analyse the interview and double-check that I haven't drawn a wrong, hasty conclusion, but I am almost sure I haven't. Based upon what I have seen and heard this afternoon, I am ninety-five per cent positive that Kevin Smith is innocent.

27

Donna

Ricky refused to talk to Donna after the police left. It was as if he were a clam, retreating into his shell and pulling the lid firmly shut. Donna would have preferred to have had a furious argument to clear the air, to let her know what the hell is going on. Instead he went out and started hammering in the backyard. Donna couldn't work out if Ricky was actually working on the extension or just venting his fury on a load of bricks. Eventually, long after it had got dark, he came inside, made himself an omelette and went to bed, turning his back towards Donna and shrugging her off when she tried to reach out and touch him. His silent attitude was new, and Donna hated it. She felt totally alone, as if she was losing her husband as well as her parents.

She lay in bed for hours, imagining what her replacement looks like. Long blonde hair that falls down her back in lustrous waves; big perky tits; clever; straight teeth; posh; a confident twenty-something who has fallen for Ricky because he's her bit of rough on the side. Or maybe not on the side. Maybe they've fallen in love and Ricky's going to move to London and leave Donna and the kids behind.

She fell asleep eventually, but she dreamed of Leanne and Kevin, both dead again. But this time there wasn't any blood; she was just looking at them both lying prostrate in their coffins, rivers of tears flowing down her face.

Donna makes the children their breakfast and gets Benjie ready for nursery.

The little boy reaches up to his mother's cheek and strokes it. 'Don't be sad, Mumma.'

Donna pulls him into a big hug, but he wriggles free. She's just finishing changing Skye's nappy when her mobile phone pings with an incoming message. Expecting it to be Kerry telling her she's running late, she grabs the phone with one hand, the stinking nappy in the other. And then she drops the nappy.

Hey, Donna! When r u getting the lottery money?

As if the night wasn't bad enough, as if Ricky going off to work without saying goodbye wasn't hurtful enough. And now she's got another message from Oedipus. So, he is after money. Donna stands stock-still, staring at the nappy on the floor. And then she texts back.

I've got no money. Leave me alone.

She looks at the nappy, thinking that it sums up her whole stinking life. She'll have to tell Ricky and the police. Janet Curran maybe. But then another text pings.

Remember. Don't tell Ricky or the police; otherwise I'll tell about your affair.

Donna drops the phone. She bends down and picks up the nappy but leaves the phone on the floor. And then the doorbell rings. She glances at her white watch with its face encircled with lots of little fake diamonds. She hurries to the door and opens it.

'Shit, Donna. You look terrible.' Kerry peers at her friend.

Declan and Benjie are racing around the living room, screaming at the top of their voices. Donna and Kerry are in the hallway, where there is barely enough space to stand, in amongst the clutter of pushchairs, coats, discarded shoes in various shapes and sizes, Ricky's gym bag, which he dumped there yesterday, and Donna's large shopping bags from Lidl, Aldi and IKEA.

Donna sniffs. 'Bad weekend.' She can't tell Kerry about the messages from Oedipus; otherwise she'll have to tell her about Mike and the bloke she snogged all those years ago. Nothing's happened with Mike, but Donna thinks she wants it to, and that's a secret she isn't ready to tell even her best friend.

'What happened?' Kerry puts her hand on Donna's arm. 'Would you rather I stay here and keep you company? The boys don't have to go to nursery. They can play in your garden.'

'Yeah, maybe,' Donna says, and turns around to walk to the kitchen. But as she does so, she can see through the window and notices Mike has just arrived. He is peeling off a sweatshirt, his muscled torso straining against a black T-shirt. He bends down to pick up a tool. Donna swivels in the doorway, blocking the view into the kitchen and out through the kitchen window. She comes nose to nose with Kerry.

'What's up?' Kerry is forced to take a step backwards.

'Actually, I'm fine. It's a total tip in there, and I could do with a bit of time to tidy up. If you could still take the boys, that would be great.'

Kerry hesitates. 'Yeah, okay.'

* * *

Normally Donna hates cleaning, but today it's a good distraction, and she finds it therapeutic to turn the kitchen into a place of calm in contrast to the turmoil in her mind. Besides, she doesn't want Mike to see her kitchen looking like a hovel. She tries not to watch him as he's working, but her eyes are drawn to the window like a magnet. Twice Mike catches her staring. The first time he raises a hand and mouths, 'Hello.' The second time he winks at her, and Donna wants to crawl into a little hole with embarrassment. She's never had men fawning over her; she knows she's no great beauty, but she had a good figure before the children were born, and Ricky used to compliment her on her lips with their perfect little Cupid's bow, as he described it.

Mid-morning, she's finished cleaning the floor, the worktops are sparkling, and a load of laundry is in the washing machine. Skye is quietly cooing in her rocking chair, playing with a mobile. Donna reckons it's time for a cuppa. She puts the kettle on and pokes her head out of the back door. Mike has his back to her. He's mixing cement in a wheelbarrow and leaning forwards. His T-shirt has ridden up and his trousers have slipped down an inch or so, exposing the crack at the top of his buttocks. There is something strong yet delicate about that notch at the bottom of his spine and the pale skin, devoid of hair. Donna's stomach does a little somersault.

'Would you like a drink?'

Mike stands up and pulls his trousers up, tightening his belt. He gazes at her for a moment just a little too long. Donna bites her lower lip with her front teeth, then brings her fingers to her lips, stroking them a couple of times. She can't help herself.

'Sure. What's on offer?' Mike grins.

'Tea, coffee – only instant though. Squash?'

'A cup of tea, please.'

A couple of minutes later they are seated at the kitchen table. Donna wants to tell Mike about Oedipus, but she's not sure if she should.

'How was your weekend?' Mike asks, swilling the burning-hot tea in his mouth.

'I've had better. How was yours?'

'Quiet.' He looks at Donna as if he's reading her mind. 'It looks like you've got the weight of the world on your shoulders.'

'There's been some stuff going on. Ricky was questioned by the police again yesterday, and I've been getting these…' She shakes her head. 'Never mind.'

'No, go on. I'm a good ear!' Mike leans across the table and puts his hand over Donna's.

'I'm sorry I ran out on you on Saturday,' she says, her eyes fixed on her mug of tea.

'It's alright.' Mike removes his hand from Donna's. 'Tell me what's been happening. I'm good at keeping secrets.'

Donna glances up. 'You won't tell Ricky, will you?'

'Of course not. Don't see much of him these days, anyway.'

'I've been getting these anonymous texts from someone called Oedipus. They're freaking me out.'

'They're not anonymous if you know who they're from!' Mike chuckles.

Donna looks at him in surprise.

'Go on,' Mike urges as if he realises what he's said is inappropriate.

'He wants my money, but it's not my money yet, it's Mum's. The solicitor said she left it to me in her will, but I'll make sure Dad is sorted. Of course I will.' Donna hangs her head. 'No one knows I'll be getting the money. Not even Ricky. The worst is, I don't think Dad knows either.'

'That's awful, and I'm really sorry about your mum,' Mike says. 'Do you know who this Oedipus is?'

Donna shakes her head.

'But why can't you tell Ricky? Why haven't you gone to the police?'

Donna looks away and reddens. 'He took a photo of me and you the other day when we hugged. We know it was nothing, but it doesn't look like that. And he's threatening to tell Ricky.'

'Fuck!' Mike murmurs, and after a while he asks, 'Can I see the texts?'

Donna gets up, smooths her leggings and goes upstairs to look for her phone. She finds it on the floor, where she dropped it earlier. As she's walking back downstairs, she turns it around and notices she's got another text.

'Oh!' She lets out a little scream.

'What is it?' Mike jumps up and comes into the hallway to meet Donna. He extends his arms and is just about to pull her into an embrace when the doorbell goes. They look at each other, pausing in the moment. Mike lets his arms swing back to his sides while Donna throws him a rueful glance and turns towards the door. Her mind is consumed with Mike as she opens it.

'Dad!' she yells as she sees Kevin on her doorstep before throwing herself against his enormous stomach. Donna bursts into tears, the surprise at seeing her dad, the relief that he is there to look after her, and the emotion of all the events of the past few weeks all coming to the surface. Kevin hugs his daughter tightly, the first time in twenty years.

'Are you going to let me in?' he says eventually.

'Yeah, sorry, Dad. Come in. Skye's here, but Benjie's at nursery. Did they release you?'

Kevin nods. 'I'm out on bail. I didn't do it. You know that, don't you, love?' He holds Donna by the shoulders and looks earnestly into her eyes.

'Of course I know that, Dad,' she says, tugging him into the house.

'Fuck, I'm happy to be here,' Kevin says.

Donna gives him a lopsided grin. 'They didn't tell me you were getting out.' Donna smiles at him. 'Would you like a cuppa?'

'I'd prefer a beer,' Kevin says.

'It's a bit early, Dad!'

'Haven't had a beer since…' His voice trails off. 'I miss your mum!'

They look at each other, their bottom lips quivering in harmony, eyes brimming with tears.

'Got a visitor?' Kevin asks, eyeing the second mug on the table.

'No, it's just Mike. He's helping Ricky on the extension.'

'What, on a Monday? Doesn't he work?'

'I think he's between jobs,' Donna mutters as she puts the kettle back on and then searches in the fridge for a can of beer.

'Are you spending my money employing labour to enlarge your house?'

Kevin's eyes are narrowed and Donna squirms.

‘No! He’s doing it for free, as a favour to Ricky.’

‘No such thing as a free lunch, Dons,’ Kevin says. ‘I’m so happy to see my little girl, and the littler one.’ He leans over Skye’s chair and tickles her under the chin. Skye doesn’t like it and twists away before letting out a little grizzly cry.

And then there’s a knock on the back door and it opens. Mike pokes his head around the door. ‘Donna, can I fill up a bucket of…?’ His words trail off.

‘Sure,’ she says, but then she sees the way Mike narrows his eyes at Kevin. There’s something not right about Mike’s expression, but she can’t work out what it is. Her stomach clenches; she is confused. But then Mike retreats out of the back door, shutting it behind him. She watches him pick up his sweatshirt, tug it on over his head, move his tools to the edge of the wall, and then he leaves, disappearing out of view around the side of the house.

‘Do you know Mike?’ Donna asks her dad.

He shakes his head, his chin wobbling from side to side. ‘Never seen him before!’

28

Pippa

'What do you think?' Joe asks eagerly once we're outside the police station.

'I'd like to reserve judgement until I've studied the tape and transcript,' I say.

Joe looks at me askance. 'Anything we can use at the bail hearing tomorrow?'

I shake my head. There is an awkward moment as we search for things to say to one another, and then we both speak at the same time.

'I'd better get going,' I say. 'I'd like to catch the train before rush hour.' I hope Joe doesn't offer to give me a lift. I need to be alone to think things through.

'Sure. I've got some bits and pieces to tie up here. Let's stay in touch.'

We smile at each other, and I turn to walk towards the Tube station. After ten metres or so, I glance back over my shoulder. Joe is still standing there watching me. I give a ridiculous little wave and hurry away, burying myself in a crowd of German tourists.

It's a relief to get into my car at Pulborough station. My head is pounding. Rush hour seems to start earlier and earlier, and I had to stand for thirty minutes before getting a seat on the train. I call George's mobile, but it goes straight to voicemail. I then try Marie's, and it does the same, so I call the hospital instead. No change in George's condition, which must be a good thing. I ask the nurse to tell him that I rang, to stress how concerned I am about him. I call the maternity ward to ask about Marie, but she has been discharged. Again, that is positive news, but I wonder where she and her parents are and chastise myself for not asking where they are staying, for not offering them a bed.

It is dark by the time I pull up outside home. Mungo must be starving. I hurry up the garden path, grateful for the security lights, and put my key in the front door. It doesn't turn. I try again. Same thing. I push the door and it swings open. 'Damn,' I mutter. Harriet must have forgotten to lock the door behind her when she left.

'Mungo! Mungo, darling. I'm home!'

The dog doesn't appear. I hurry through to the kitchen, where Mungo sleeps, but his bed is empty. I feel a kernel of panic. 'Mungo!' I yell now, hurrying through the house, upstairs and down again. Then I open the back door and peer out into the garden, shouting for him. But there is silence, and no dog appears. I try to calm myself. Harriet must still have him. She doesn't normally work this late, but perhaps she hung on to him and is waiting for me to get home.

I fumble with the phone in my hurry to call her. This time she answers.

'Harriet, it's Pippa Durrant. Have you got Mungo?'

She hesitates. 'No,' she says in a questioning tone. 'I dropped him back at your house at least two hours ago. What's happened?'

Panic grips my throat, and my voice sounds strangled. 'The front door wasn't locked and Mungo is nowhere to be seen. Did you lock the door properly after you left?'

'Of course I did, Dr Durrant. This is my livelihood, and if I didn't lock up properly or didn't care for the dogs, word would get around in no time and I'd have no business. I promise you I locked up.' She sounds both indignant and upset. 'I made sure he was settled in his bed and then I left. Are you sure no one else has been in the house?'

No, I'm not sure. I don't have an alarm and have no means of knowing what has happened. But Harriet is the only person who knows where I leave the key. The key! Of course. I haven't looked to see if it is still there.

'Don't worry, Harriet. I'm sure he'll turn up.'

'Dr Durrant, if you can't find him, please call me back. I'll come over and help you look for him. He's a gorgeous dog, one of my favourites.'

'Thanks, Harriet. Will do.'

I rush to the side of the house and lift up the blue flowerpot. There's not much light, so I run my fingers over the paving stone, but there's nothing there except dampness, bits of soil, and leaf residue. I lift up the adjacent flowerpot, the terracotta one that holds my sad little bay tree. There is nothing under that either. My heart is thumping as I run back into the house and press redial on the phone.

'Have you found him?' Harriet asks breathlessly.

'No, and the key isn't under the flowerpot. Did you leave it there?'

'Yes. I put it back in exactly the same place I found it. Hold tight, Dr Durrant. I'm coming over. I'll be with you in ten minutes.' She hangs up before I have a chance to reply.

I don't know what to do with myself. Mungo is like my third child. Sometimes I think I love him even more than I have ever loved any human. It sounds terrible to say that, but with Flo gone and George so distant, Mungo has been quite literally my lifesaver. I pace the house, calling him half-heartedly now, as I know he isn't there. We'll have to go door to door, asking the neighbours if they've seen him. I'll call the police, but what should I tell them? That I've had a break-in? The key is gone, my dog is gone, but the house appears totally untouched.

I pace from room to room, checking that everything is where it should be. My laptop is on the kitchen table. The television is in the living room. My jewellery is stashed at the back of the chest of drawers in my bedroom. The door from the hallway into my office is locked; the key is hanging up behind the curtain in the living room, where I always leave it. I unlock the door, glance around, check my filing cabinet is still locked. Everything is exactly as it should be. But at this point I would give up everything I own in exchange for the safe return of Mungo.

'Dr Durrant!' Harriet is at the front door. She is flushed, as harassed-looking as I feel. 'Any news?'

'No. I'll ring a couple of neighbours, but I think we should do a door-to-door.'

'I agree. Have you looked everywhere? The house, the garden? He's not a young dog. He seemed in good health, but you never know.'

I stifle a sob. 'I haven't had a good look in the garden.'

'Let's go,' she says. She's a practical, head-girl type is Harriet. A farmer's daughter, rosy-cheeked, no nonsense, early thirties. She's brought a strong torch, which she shines around the small garden, peering behind bushes, all the time calling his name. There's nowhere for Mungo to go. He can't get out of the courtyard garden. It's one of the many reasons that attracted me to the house in the first place: a walled garden with borders crammed with English country-garden-type flowers: delphiniums, peonies, foxgloves, cornflowers, roses, dahlias – plenty of colour in the summer.

'I've never really got to know the neighbours,' I admit.

'Don't worry, we'll find him,' she says determinedly.

We walk back through the kitchen door, through the kitchen, and pause in the hallway. I reach for my coat before realising I'm still wearing it.

'Why don't you do the houses on the right, and I'll do the ones on the left?' Harriet says. 'Leave your mobile on. Let's touch base in thirty minutes, assuming neither of us have found him before then.'

'Okay. But should we call the police?'

I think of Joe Swain and wonder whether Mungo's disappearance has got anything to do with the case. But how? It doesn't make sense. Could Ricky have Mungo? Or has someone injured my son and taken my dog in order to hurt me? I pinch the back of my hand. Paranoia is getting the better of me.

It's gone 6.30 p.m. by now, so most people are at home when I ring their doorbells. The answers are all the same.

'Sorry, love. No.'

'I've only just got home from work. Haven't seen him.'

'No, can't help. Why don't you put up a notice on the lamp posts?'

I want to scream. After reaching the end of the street, I stride into Buckhurst Lane. There are fewer houses here. The answer is still the same. A shake of the head, a look of woe, of sympathy. And then I reach The Kings Horse pub. I've only been in once before and came straight back out again. It's more of a workingman's pub than a country inn, full of old men watching sport on the television, tipping back glasses of beer, jostling each other loudly. They don't serve food. The place is practically empty; not surprising considering the early hour and the fact it's a Monday evening. No one looks up as I walk in, my nostrils twitching from the unpleasant smell of stale spilled beer. The barman looks barely old enough to be drinking in a pub let alone serving in one. His eyes are firmly glued to his mobile phone.

'Excuse me,' I say, coughing.

He glances up, eyelids heavy. 'Yeah?'

'Have you by any chance seen a black Labrador?'

'Yeah.'

I gasp and then control myself. 'Is that a yeah, you've seen him?'

'Yeah,' he says, showing no further emotion.

I want to shake this boy. 'Where and when did you see him?'

'He's out the back. Dad's got him.'

'Mungo's here!' I clap my hands. 'Oh, that's wonderful.'

The boy slides off his bar stool and ambles slowly to a door at the back of the bar. *Hurry up*, I want to scream.

'Dad! Dad! A woman's here for the dog.'

The lad returns to his bar stool, not once looking up or asking me if I'd like a drink or offering any further nuggets of information.

I wait, my foot tapping the floor, chewing my fingernails. Eventually a man appears from behind the bar. He walks as slowly as his son, but I can forgive him. He has a severe limp and a livid scar that runs down his left cheek.

'Is he yours?' he grunts.

'If he's a black Labrador. My telephone number is on a tag attached to his red collar.'

'Didn't see no tag. I've rung the RSPCA. They're going to pick him up in the morning.'

'But he's mine!'

'So you say.'

I want to scream. 'Where did you find him?'

'Old Jimmy found him. The dog was with some bloke who was holding his collar, not even on a lead. The bloke let the dog go and walked away. The dog was trotting around aimlessly, so Jimmy brought him in. We've given him a drink and a bag of crisps.'

Clearly this man has no idea how to look after a Labrador. I try not to wince.

'Can I see him? When he sees me, you'll see from his reaction that he's my dog. Please?' I beg.

'Alright then. Pete, go get the dog,' he shouts at his son.

A long few minutes later, Pete comes out. They've attached a piece of string to Mungo's lead, but when Mungo sees me, he bounds forwards with such force that the string breaks. I bend down, and my beautiful dog jumps up on me. I throw my arms around him, and despite the fact I loathe being licked on my face, I let him lap up my tears of relief.

'Thank you,' I say as I stand up. 'Do you think Jimmy would be able to give me a description of the man who had him?'

'Dunno,' the owner of the pub says. 'He's over there. You can ask him yourself.'

I walk towards the aged man wearing a frayed jumper sitting at the far end of the bar, huddled over a beer.

'Well, look who it is! The black dog! Hello, dog!' He leans down and gives Mungo a rub on the back.

'Thank you for rescuing Mungo. Do you know who had him?'

He shakes his head. 'I saw the man walk down your garden path, away from the house, holding on to the dog's collar. When he got on to the road, he let the dog go. Just walked off in the opposite direction.'

'How do you know where I live?' I ask.

He shakes his head at me. 'You're notorious, young lady,' he says, laughing. 'When one of our folk are in papers, we all know where you live.'

I nod. This is a small town, after all. I shouldn't be surprised.

'Could you give me a description of the man?'

'Youngish, medium height. My eyesight ain't so good these days.' He rubs his rheumy eyes as if to give credence to the statement. I thank him anyway, call Mungo to heel, and the two of us race back home.

I telephone Harriet. 'I've got him!' I exclaim. I don't know who is more relieved, her or me. Now I just need to work out who took Mungo. And who has the key to my house.

29

Donna

Donna is in a wonderful mood when Ricky gets home from work. As soon as he steps inside the front door, there she is, throwing her arms around him, giving him a big kiss on the lips.

'I hate arguing with you,' she says, dancing around as if they are lovers making up after their first tiff.

After Kevin left, she decided she needs to rally round her family, be the glue that brings them all together, because they're all she has. She resolves to stay away from Mike, and when the time is right, she'll tell Ricky about the messages from Oedipus. But in the meantime she needs to make Ricky fall back in love with her again, and hopefully fall out of love with his bit on the side.

Ricky is suspicious. They haven't spoken properly in forty-eight hours and she's acting as if nothing is amiss.

'I've cleaned the house and made your favourite, toad-in-the-hole, for tea. Would you like a beer?' She pulls him into the kitchen and grabs a beer out of the fridge. 'Benjie, come and say hello to Daddy! How was work?'

'Fine,' he says, sitting at his normal place at the kitchen table. He can't recall seeing the kitchen this neat and tidy since they moved in. She takes the tray out of the oven and places it on the table, then cuts Ricky a large slice.

'Here you go! Hope you like it,' she coos.

After Ricky has eaten half of what is on his plate, Donna puts down her knife and fork. 'I know you won't think this is great news, but I do. And he's my dad, so please be kind. He was released from prison today. Obviously they don't think he did it!'

'What do you mean?' Ricky's fork hovers in the air.

‘Dad’s been released!’

‘Released released, or released on bail?’

‘I think he said on bail, but that’s great news, isn’t it?’

Ricky lets his fork drop. ‘No, it’s not. They think he’s guilty as hell, but he’s been let out of jail until the trial. And then when he’s found guilty, he’ll be put away for the rest of his life.’

‘They wouldn’t have let him out if they thought he was a murderer,’ Donna cries.

‘Don’t be so bloody stupid. They let everyone out, even suspected murderers, so long as they don’t think they’re likely to kill anyone else whilst on bail. Or if they’ve got previous.’

Donna’s face falls. ‘But Dad isn’t guilty. He loved Mum.’

‘Don’t be so naive, Donna. I know you don’t want to believe he’s a murderer because he’s your dad, but Kevin killed your mother.’

‘You’re wrong, Ricky. I looked him in the eye this afternoon and asked him if he did it. He took my hand, placed it on his chest and said he’d never touched Mum.’

Ricky thumps his fist on the kitchen table. The cutlery makes a loud clatter, and Donna grabs her wine glass to stop it toppling over.

‘Did Kevin come here?’

Donna nods as a knot of fear grows in her throat.

‘I forbade you from seeing him! Which part of that do you not understand?’

‘You can’t forbid me from seeing my own dad! I love him. Besides, he came here, just turned up. I didn’t go to him or anything.’

‘Kevin is a dangerous man. You are not to see him!’ Ricky yells. ‘Do you understand?’ That tendon is flickering in his jaw again, and his eyes are narrowed.

‘Dad wouldn’t hurt a fly,’ she says. ‘You don’t know him like I do.’

Ricky stands up, shoving his chair backwards so hard that it topples over. He strides around the table and holds Donna's face between his hands. 'Donna, I love you. I want what's best for you, for us. You must promise to stay away from Kevin. I don't want him anywhere near you or the babies. Do you understand?'

Donna nods, but she doesn't understand. Ricky releases his grip and gives her a quick kiss on the forehead. She knows Ricky has never liked her dad, but she has never seen him display this level of animosity towards him.

'Mum would never have wanted you to stop me from seeing Dad,' she says quietly, almost to herself.

'You didn't know your mother, and you certainly don't know your father!' Ricky says.

'Of course I knew Mum!' Donna raises her voice now too. Speaking about her mum seems to give her strength.

Ricky can't help himself. The words just slip out. 'So you knew she was having affairs for years? You knew about Abdul, did you?'

Donna pales. 'What do you mean?' she whispers.

'I'm sorry love. You think you know your parents so well, but you don't. Your mother had affairs, and your father found out and killed her.'

'Fuck off! Just fuck off!' Donna screams.

And Ricky does. He walks out of the kitchen and then she hears the front door slam, a noise that ricochets through the house, causing Skye to cry out in her sleep. Donna looks at the intercom but doesn't move. Then she hears the van cough and Ricky is gone. *Let him go into the arms of his whore*, she thinks. *Good riddance!*

Skye whimpers a little and then falls silent. Donna stays seated at the table, her eyes overflowing with tears, her body trembling with shock and disappointment. She thought she loved her family, but now she wonders whether in fact she hates them. She needs to talk to someone, Mike preferably, but as she hasn't got his number, Kerry will have to do.

She stumbles upstairs, trying to stifle her sobs so the little ones don't hear. She retrieves her mobile phone from the stairs, and only when she puts in her passcode does she remember that she received another text from Oedipus. A text that she hasn't read because she got distracted by Mike and her dad. She reckons the day can't get much worse, so she clicks on it.

Account number: 94508272 Sort code: 339914 Transfer £100k by Friday 9am; otherwise I'll tell Ricky. Get the dosh off your dad. Go to the police or tell ANYONE. You're DEAD.

Donna drops the phone. This sort of thing only happens in films. It's a joke. She hasn't got one hundred quid, let alone one hundred thousand. The money isn't hers. Not yet anyway. She wonders if her dad has access to it. But what should she tell him? As much as she loves Kevin – or at least she thinks she does – he's tight. The chances he'll lend her that kind of money, assuming he even has access to it, are slim indeed.

Donna has never felt so lost, so terrified. She crawls into bed, fully clothed, and holds the pillow to her stomach, keening backwards and forwards, sobbing for her mother.

'Why is Ricky saying such horrid things about you?' she cries. 'I love you, Mum. I miss you.'

* * *

When Donna wakes up, the light is pale grey. For a moment she is confused. The curtains are open and Ricky's not there. She glances at the alarm clock. 4.52 a.m. She's still in yesterday's clothes, feeling hot and sweaty. Last night comes back to her. There's an empty wine glass on her bedside table. She swings her feet out of bed. Giddy and nauseous, she makes her way to the bathroom. Her lips are stained dark red from the wine; stripes of black mascara line her cheeks.

After drinking from the bathroom tap and slapping her face with cold water, she wanders around the house looking for Ricky. He's not there. His van isn't outside either.

She's terrified of her phone now, wondering if she's got another threatening text, but she needs to use it, to ask Kerry to take Benjie to playgroup. There's no way she can face the world. Besides, she needs to go and see Kevin to ask for the money. With her heart thumping hard, she switches it on. But there are no messages, no missed calls. She turns on the television, and to her dismay, her dad's release on bail is on the news. It's only on Southern, but still. And they're showing the picture of that psychologist woman. Once again, Donna wonders what the hell she's got to do with it.

There's a loud noise out the back. It sounds like something metal has crashed to the ground where the building work is going on, where their new extension is. Thinking it must be Ricky stumbling home after a heavy night drinking, she rushes to the back door. But she can't see anyone. She tries to be rational. It's a windy day. Something must have fallen down. No need to worry.

30

If I was careful last time, this time I'm being pedantic. I check and double-check the contents of my backpack. Latex gloves, disposable paper suit, shoe covers, balaclava, alcohol wipes, bin liners and a hammer – all there. I take one of those sticky lint clothes rollers and roll it up and down every inch of my trousers, my hoodie, the backpack and even my hair. I can't risk a single little fibre or a hair inconspicuously falling to the ground, ready to be pounced upon by the forensics. I may not get the chance to change into the paper suit, but if I do, I've got my story all ready. Pest control. Perhaps in another life I'd make a good rat-catcher.

It's cold outside, so no one glances at me dressed in my hoodie and leather gloves and sneakers carefully chosen to make sure they don't squeak. I'm lucky because it's blowing a gale, but it's not raining. Not yet. I'll abort my mission if it starts raining. The rain washes away footsteps outside, but there's too much of a risk I might bring the wet inside. Besides, they'll be a different sort of wet soon enough. I chuckle to myself as I think about it.

I walk slowly. Patience is one of my virtues. Everything comes to those who wait, and if it doesn't, then what's the harm in speeding things up? My heart beats a little faster than usual.

It must be the excitement. The anticipation. The knowing that I am in control.

I stop at the end of the street, looking. Really looking. Not like most people who think they see but miss the most important bits. That's why ordinary people make such lousy witnesses. They see what they want to see, what they think they should see. Not me. I go through my mental checklist, and when I'm sure the time is right, I step forwards and walk briskly towards the house, a little anticipatory grin playing at the corners of my mouth.

31

Pippa

I ring a locksmith but just get a voicemail, so I leave a message. I bolt the front door top and bottom.

I'm too wired to sleep, so I switch on my laptop, take it to bed and find a stupid romcom on Netflix. Normally Mungo sleeps downstairs, but tonight I've brought his bed upstairs and placed it next to mine. I need his company. He is thrilled and is happily lying on his back with his legs in the air, snoring contentedly. A ping alerts me to an incoming email, so I pause the film and hope it isn't yet another client cancellation.

It's from Joe. He's sent me the transcript of the interview and promises to drop off the video in the morning. Switching off Netflix, I set to work on my analysis. I'm looking for nonspecific denials, outright failures to deny, unnecessary words, embellishments, and all sorts of other phrases that suggest the speaker has said one thing but means something totally different. I highlight every sentence, looking for clusters of evidence within each response. The trouble is, I just can't find them. I know Joe thinks Kevin Smith is guilty, but in this interview, he doesn't appear to tell a single lie. And if Kevin is telling the truth, then he is not guilty. He didn't kill his wife and he hasn't got a clue who I am.

I'll wait to get the video to be doubly sure, but I know what I saw, and I know what this transcript suggests. The truth.

The more I think about it, the more I think that Kevin is innocent, but from what I have seen of Ricky, he is guilty. I wonder if it was Ricky who broke into the house earlier, who stole Mungo. If only dogs could talk!

* * *

I awake to find two texts on my phone. The first is from Brent, asking if he can come and see me. I worry for Brent. Perhaps he isn't as together as I hoped. Perhaps the rejection by his birth mother has hit him really hard. It wouldn't surprise me.

The second text is from Joe.

Bail hearing at 10am. Any info for me before then? J

I reply.

Not what you're going to want to hear, but think K is innocent. Couldn't detect any lies from the transcript.

I hesitate about whether to sign off with an *X* but decide that would be unprofessional and suited to a young person, not me. I wait for a reply, but I don't get one.

I telephone the hospital to ask after George. The nurse speaks kindly, with a sing-song Indian accent.

'Yes, Mrs Durrant. Your son was in discomfort last night. He will have another CT scan this morning to rule out any further problems. Please don't worry.'

But I do worry. Of course I worry. I'm his mother.

I text Brent.

Sorry can't meet this morning, need to go to the hospital to see George. Perhaps later on today? I'll call you. Hope all's ok?

My next phone call is to Harriet.

'Any chance I could drop Mungo off at your house today?'

I know it's not her normal service, but she doesn't hesitate. 'Yes, of course. Bring him over whenever it suits.'

* * *

George is asleep. Both arms are connected to drips; his face is pale underneath a couple of days of stubble. I look at this man, who looks so much like my own father, my heart full of love. A nurse arrives to take his blood pressure and to give him pills.

'Has he had the CT scan yet?' I ask.

She glances at a chart hanging off the end of his bed. 'No. It's due today, though. He had a busy time yesterday. His fiancée and her parents were here most of the afternoon, and a friend of his popped by in the evening. George was asleep by then, so the friend didn't stay long.'

I am confused. Who would know that George was in hospital? I wonder for a moment if it was Trevor. He might have said he was a friend so as not to upset the apple cart. But that's not Trevor's style. He would be proud to be George's father.

'What sort of age was the friend?' I ask, trying to keep my tone casual.

'Everyone is young to me these days!' The nurse chuckles. 'I'd say about the same sort of age as your son. Maybe a tad older – thirty-ish.'

'Do you keep a register as to who comes in and out?'

She shoots me a look. 'No. There's a trolley that comes around a bit later if you want a cuppa.'

It's a bit of a non sequitur, but I smile at her. And then she is gone, bustling from bed to bed. One of the NHS's true heroines.

After an hour or so, during which I try and fail to read *The Times*, George wakes up.

'Hello, love, how are you feeling?'

'Not great,' he says, sighing.

'Is Marie due to see you today?'

He shakes his head. 'Her parents insisted she go home with them. If she doesn't go now, she won't be able to fly, and she'd have to have the baby here. At least if she's in

Geneva, they can look after her.' George turns his head away from me, but I can sense the pain.

'You'll be out of here in no time, darling. And then you'll be back with her for when the baby is born.'

He doesn't answer, and I hope I haven't made a false promise.

'Who was the friend that came to visit you last night?' I try to keep the question light in tone.

'No idea,' he murmurs.

'Do any of your friends know you're here in hospital?'

'Wouldn't have thought so. Don't have many friends in the UK. Kind of lost touch with them all.' He closes his eyes and his breathing settles. But as he calms, I feel increasingly uneasy. Who was it that visited George? Was it Ricky, and if so, what the hell did he want? I debate calling Joe, requesting police protection for George. Is that ridiculous? I just don't know.

As it turns out, Joe calls me. George is in a deep sleep, and there's nothing much for me to do, so I tell the duty nurse I'll be going into town for a couple of hours and will be back later.

'Kevin's got bail,' he says dejectedly.

'I think Ricky might have visited George in hospital yesterday evening,' I say.

Joe laughs. 'Come on, Pippa! Why would Ricky visit George?'

This infuriates me. 'He ran George off the road, so he probably popped in to find out how his victim is doing! That's what sick people do, isn't it?'

'You're the psychologist; I'm just a policeman.' He pauses. 'The thing is, Pippa, Ricky didn't run George's car off the road. It wasn't him.'

'How do you know?' I exclaim.

'We ran number plate checks, and Ricky was where he said he was, and it wasn't anywhere between Storrington and Gatwick. He was in London.'

I don't know what to say. I was so convinced it was Ricky.

'Was it an accident or deliberate, George's collision?' I ask eventually.

'We don't have any evidence to suggest it was anything but an accident. Witnesses are notoriously unreliable on the whole, as I'm sure you know. It's quite possible that the witness thought he saw something he didn't. The trouble is, we only have a partial plate, and being a rural road, there are no cameras in the vicinity.'

'How partial?' I ask.

'Two digits,' he says. 'We're going to have to let it go.'

'Someone broke into my house yesterday.'

'What?' Joe exclaims. 'Why didn't you ring me?'

'Well, they didn't break in exactly. The key has gone from under the flowerpot, and they took my dog. Let him loose on the street. I recovered him from the pub.'

Joe laughs. That infuriates me. I know it's not a serious crime like murder, but it is still deeply upsetting.

'What was the dog drinking, beer or spirits?'

'Ha ha.'

'You shouldn't leave a key under a flowerpot, Pippa. It's not safe.'

I sigh. 'I'm changing the locks.'

'Good. How's George doing?'

'I'm in Redhill now. Not so great. We'll know more later.'

'Would you like me to drop off the video?'

'At my house?' I ask.

'Yes. I can come by after work if that's convenient.'

'Sure. See you later.'

* * *

George has had his CT scan by the time I return to the hospital, and although he's in a lot of discomfort, the doctor isn't worried about him. I am more concerned about who will turn up to visit George when I'm gone, as he lies there incapacitated.

'Are you prepared to see Dad?' I ask George. 'He's really worried about you and would desperately like to visit.'

'No,' George mutters, and turns his head away from me. I don't push it and am still hopeful that when he's feeling a bit better, he might relent. As much as I dislike how my ex-husband behaved, as much as I think he deserved the ostracising at the time, animosities have gone on for too long. I want George not to forget but to forgive.

'I don't think my son should have any visitors except immediate family: his father, his uncle and me,' I say to the matron as I leave the hospital.

She frowns.

'We're still not sure if it was an accident or deliberate,' I explain.

She goes on to a computer and scrolls through some documents. She looks up at me, peering over the top of her spectacles. 'There's nothing on file to say that George needs protection. But don't worry, there's someone here all the time. Nothing goes unnoticed in this place.'

Unconvinced, I give a half smile and promise to return in the morning.

I stop by at Harriet's to collect Mungo, and by the time I pull up outside home, the light is fading fast. The rain has stopped, but it's still a miserable autumnal day. There is a person leaning against the side of my house, just by the front door porch, half in the shadows. I catch my breath. Holding Mungo on the lead, I get out of the car. I can see it's a man with a pale face, so not Joe. Mungo growls and my heart misses a beat. The man stands up straight as we approach, and when we're about ten metres away, he bends down and holds open his arms.

‘Hello, Mungo! Haven’t seen you in ages.’

Mungo wags his tail and I let out a sigh of relief.

‘You gave me a fright, Brent,’ I say. ‘I wasn’t expecting you.’

He stands up. ‘Sorry about that. I need to talk to you. Can I come in?’

‘Of course. Have you been waiting long?’

‘No. Half an hour or so.’

That’s long, I think to myself. *He must really need to see me.*

I lead Brent through the house, open up the office, and tell him to take a seat whilst I feed Mungo and make us both a cup of tea.

‘What’s going on?’ I ask as I sit down in my chair and swivel to face him.

‘I’ve split up with my girl,’ he says.

‘I’m sorry to hear that. What happened?’

He rolls his eyes. ‘Usual. She got too clingy and I pushed her away. How’s George doing?’

‘Making reasonable progress,’ I say.

‘Would you like to talk about your birth mother?’ I ask gently.

‘I didn’t tell you everything before,’ he says, looking everywhere except at me. ‘She’s dead.’

I frown. ‘You said she told you to go away, that she didn’t want to know you.’

‘Yes. And then she died.’ He sniffs. ‘So there’s no hope now.’

‘What happened?’

‘When I found her, she was in a hospice. Cancer. Dying. And now she’s dead.’

I lean forwards. ‘I’m so sorry, Brent. You don’t deserve this.’

‘All I wanted was a fucking family. To at least be acknowledged.’

'Of course you do. Anyone would want that. Tell me more about how that feels.'

But we're interrupted by the doorbell. I glance at my watch.

'Would you excuse me a moment?' I stand up and peer out of the window to check who it is. It's Joe, looking as debonair as always.

Hovering by my chair, I turn to Brent. 'I'm sorry, Brent. I'd forgotten that a colleague was dropping off something for me. Can you hang on for five or ten minutes?'

He nods.

Joe is at my front door, not my client door. I open it.

'Come in,' I say, smiling. 'I've unexpectedly got a client. Would you like to stay? I don't know how long I'll be.'

'No. I was just going to drop this off.' He hands me an envelope. 'I've got a lot of paperwork to catch up on this evening. How about a drink later in the week? You can give me your thoughts on Kevin Smith in person.' He grins.

'I'm not sure you'll like my analysis,' I say, 'but I'd be happy to have a drink.'

We agree on Thursday evening, which will give me plenty of time to finish the report. He waves his hand awkwardly and disappears down the path to his sleek car. Beaming, I go back inside and into my study. I do a double take.

Brent has gone.

32

Kerry

'Hiya, Donna! Anyone home?' Kerry shouts through the letter box. It's gone 4.30 p.m. and she's brought Benjie back from playgroup. She's in a hurry to get home, to give Declan his tea so she can get ready for a date with her new boyfriend, a plumber from Worthing. Donna's hallway looks like a bomb has exploded, as it always does. She presses the doorbell again and tries to quell the kernel of concern in her stomach. Why isn't Donna answering? Then she hears the cry of a baby – not a cry, more like a desperate wail.

'Wait here.' She bends down to the little boys. 'Can you be super-good, boys? Hold hands and stay here until I get back? If you promise not to move, I'll give you both a chocolate bar, okay?'

They look at her with big eyes, mouths salivating. Both Benjie and Declan nod their heads earnestly.

She walks around the left of the house. The side gate is ajar. She manoeuvres between the piles of bricks and bags of concrete and wheelbarrows and poles of scaffolding. She peers into the kitchen and sees it as it always is. Yesterday's dinner plates are piled up next to the sink. This morning's breakfast and lunch paraphernalia is still on the table. No sign of Donna.

She returns to the front door, knocks on it and shouts for Donna again. When there's no answer, she tries the back door, and to her surprise it opens. Walking in gingerly, she carries on shouting for Donna. If she was on the toilet, she'd be out by now, wouldn't she?

Baby Skye is wailing. Hesitating no longer, Kerry runs through the house, skipping over discarded clothes, stray Lego pieces and an empty mug. There's no one downstairs.

She takes the stairs two at a time and races into the children's room. The walls are painted pale blue. There's a yellow blind at the window that is half down. Benjie's bed is unmade, his toys scattered on top of the duvet and on the floor. Skye is whimpering now, trying to pull herself up in her cot. But Kerry senses the baby is exhausted.

'You poor little thing!' she says as she lifts the infant up. 'Wow, you're stinky, aren't you?' She tries not to inhale the stench of excrement coming from Skye's nappy. She wrinkles her nose as she notices the stained, urine-drenched bedclothes. 'Let's get you changed,' she says. She shoves some toys to one side, lays Skye down on the changing mat on the floor, adeptly removes her nappy, and wipes her bottom with several wet wipes. The baby stops crying for a moment but then starts wailing again. Kerry puts a clean nappy on her and holds Skye up in the air.

'Are you hungry, darling?' she asks. 'Where's your mum gone? It's not like her to leave you all alone.'

Kerry puts the changing mat on top of the wet bedclothes and places Skye back into her cot. The baby starts screaming again. Her face is raspberry red, and yellow snot cakes her nose.

'I'll warm you up some milk,' Kerry says. 'But I need to bring the boys in and go and find your mummy first. I'll be as quick as I can.'

Kerry leans out of the window. To her relief, she can see the little boys sitting on the doorstep, chatting away earnestly.

'Stay there, boys!' she yells. 'I won't be much longer.'

She rushes out of the children's room. The door to Donna and Ricky's bedroom is closed. Kerry has been in once or twice before, when she and Donna were getting ready to go out. It's a nice enough room, with a large pine bed, green-and-white floral curtains and a large fake wood wardrobe, one of those modular ones sold at IKEA. Kerry hesitates and then knocks on the door.

'Donna, are you awake?'

Silence.

Kerry turns the door handle and gingerly peers inside.

Her screams reverberate throughout the whole street, shattering the mundane tranquillity of an ordinary neighbourhood on a quiet Tuesday afternoon. A Tuesday afternoon that should have been just like any other Tuesday afternoon.

But is not.

It's the blood that Kerry sees first. Scarlet-red blood everywhere. Up the walls, on the curtains, soaking the duvet. So much blood. The stench of blood and faeces is overwhelming. She can't recognise Donna's face, because it is a red mush of blood and gore and bone. But she recognises those leggings, those Ugg boots. And she recognises the face of the woman on the photo that has been placed so very carefully on Donna's stomach.

Kerry runs to the staircase and vomits, retching again and again, leaving a trail of rancid puke all the way down the stairs.

Her screams mingle with the screams of the baby and the cries of the little boys, who have no idea what has happened but inherently know that no adult should ever make a noise like that.

33

Ricky

The police receive four phone calls reporting an incident on Ridings Lane, Horsham. Three are from concerned neighbours, too scared to go and investigate themselves; the fourth is from Ravi, a passing Amazon delivery driver, who nearly runs Kerry over as she zigzags into the road.

'It's not natural, a noise like that,' old Mrs White tells the police when she gets through to 999. 'A woman is screaming as if something really terrible has happened. I'm bolting my doors.'

At first the Amazon driver is angry with Kerry.

'What yer doing nearly getting run over?' Ravi shouts as he jumps out of his van. But when he realises the state she's in and hears the wails and notices her inability to form a coherent word, he gets scared.

'Get the police here right away!' he tells the operator.

And then Ravi sees the two little boys clinging to each other on the doorstep, their faces as pale as the moon in the dusky light. He parks the van on the side of the road a few doors up.

'Get in,' he instructs Kerry. 'Wait here until the police arrive. I'll go get the little boys.'

'Declan!' she says, moaning, bending forwards as if she's been stabbed in the stomach. Ravi hopes she won't be sick in his van.

He paces over to the two boys and crouches down. 'What are your names?' He tries to sound child-friendly, but at twenty-five, with no experience of children, he wonders if he sounds scary instead. The boy with the crew cut wearing a bright-blue anorak looks at him with big eyes.

'Benjie,' he says.

The other lad doesn't look up at all. Tears are dripping down his face.

'Cheer up,' Ravi says, winking, before plonking himself down on the doorstep next to them. The front door behind them is ajar, and he can hear a baby screaming from inside the house. But he isn't going to go in. The last thing Ravi wants is to get involved in some strangers' mess.

Ravi looks up in alarm as two men stride towards him.

'What's going on? What are you doing on the doorstep of my house?'

'Sorry.' Ravi stumbles to get up. 'There's a lady screaming her head off. Nearly ran her over, I did. She's sitting in my van. And these two little 'uns were sitting here all alone. I've called the police.'

Mike sizes Ravi up whilst Ricky shakes his head as he absorbs what Ravi has said. Then as if a switch has been flicked in his brain, he spits, 'What the fuck?'

He scoops Benjie up. Declan starts yowling. They can all hear the baby screeching from inside the house.

'Give me Benjie,' Mike urges. 'I'll look round the back whilst you go in.'

Ricky nods and shoves Benjie into Mike's open arms. Benjie starts wailing too. A few moments later there's the *eeh-awh* sound of a police siren, which increases in volume, getting louder and louder until the vehicle is blocking the road right in front of 41 Ridings Lane. Two policemen in uniform jump out, the car's blue lights still flashing. Kerry stumbles out of Ravi's van and weaves towards the policemen as if she's drunk.

'Donna,' she moans before crumpling to the ground like a marionette with cut strings.

The smaller of the policemen, with an egg-shaped head and bushy moustache, radios for an ambulance and backup. The taller, younger man rushes into the house and puts his arm around Ricky, who is standing at the top of the stairs making animal noises.

Thirty minutes later, Ridings Lane is the scene of a major incident. Police cars are positioned either end of the street, cordoning it off. The neighbours who are home are gathered in small groups, muttering behind hands, eyes wide, necks craning. They've been told to remain in their homes, but no one wants to be alone at a time like this, so they flock together like sheep. Large crowds stand at either end of the street, people furious that they can't get home. No one knows what's going on, other than it's serious. With the number of police cars and three ambulances, it must be serious.

Janet Curran is on the scene quickly, taking charge of Benjie and Skye.

'Where are you taking them?' Ricky lunges towards her.

'They'll be kept somewhere safe tonight,' another policeman says. 'It's bctter they're not here.'

Benjie is screaming, clutching BaaBaa to his chest, and Janet is struggling to keep hold of his hand.

'They're my children! Give them to me!' Ricky dives forwards and swipes Benjie's hand from Janet's.

'I want Mama!' Benjie howls. Ricky bends to his knees and sweeps Benjie into an embrace. The little boy sobs into his shoulder.

* * *

Kerry is seated in the back of an ambulance, a tinfoil blanket around her shoulders. A mug of sugary tea has materialised from somewhere. An ambulancewoman is trying to get her to drink it, but she's shaking too much to hold the mug.

'Where's Declan?' she asks again and again.

'Your mum's got him,' the paramedic replies, patiently answering the question that Kerry has asked nearly ten times. It's as if nothing can penetrate her mind, as if she can't retain any information. Donna's mutilated body and that sea of blood have wiped most of Kerry's cognitive functions.

* * *

Detective Sergeant Joe Swain and various of his colleagues appear, taking charge of the scene.

Janet Curran is standing next to Ricky and Benjie, gently swinging the sleeping baby in her car seat backwards and forwards, backwards and forwards. She has given Skye a bottle, and despite the commotion, the loud voices, the police sirens and flashing lights, and the street full of strangers, Skye is fast asleep, oblivious to the fact that she has been traumatised. Janet has a phone pressed up to her ear and is speaking in a quiet but authoritarian manner.

'Kevin,' Ricky mutters, shaking his head as if he's trying to dispel what he's seen.

'We've put out an arrest warrant for Kevin Smith, and officers are on their way to his house as we speak,' Joe Swain confirms. 'I'm very sorry.'

Ricky screams, jabbing his finger at Joe's chest. 'If you'd done your fucking jobs properly, that bastard would still be behind bars and my wife would be alive. It's your fucking fault!'

Benjie starts screeching again. Janet Curran bends down and tries to calm him, but Benjie just kicks her and thumps her chest with his little fists.

Joe feels like hanging his head, but he knows he can't admit liability.

'Can you take this gentleman to my car?' he instructs a uniformed policeman standing to his left. He needs Ricky off the street so no one can hear the accusations. He beckons to the policeman and they step to one side.

'Yes, sir. I've already taken Ricky Wiśniewski's statement. He's got alibis for the whole day, and we're getting them checked out now. He says he left home at 7.30 a.m., spent the day at work on a building site down on the coast, went out for a drink straight after work, and arrived back home just after we were called.'

'Thank you,' Joe says.

Mike puts his hand on Ricky's arm and leans in sympathetically. 'Come on, mate. We'll take the kiddies.'

'Who are you?' Joe Swain notices Mike standing a few steps behind Ricky.

'I'm a friend of Ricky's. Helping him build their new extension out the back. I've already given a statement to one of your colleagues. I arrived here with Ricky, didn't I, mate?'

Ricky nods, but it's clear he isn't taking in a word anyone is saying.

'We met up for a quick and early drink before arriving back home, and then we were going to do a couple of hours on the extension. I've already given one of your colleagues my name and address,' Mike explains.

Another uniformed officer interrupts Joe. 'We're letting the gentleman over there go.' He points to Ravi. 'He's an innocent bystander, a good citizen, just trying to help.'

Mike holds out his hand to take the car seat from Janet. She looks up at him, her mouth open, as if she's about to resist, but one glance at Mike's narrowed eyes and pursed lips and Ricky's face of stone and she takes a step backwards and swallows her words. Ricky picks up Benjie and follows Mike and the policeman to Joe Swain's car, glancing back at his home, which is no longer a home but a house that is floodlit, swarming with strangers: men and women dressed in white overalls, shoes hidden within paper covers, wielding cameras, carrying holdalls, taking things in and removing things from the house. And then a black van arrives, let through the cordon, manoeuvring between the police cars, pulling up level with Ricky's front door. Two men open the rear of the van and take out a stretcher. Mike is shocked by the ferocity of Ricky's scream, which fills the police car with a deafening, heart-wrenching roar.

'Donna! No!'

34

Ricky

Joe Swain has turfed Ricky, Mike and the kids out of his car. He needed to make a telephone call in private, so now they are standing at the side of the road once again.

Ricky has no choice but to stay with Mike. His home is a crime scene, and the police can't tell him when he'll be allowed back in. He is broken and lacks the capacity to make decisions.

'That's what shock does to you,' Mike says. 'Have you got any family you can stay with?'

Ricky shakes his head. The police officer doesn't look surprised.

Another thing we've got in common, Mike thinks. Mike's not keen on physical contact, but he puts his arm around Ricky's quivering shoulders.

'Let me help you out for a few days. Come and stay with me. I've got space for you and the kids. It's no bother.'

No one suggests that Ricky should collect any belongings from his house, so he just follows Mike and slips into the passenger seat of Mike's van wearing the scruffy, sweat-smelling clothes he's been wearing all day.

Janet appears with an old holdall that Ricky used to use for taking stuff to work. The zip is broken, and Ricky can see it's full of nappies and wipes and clothes for Benjie and Skye. Janet puts it in the boot of the van. Mike shoves his tools around and lifts up the back seats. Janet straps Skye's car seat into the rear and magically produces Benjie's car seat. *The cow does have some uses*, Ricky thinks fleetingly. Exhausted from so much crying, Benjie has fallen asleep on Ricky's shoulder, and it's easy for Janet to transfer him to his car seat.

As Mike starts up the engine, she lamely lifts up a hand as if to wave goodbye.

Ricky doesn't even notice where they're going. Five minutes later, Mike has parked up and is opening the passenger door.

'Out you get, mate.' Mike leans into the back and lifts the sleeping Benjie out, handing him to Ricky. He carries Skye's car seat and the holdall. There's a street lamp outside the low-rise red-brick building that Mike leads them into. The communal entrance hall smells of boiled vegetables, and it makes Ricky gag.

'You alright, mate?'

Ricky nods, but of course he's not alright.

There are four keyholes on Mike's door. Ricky wonders why. He didn't think there was anywhere in Horsham that was dangerous enough to warrant four locks, but he hasn't got the energy to query Mike.

He follows him inside. It's a first-floor, one-bedroom flat. The living room has a kitchenette along one wall, but the thing Ricky notices is how empty the place is. It is such a contrast to the happy mess of his own home that it chokes him. He tries to keep the tears at bay and clears his throat a few times. There's a white plastic table and two mismatched wooden chairs, the sort you pick up at a charity shop; a sagging sofa with a torn, green cover that looks like it's been rescued from a skip; an old silver kettle and toaster; and a small microwave that's seen better days.

'What would you like to eat? Haven't got much. Just a pizza or some bread. I might have some eggs for an omelette.'

'Nothing. I don't feel like eating.' Ricky's stomach clenches.

'You sure?'

'Yeah.'

'Follow me, then. You can sleep in here with your little ones,' Mike says, opening the door to a bedroom that is just large enough to house a small double bed and a slim wardrobe. The bed is neatly made, with a navy-blue duvet pulled up and over a matching pillow.

'It's okay, I'll take the sofa,' Ricky says. 'Benjie can sleep with me, and Skye can stay in the car seat.'

'No. I insist. I always give guests the bed,' Mike says. 'Besides, you need to sleep. The ambulanceman gave me a sleeping pill for you.' Mike extracts a little foil strip from his pocket. Ricky doesn't remember that, but he nods anyway. Mike places Benjie on the bed and removes his shoes. Gently, he puts Skye's car seat at the foot of the bed.

'The bathroom's in here.' Mike steps back into the corridor and opens the adjacent door. The bathroom is in fact a shower room just large enough for a small shower with a grey plastic shower curtain, the base lined in dark mould, a toilet with the lid up and a small sink. There is a glass with a worn toothbrush and toothpaste in, and a razor and a can of shaving foam on the ledge under the sink. It smells musty and damp. Mike hands Ricky a towel.

'Have a shower or go straight to sleep, whatever you want. I'll leave a clean pair of briefs and a T-shirt on your bed.'

Ricky shuts the door and sits down on the loo. He doesn't know how long he sits there, but eventually there's a knock on the door.

'You alright?' Mike asks.

'Yeah,' Ricky replies. He strips off his clothes, dumps them in a pile on the floor, gets into the shower, and turns it up to full heat. Even when it's on maximum, it's still not warm enough to put any heat into Ricky's bones. When the water begins to cool, he dries himself mechanically, then wraps the towel around his waist. The mirror is totally steamed over. Ricky is glad. He doesn't want to look at himself. He'd be happy never to look at himself ever again.

Ricky leaves Benjie fully dressed, just pulls the duvet over him. The bed is hard and the pillow smells strange. All

Ricky wants is to go home. He sits up in bed, but even when his eyes are open, he sees Donna, her face unrecognisable and all that blood. *How did they get to that?* he thinks. How did they ruin everything when they could have had so much?

It's after 1 a.m. when Ricky gives up on sleep. He told Mike he'd take the pill, but he hasn't. Ricky doesn't do drugs. He knows too well how they screw up lives. He doesn't do medicine either. Deep Heat is the only thing he's prepared to use on his aching muscles at the end of a hard day on the building site. Ricky throws back the duvet and uses the torch on his phone so as not to wake the children. He's naked. He looks at the T-shirt and briefs that Mike left out and pulls them on. It's the lesser of two evils wearing someone else's clothes rather than putting back on his filthy old gear. He can't go out in underwear, so he carefully opens Mike's wardrobe and extracts a pair of jeans and a sweatshirt. As the trousers are too long on him, he turns them up at the ankles. He finds an empty bag dumped at the base of the wardrobe, and he shoves his old clothes in it, putting his wallet in the pocket of Mike's jeans.

He pauses for a moment, wondering if it's alright to leave his sleeping children. Leaning over them one at a time, he gives them a gentle kiss on the forehead. With his shoes in one hand and the bag with his clothes over his shoulder, he tiptoes into the corridor. The door is locked and bolted, but Mike has left the keys next to the microwave. Holding his breath, Ricky picks them up as carefully as he can, all the time watching Mike, checking that he is still asleep. Gently, he slides the bolts across the top and bottom of the front door, turns the key in the lock and opens the door. It creaks and Mike stirs. Ricky remains totally still for a moment, but then Mike turns over on the sofa, facing away from the door. Leaving the keys on the floor, Ricky closes it carefully. And then he's out of there, racing down the stairs and on to the street.

He has no idea where he is and can't even remember how long it took to get from his to Mike's place, so he uses the location app on his phone. It's a one-mile walk, if that. The night is cold and still, clouds drifting in front of a bright moon. There are street lamps, but it would be light enough to navigate the streets without them. Ricky inhales the biting air and lets the tranquillity settle the adrenaline pumping through his body.

Around the corner he notices a big bin, one of those large grey communal ones. He would have preferred to burn his forever-tarnished old clothes, but that's not practical, so he lifts up the lid and, trying hard not to breathe in the filth, takes out some of the stinking black bags of rubbish. He chucks in Mike's bag and replaces the black bags on top so it's hidden from view. He's got no idea when it's bin collection day, but as the bin is practically full, he's hopeful it will be today or tomorrow. Donna was in charge of that. His job was just to put the rubbish out whenever she told him to. He stifles a sob at the memory.

Ricky jogs along the streets, only slowing down once, when the headlights of a car break the silence of the night. He wouldn't want anyone to think he was up to no good at 1.20 a.m.

He stops when he reaches the start of Ridings Lane. The police barrier has gone. He walks slowly, his head down. He crosses the road and stays in the shadows. Crouching down by the side of old Mr Jones's prized and ancient Cortina, which hasn't been roadworthy in a decade, Ricky peers at his house. He had thought there might be a policeman stationed at his front door, but the house is in darkness, and other than blue-and-white police tape strapped across the path, no one would know it was a crime scene. He stifles another sob as he notices a solitary bouquet of flowers left on the pavement, and then he turns and, rubbing his eyes, walks over to his van.

35

Pippa

I am dreaming. I am in a cavern with no door. There are photos of me covering every surface. I can hear George's voice but can't work out where it is coming from. I ricochet from wall to wall, searching for a way out, and then I wake up with a start, covered in a film of sweat, out of breath, my heart racing.

The phone is ringing. I fumble around for the light switch, but by the time I've turned on my bedside lamp, the phone stops. I am shaking. It's just before two a.m. George must have deteriorated. *Please, God, don't let me lose both my children.*

I lean towards the phone, and as I do so, it starts ringing again.

'Yes,' I say breathlessly.

'Pippa, it's me. Joe. I'm parked outside your house. We need to come in.'

'Why?' I pull my knees up to my chest.

'There's been another murder, and we need to talk to you.'

I am speechless. Who has been killed? And who is 'we'? And why do they need to speak to me at two o'clock in the morning? My gut clenches at the thought that it might be George. Surely no one would hurt George in the hospital. I swing my legs out of bed, slip my feet into my furry slippers, pull on yesterday's jumper, which I discarded on my antique rocking chair, and tie my white waffle dressing gown firmly around my waist. The doorbell is ringing before I've had time to go to the bathroom or run my fingers through my hair.

Mungo lets out a sleepy bark. I hurry downstairs, undo the bolts and then double-check through the front door peephole that it is indeed Joe. He is standing there with Mia Brevant.

'Come in,' I say, and gesture for them to go into the living room, switching on all the lights.

'Sorry to wake you,' Joe says without his normal smile. His eyes are bloodshot.

Mia and Joe sit next to each other on the sofa, Joe slumping backwards, Mia leaning forwards, her elbows on her knees. I perch on my favourite armchair, facing the television. Mungo ambles in, gives a quick woof and collapses at my feet. I try to stop my knees from shaking and am glad that the dressing gown is too big and too long for me.

'Donna Wiśniewski, Leanne's daughter, was found dead this afternoon.'

'Oh God!' I grip the arms of the chair, relieved that they are not here to talk to me about George, but I am shocked that another member of the Smith family is dead.

'What happened?' I ask.

'We have two immediate suspects. Kevin Smith, the deceased father who was released on bail today, and Ricky Wiśniewski, the deceased's husband.'

'I'm afraid to say that your photo was found on her body. A different photo – a picture of you and, we assume, your son.' Joe takes his phone out of his pocket. I pray he's not going to show me a picture of Donna's dead body.

'Look,' he says, leaning forwards and holding his phone up so that I can easily see its screen. My teeth are chattering and there's nothing I can do to stop the trembling. I glance quickly, ready to remove my eyes should there be blood and gore, but the photo is simply of a photo. It is me and George, George leaning down to give me a kiss. I'm wearing the white shirt and silver necklace I wore on Sunday. The photo must have been taken when George and Marie arrived at The

Duck and Pheasant, when we first greeted each other. I try to recall who else was in the pub. Were there any people behaving strangely? But I draw a blank. We were there early and there weren't many other diners.

'Yes,' I whisper. 'It's me and George. Taken on Sunday.'

'How do you know it was taken on Sunday?' Mia asks.

'I've been estranged from my son. I haven't seen him properly in several months. We met for lunch at The Duck and Pheasant, and I was wearing those clothes. And then later that afternoon he had the accident. But it probably wasn't an accident, was it?' I turn to face Joe, feeling the blood rush from my face.

'We don't know anything at this stage,' Joe says sheepishly.

'There is a message written on the back of the photograph. What does the message say, Mrs Durrant?'

I look at Mia and Joe in confusion. 'I don't know!'

'Where were you this afternoon between two and four thirty p.m.?'

'In Redhill, then at the hospital seeing George. I drove home around four p.m. and collected Mungo, my dog. A client was waiting for me when I got back here, and then you, Joe – I mean, DS Swain – arrived. I don't know the exact timings, but that was my afternoon.'

'So you could have stopped off in Horsham on your way home,' Mia says.

'I could have done, but I didn't!' Anger and indignation are rising through my veins. *Stay calm*, I say to myself. I know enough about questioning techniques; I just need to apply them the other way around, where I am the interviewee.

'The message on the photo said *You're next*,' Joe says quietly.

'I'm next?' I ask. 'Or George?'

'We don't know,' Joe says. 'We need to get to the bottom of your involvement in this case.'

‘Believe me, there’s nothing more I want too.’

‘At this stage, our primary suspect is Kevin Smith. We are bringing him in for questioning,’ Joe says.

I purse my lips. Immediately doubt sets in. Could I have been wrong about Kevin? Maybe he is guilty. But what father would murder his wife and daughter in cold blood, placing a photograph of me on their bodies? And why me?

‘Is there anyone who you can stay with tonight, or who could come and stay here with you?’ Mia asks.

‘I could ring my brother, I suppose.’ But I can’t. Not really. Rob has done enough for me. The last thing he needs is me waking him up in the middle of the night or, worse still, bringing danger into his home. Joe must sense my reluctance.

‘We’ll get the local constabulary to drive past regularly, and you’ve got my mobile number. My phone is always on.’

I nod at him gratefully. ‘And George? Who is going to keep an eye on my son?’

‘We’ve already had him moved to a private room. He’s safe in the hospital,’ Joe reassures me.

Mia and Joe stand up. Mungo lifts his head, gives a little growl and promptly falls asleep again. I get up too and tighten my dressing gown belt. I feel so vulnerable in my nightwear and my bare face and bed hair.

‘We’d like you to come into the station and make a formal statement tomorrow,’ Joe says.

‘And will you keep my name out of the press this time?’ I can’t help the edge of sarcasm in my voice.

‘We will do our best,’ Joe says, grimacing. I sense it is out of his control, and his expression is setting me up for the worst. ‘The murder will inevitably be reported in tomorrow’s newspapers. There’s not much we can do about that.’

They walk towards the door. Joe has his hand on the front door handle, and then the thought hits me.

‘The words *you’re next* on the back of the photo. Were they handwritten or typed?’

Joe pivots to face me and wrinkles his nose. ‘Handwritten. Why?’

‘Never mind,’ I say, shaking my head. I’ll tell him tomorrow, I decide. I can’t imagine the police will give much credence to my ability to analyse handwriting. I tend to leave off graphology from my professional profile, as few of my colleagues give it any credibility. Nor do I give it credence in isolation, but when used in conjunction with other analytical tools, graphology can be very helpful indeed.

36

Pippa

I listen to Joe's car rev up and drive away, the car engine cutting through the tranquillity of the night. Mungo is snoring softly, but there is no way I can sleep. I shuffle around the house, making sure all the doors are bolted and windows locked.

Trevor insisted we had a house alarm when we were married. One of those Redcare systems that link into a monitoring station and, if the call centre workers suspect the house has been broken into, alert the police. The wealthier Trevor became, the more he spent on art and the latest technology. We had things worth stealing in those days. Not that we were ever the victims of theft. When we divorced, I had no desire to take half of all of that stuff. I don't even like the postmodernist paintings he has such a penchant for, and what would I do with the latest Bang & Olufsen speaker system designed for a large home theatre? I debated putting in an alarm when I moved into the cottage, but as the equity was in the property itself rather than the chattels within it, and I have neighbours both sides plus a dog, I reckoned it was an expense I could avoid. But tonight I regret that decision. I wish I had a little panic button by the side of my bed. I wish I had made more of an effort to befriend the neighbours. I wish there was someone else upon whom I could offload my feelings of panic.

I lie in bed, my heart juddering every time I hear a creak in the timber of the old building or the slamming of a door in the distance. As the faint light of dawn creeps through the curtains, I give up on sleep and load the video of Kevin Smith's interview on to my laptop.

I want him to be guilty. I want to feel safe knowing he's locked up behind bars and can't hurt George or me. The trouble is, I am as sure as I can be that he was telling the truth.

Over and over again I play the section of the interview where Joe asked him, 'Do you know who killed Leanne Smith?' and Kevin answered, 'No.'

I look at the fleeting physiological response immediately before he replied. He was angry. His eyebrows lowered and squeezed together; his eyes were tight and focused on Joe with narrowed pupils; his lips were tightly closed in that fraction of a second before speaking. It makes sense that he was angry. He was being falsely accused.

I look for verbal and nonverbal disconnect, where his physical movements may be inconsistent with what he is saying. He doesn't do any throat clearing or extra swallowing. His hands don't touch his face or adjust his sleeves or hide his mouth. And he doesn't move around in the chair.

There are no verbal clusters suggesting falsities. Sighing, I shove the laptop to the side of the bed and try to close my eyes.

* * *

At 8.30 a.m. I put on a coat, and Mungo and I trot off to the newsagent. Donna's murder is front-page news. I buy copies of *The Times*, *The Guardian*, *The Daily Telegraph*, the *Daily Mail* and *The Sun*, hoping they will give me a broad cross section of what has been reported. Debbie, who runs the shop, raises her eyebrows at my pile of papers, but she doesn't say anything. We recognise each other but have never exchanged more than basic niceties.

‘You take care.’ She throws the sentence out to me as I’m leaving, much like a fisherman chucks a rope to the quayside. I hope that the kind comments can safely deliver me to shore.

Rob calls me.

‘I hate that you’re embroiled in all of this,’ he says. He tells me that he visited George and how much better he seems. ‘Come and stay with me,’ Rob insists. I decline. For now, anyway.

I scour the articles and switch *South Today* on the television, turning up the sound when the pretty blonde reporter stands at the end of the cordoned-off street in Horsham, reporting that another death has taken place, which the police believe is murder. The papers don’t tell me anything I don’t already know. The daughter of the murdered lottery winner has been found murdered too. She leaves behind a husband and two very young children. The police are seeking a fifty-five-year-old man whom they believe will help them with their investigations. And then I spot it. The body was discovered by Donna’s best friend, Kerry Moore, a hairdresser from Horsham, who is too distressed to talk to journalists.

Here is a name I haven’t come across before. I wonder what Kerry knows. Donna is dead and I fear Ricky. I need to talk to Kerry. Today.

But first I need to speak to Joe. I send him a text message suggesting I come to the police station. It’s a pain to have to drive to Crawley, but it will be easy to pop into Horsham on my way home.

After collecting me from the reception area, Joe takes me into the beating heart of the station, a large open-plan office buzzing with people on the phone, talking animatedly in groups of twos and threes, hunched over computers. I’m not sure what I expected, but it wasn’t this. Joe’s desk is in the far corner, situated under a window, the luxury of views on to the street being, I assume, a reflection of his seniority. His desk is a mess: haphazard piles of paper, two coffee mugs, a computer and a keyboard and an overflowing in tray. I'm surprised. I had assumed someone who dresses as smartly as he does, who superficially seems so organised in his thinking patterns, would exhibit similar tendencies of perfection throughout his life. Just goes to show that even a seasoned psychologist such as me can get it wrong.

A couple of people pass by and do a double take when they see me. I assume my photograph must be pinned on a noticeboard somewhere for everyone assigned to the Smith murders to see.

'Kevin Smith. It's too much of a coincidence that Donna dies the day he's released from prison, don't you think?' Joe leans back in his chair and steeples his fingers.

I sit down opposite him.

'He's innocent,' I say blandly.

'What?' Joe leans forwards as he frowns.

'I don't think you're looking for the right person. I've studied the transcript and the interview, and during the interview we had with him, Kevin didn't once tell an untruth.'

'Oh, come on, Pippa!' Joe says, glaring. 'Don't spin me nonsense.'

I prickle. 'Are you calling my analysis nonsense?' I spit.

'No, of course not.' He leans towards me and uncrosses his legs. 'It's just all the evidence suggests it's Kevin. And – well, I don't mean to be rude, but all of this micro-expression stuff and body language and semantics, it's not exactly evidence based, is it?'

If we weren't in an open-plan office, I would shout at Joe. But as we are, I try to rein in my fury.

'Joe, I'm a scientist. Everything I do is evidence based,' I hiss.

'Number one, Kevin's DNA and fingerprints are all over the golf club that is believed to be the murder weapon used to kill Leanne. As of now, we haven't found the weapon used to kill Donna, but Kevin's DNA and fingerprints were found at her house.' He ticks his list off on his fingers. 'Number two, motive.'

'What motive?' I interrupt. 'Why would Kevin kill his own daughter? And so brutally?'

'His motive for killing Leanne was jealousy and money. Searching through her text messages, we discovered she was having an affair, and she had the lottery money. Leanne was seeking a divorce, and according to her solicitor, she didn't want Kevin to receive any of the lottery money. When he found out about the impending divorce and that he would have to fight Leanne to get any of the winnings, he killed her. Motive for killing Donna is the money. Kevin is the only person who knows that Leanne bequeathed the money to her daughter rather than him. So there you have it. Greed and jealousy. The two oldest motivators for crime in the book.'

'And—' I try to butt in.

'And opportunity. Kevin's whereabouts are unaccounted for at the time of both murders.'

'Where was Ricky?'

'At work. He has an alibi.'

I shake my head. 'I think you're holding the wrong person, and as such you're putting George's and my lives at risk.'

Joe laughs. It's a thin, fake laugh, but still it's a laugh. I look at this man who I thought I was beginning to know and like, and I am horrified. I stand up, grab my handbag and coat, and walk away.

'Pippa, wait.' He gets up and chases after me. A few people turn around to look. I hope I'm heading in the right direction, towards the stairs rather than deeper into the office. I glance over my shoulder as I'm pacing. Joe has stopped. He's talking to someone. I'm forgotten, I assume.

'Is this the way out?' I ask a young woman dressed in a skirt that I deem to be much too short for work.

'Yeah.' She points towards an exit sign I hadn't noticed.

I roll my eyes conspiratorially towards her and hasten forwards. As I turn out of the office into the corridor, with a bank of lifts to the right and the stairs to the left, I swivel to look again. Joe is facing me now, his eyes fixed on my face. I scowl and walk away.

So much for him looking out for me. Once again I'm reminded that the only person who can help me is myself. It's a sobering thought.

Next step: track down Donna's best friend.

37

Pippa

I do an online search for Kerry Moore. She is listed as one of the stylists working for Cut & Curl Hairdressers, in Horsham. I am surprised and relieved that there is only one Kerry Moore living in the Horsham area listed on 192.com, so it shouldn't be difficult to find her.

I start with Cut & Curl, which is located at the far end of town in a small precinct called Shields Way. Three of the six shops in the precinct are empty, with large estate agency 'To Rent' signs positioned outside. On the far left is a tatty-looking charity shop, with a phone-repair shop adjacent. Cut & Curl Hairdressers' sign is lurid pink with black writing. There is a handwritten sign in the window stating 'Half-price cuts today! No booking required'.

The door jingles as I push it open. There are four black leather chairs with mirrors in front, and two sinks towards the back. One wall is painted the same lurid pink as the sign on the outside. Loud, thumping music is playing, but other than the young woman behind the reception desk, who is tapping away on her phone with long bright-yellow talons, the place is empty. She doesn't look up until I'm standing right in front of her.

'Yeah,' she says. She has purple lips and platinum hair cut short on one side and long on the other.

'I was wondering if I could make an appointment with Kerry.'

'Kerry who?' she asks. Her eyebrows almost meet in the middle, giving the effect of one long line stuck across her forehead.

'Kerry Moore? She's one of your stylists, I believe?'

‘Oh, that Kerry. Nah. She only works Saturdays. Do yeh wanna book for this Saturday?’

I can’t wait another four days to talk to Kerry, so I shake my head. ‘I need to get hold of her sooner than that. She promised to do the hair for my daughter’s wedding.’

I can’t think where that lie came from, and as soon as I say the words, I feel sick. ‘Any chance you could give me her number?’

I can see the cogs turning in the young woman’s brain.

‘It’s against company policy,’ she says eventually.

‘That’s very sensible,’ I say, nodding sagely. ‘Tell you what, why don’t you call her and let me speak to her? It doesn’t look like the salon is very busy, and I’m sure your boss would be very unhappy if you lose a big booking like mine, don’t you think?’ My smile is saccharine. The young woman glowers.

I lean on the counter and watch as she removes a telephone book. She dials a mobile number. I hold my breath, hoping Kerry will answer.

‘Kerry, it’s Jazzy from the salon. Got a woman here who wants to talk to you about a wedding.’ There’s silence for a moment, and I can’t hear what Kerry is saying. I hold my breath. ‘Yeah.’

Jazzy hands the phone over to me. I turn my back to her.

‘Hello, Kerry. My name is Philippa Durrant. I’m the woman in the photo. I assume you know what I mean.’

There is a sharp intake of breath before she whispers, ‘Yes.’

‘Can I come and see you? I think the police have got it all wrong.’ I’m taking a big gamble telling her this, but my view is that honesty is the best policy. Kerry is never going to open up to me if I trick her into talking to me.

‘Thought you said you wanted to talk to her about wedding hair?’ Jazzy interrupts, invading my space and jutting her chin out towards me. I turn my back on her again.

There is a long pause on the end of the phone, and eventually Kerry says, ‘Okay. When can you come?’

‘Now, assuming you live in Horsham.’

‘Broadbridge Heath,’ she says, and gives me her address.

I hand the phone back to Jazzy. She scowls at me, but I am out of the hairdresser’s before she can utter any words.

Barely ten minutes later I park up outside a red-brick block of flats in a large new development in Broadbridge Heath. It’s just two streets away from Leanne and Kevin’s house, and for some reason being so close by makes my mouth dry. Number one Wilders Place is on the ground floor. The communal door is open, and there’s a child’s pushchair outside Kerry’s door. I ring the bell. I can hear shuffling on the other side, and eventually the door is opened just an inch, the chain in place.

‘Yes?’ Kerry says.

‘It’s Pippa Durrant. We spoke a few moments ago.’

‘How do I know you’re not a journalist?’

‘Do you recognise me from the photo?’

She grimaces and rubs her nose. ‘Yes, silly me. It’s all been too much the last twenty-four hours.’ She releases the chain and opens the door.

Kerry’s jet-black hair is tied back in a ponytail. Paler roots are showing, and I reckon her hair is several shades too dark for her pale face. A tiny diamond nose stud glistens on her left nostril. If she didn’t have red, puffy eyes, a sore, swollen nose and weeping cold sores on her upper lip, she would be a pretty girl, with delicate symmetrical features.

‘I’m very sorry about Donna,’ I say as I walk into her neat living room. Her eyes well up, and she tugs at the sleeve of her long-length black T-shirt. She looks skinny and lost, as if she could do with a big hug. But that’s not my job.

‘Do the police know you’re here?’ she asks.

I shake my head. ‘Did you know they’ve got Kevin Smith in custody?’

'Yes.' She sits down on a bright-red sofa with chrome legs and wraps her arms around her legging-clad knees, pulling them tightly up to her chest. I perch on a navy-blue armchair.

'You can't stay long,' she murmurs. 'Mum's taken Declan out – he's my son – but they'll be back soon.'

'It's okay,' I reassure her. 'I just want to ask you a few questions about Donna.'

She poses the first question: 'Why was your photo on Leanne's body and Donna's?' She shakes her head as if she's trying to dislodge the memory.

'I don't know, and that's why I want to speak to you. To see if we can work out any connections.'

I lean forwards, open my palms towards her and smile gently. 'I want to find out who killed Leanne and Donna as much, if not more, than you do. It's destroying my business and destroying my life. I didn't know Leanne or Donna, but somehow or other I'm entangled in this, and it's imperative I work out how and why.'

'You don't trust the police either?'

I wince as I think of Joe. I trust him, but do I think he's right? No. I sidestep the question. 'Obviously Donna must have been devastated about her mum's murder.'

Kerry nods and sighs.

'How were things with Ricky, her husband?' I ask.

'They've been arguing the last few days, but generally alright, I think.'

'Was she worried about anything in particular?'

Kerry shuts her eyes and exhales so much, her shoulders sag by several inches. 'Oedipus.'

'Sorry?'

'Oedipus. She was getting these texts from someone called Oedipus.'

I am nearly off the edge of the chair, I lean forwards so much. 'Who is Oedipus?'

'She didn't know, or if she did, she didn't tell me.'

‘What did he want?’

‘He threatened to tell Ricky she was having an affair.’

‘Was she?’

Her ponytails swings from left to right as she shakes her head. ‘I don’t think so. She really loves Ricky.’

‘Have you told the police this?’

Kerry’s bottom lip trembles. ‘Yes, but I didn’t tell them about the threat to tell Ricky she was having an affair.’

‘Why?’ I ask gently.

‘Because she wasn’t having an affair. I’m sure she wasn’t. And what good would it do if that’s Ricky’s last memory of Donna? You know what the police are like. They’ll twist things.’

We are both silent for a while, and then she hangs her head and says, ‘And I looked at Donna’s phone when I shouldn’t have. She didn’t show me the message, so I’m not meant to know. Her phone was lying on the table and it buzzed. I read the message. I’m sorry,’ she says, sobbing.

‘I know you want to protect Donna and Ricky, but it’s really important that the police find this Oedipus. He could be the killer.’

Kerry blinks several times, her eyes widening. ‘But the police couldn’t find her mobile phone. That tall black guy, the boss policeman, he asked me if I knew where it was. So you see, even if I tell the police, if they can’t find her phone, they won’t be able to track down the messages.’

I don’t know anything about mobile technology. Perhaps the police can read messages even if the phone is lost. I assume it needs to be switched on. I will have to ask Joe.

‘Do you think Kevin Smith killed Donna?’ I watch Kerry very carefully as she processes her answer.

‘No. He was a dick and a useless father, but no, I don’t think he’s a killer. Donna was sure he didn’t kill her mum.’

‘If Kevin didn’t do it, what about Ricky?’

For the first time Kerry laughs. ‘Ricky! He’s a total softie. He loves Donna. He’d do anything for her. It can’t have been Ricky.' And then she gulps. 'It wasn't Ricky, was it?' She looks at me in horror.

I lean back in the chair. 'I've no idea, Kerry. All I do know is that we need to track down the person who calls him or herself Oedipus.'

38

Pippa

Graphology is a dying skill, not because of the sceptics, but due to the fact we rarely put pen to paper anymore. When I first trained in it, CVs and covering letters were handwritten, official forms were completed by hand, people wrote letters. Nowadays everything is done with a keyboard. When Ricky turned up at my house pretending to be a client, I asked him to complete my new client form. He only wrote his name and address, but at least I have his handwriting. I need to compare that piece of writing to the words written on the back of the photograph that was left on Donna's body.

I ring Joe from the car. I half expect him not to pick up the phone to me, but he does.

'Pippa,' he says.

'Any chance you could let me see the writing on the back of my photograph?'

'Why?'

'I'm a trained graphologist, and I'd like to have a look at the writing to work out if there are any clues regarding the personality of the writer and to compare it against other samples of writing I have from clients.'

'It's evidence, so no, you can't have it.'

'Could you at least take a photograph of it and send that over to me?' I sense the hesitation. 'Joe, you owe it to me to let me help. I'm in danger. George is in danger. We need to know who wrote that note and why, and I've got the skills to do that.'

'Right. I'll email you a picture. Got to go now.' He hangs up on me without saying goodbye.

I don't feel like going home. I don't feel safe there anymore. Mungo has been as good as gold despite being cooped up in the car for most of the day.

'Fancy a walk?' I ask him. The woof and tail wag are all the responses I need.

I park the car at Tesco, and we walk down Old Wickhurst Lane, through a complex of black-and-white converted barns and down to the edge of the river. The footpath follows the course of the fast-flowing river, the riverbanks tall with nettles and wild garlic and hedgerows untouched for generations. The fresh air and escape from civilisation give me time to think and Mungo a chance to run free. We could be miles from anywhere in amongst the fields and ancient woodland. Other than the faint, distant hum of traffic and regular airplanes taking off and landing at Gatwick Airport a mere fifteen miles away, we could be in a rural idyll, the quintessential English countryside described and adored by writers throughout generations.

It crosses my mind that I am probably much more in danger out here, a woman walking all alone with a soppy Labrador for company in a woodland in fading light, than I am at home surrounded by neighbours, even if those neighbours are strangers. 'Be brave,' I say out loud to myself.

I think about Oedipus and how most people think of Freud's Oedipus complex first and rarely recall the Greek myth. I wonder if Donna's Oedipus is referring to Freud's psychoanalytic theory of a child's unconscious sexual desire for the opposite-sex parent and hatred for the same-sex parent, or whether he's referring to the Greek myth, in which Oedipus accidentally fulfils a prophecy to kill his father and marry his mother, bringing disaster to his family and city. Is Donna's Oedipus blind, or has he blinded himself with something that belonged to his mother, his mother who, when she realised what had happened, hanged herself? Surely that's too literal an explanation. I do what I've tried to avoid doing: visualise Donna's and Leanne's faces battered to a pulp. Could it be that this Oedipus has disfigured them because they are mothers? But how do *I* link in?

And then it hits me.

Brent.

Brent is the only person I know who has sought out his birth mother, whose birth mother has died. Has Brent got anything to do with this? But why and how? Brent hasn't been in trouble since he was a teenager. Am I putting two and two together and making five?

I realise I have stopped still. Mungo bounces up to me and sits at my feet, his head cocked to one side, wide almond eyes staring at me expectantly. I find a small branch and throw it for him. He leaps up and catches it in mid-air.

'Come on, Mungo. Let's go and talk to Brent.'

As I'm striding back towards the car, my phone pings with an incoming email. It's from Joe – the photograph of the words that I asked him for. *YOU'RE NEXT*. They are chilling and grab at my throat. The scrawl is childlike, as if the writer has tried to disguise his writing by using capitals. I wish I had the original so I could assess the pressure of the pen on the paper and measure the angles properly. But this will have to do.

I can't decide. Should I go and find Brent or analyse the writing first? Mungo looks at me with imploring eyes. I glance at my watch. It's nearly his teatime.

'Come on then, home it is!'

Mungo jumps into the back of the car and I climb into the driver's seat. I switch on the radio to catch the five-o'clock news. The headline story is about Brexit, followed by another humanitarian disaster in Syria. And then I nearly crash the car. *Police have announced that they are searching for a suspect in what have been dubbed The Lottery Winners Murders. Leanne Smith was found murdered in her home in West Sussex ten days ago. Her daughter, Donna Wiśniewski, was found murdered yesterday. Detective Sergeant Joe*

Swain, of Sussex Police, has confirmed they are looking for Kevin Smith in connection with both murders. Members of the public have been warned not to approach him and to call the police immediately.

Joe didn't tell me Kevin was still missing. Am I in more danger than I thought? I start playing mind games. The little demon sitting on my shoulder throws a grenade of doubt. Perhaps I was wrong. Perhaps Kevin was lying and I've lost my professional touch. Or maybe he didn't kill Leanne, but he has run off with the lottery money. But did he kill Donna? The police wouldn't be searching for him unless they had hard evidence, would they? And do the press know that my photo was found at the crime scene for the second time? The news report on the radio didn't mention me, but that doesn't mean my photograph hasn't been disseminated across the media yet again.

I don't want to be alone. I call Rob, but his phone goes straight to voicemail. I consider calling Trevor but decide against it. Instead, I carry on driving home.

'You'll protect me, won't you, Mungo?' I ask my dog, but in my heart of hearts I know a Labrador is unlikely to do anything other than lick an attacker to death.

I let Mungo out of the car and follow him up the darkening path to my front door. He doesn't bark, his fur doesn't stand up on end, so I feel confident that all is as it should be. I switch the lights on, lock the door behind me, and make my way into the kitchen. After giving the dog his supper, I print out the photo Joe sent me and get out my Emotional Responsiveness Gauge. This clear plastic card, which looks a little like a protractor, is printed with red lines that allow me to measure the slant of handwriting so I can assess how emotionally responsive the writer is. In simplistic terms, the range is anywhere from highly introverted to extremely extroverted. I also search my files to retrieve Ricky's handwritten registration form. Of course this is unethical, because I am only meant to analyse someone's writing with their permission, but under these circumstances I forgive myself.

I do a quick comparison between the two. On first glance they aren't anything alike, but experience has taught me that until I actually measure the lines and curves that make up each letter, and until I assess how everything fits together, eyeballing writing can lead to erroneous results.

Half an hour later I stretch my sore neck and try to relax my aching jaw. I am reasonably confident that the two pieces of writing have not been penned by the same hand. It's difficult to be sure, because three words are never enough to provide an accurate analysis, and I really need the original, not a photo. Ricky's writing displays an average amount of extrovertism, plenty of confidence, and a keen, analytical brain, but the threatening words of the sample Joe sent me suggest someone who is introvert, tightly controlled and with the potential for an explosive temper. The double loops in the letters *o* and *a* are indicative of deceit and, combined with the left-slanting letters, a jagged baseline and uneven pressure, suggest this person may not only be unstable but has plenty to hide. Not surprising, really, considering the tone of the note and the fact the writer is most likely to be a murderer. What is more interesting is Ricky's writing doesn't suggest any of these traits.

I sigh. I was so sure Ricky was our man, but based on this handwriting analysis and comparison, perhaps I have been wrong.

39

Ricky

'Hey, Ricky, you alright in there?' Mike stands outside the bedroom door. The racket is ear-piercing. The baby is screaming, and the toddler is sobbing, calling out, 'Mama! Come here, Mama!' He raps on the door. The sleeping pills would have knocked Ricky out, but would they have kept him sleeping through this cacophony? It seems unlikely. When he still gets no answer, Mike opens the door. The duvet is crumpled on the end of the bed, Benjie is sitting on a pillow wearing yesterday's clothes, and the baby is in the car seat, exactly where Mike placed it last night. The wardrobe door is hanging open and Ricky is nowhere to be seen.

'Fuck!' Mike screams, slamming his fist into the wall. 'You stupid bastard!'

If Ricky has done a runner, the police will come looking for him. And as they knew Ricky was staying with Mike, they'll start looking for him too. Mike gave the police a false telephone number and address, but even so, he knows they'll track him down sooner rather than later. And that cannot happen.

The toddler stops crying and stares at him with saucer eyes.

'What you looking at?' Mike says aggressively, and then paces over to the edge of the bed and sits down next to Benjie.

He sucks the blood off his knuckles. 'Are you sad your mother is dead?'

The little boy just stares at Mike and then sucks his left thumb, rubbing the ears of his toy between his right thumb and index finger. Perhaps the child doesn't understand the meaning of dead.

'Are you missing your mum?'

Benjie nods and sniffs.

'You'd better show me what to do with your sister. I've never changed a baby's nappy before.'

Benjie slides off the end of the bed and pulls his trousers down.

'What do you think you're doing?' Mike snaps.

'Done wee wee,' Benjie says, and tries to undo the sides of his disposable nappy.

'You're too old to wear those things, aren't you?'

Benjie's bottom lip quivers.

'Right. How do we stop that baby from crying? It's messing with my head.'

Benjie pulls a nappy out of the holdall, then grabs a feeding bottle and the container of dried milk.

'You stay here and look after your sister, and I'll go make the milk.' Mike needs to get away from the piercing screams of the foul baby.

Standing in his little kitchenette, he unscrews the teat, places the bottle under the cold tap and fills it up, then puts a spoonful of milk powder in it. After screwing the teat back on the top, he shakes the bottle hard and returns to the bedroom.

'It hasn't dissolved very well, but it'll have to do.' He hands the bottle to Benjie. 'You feed your sister, and I'll make you some breakfast.'

He takes the key out of the bedroom door, shuts the door behind him, and locks the children inside. With all that racket, he can't think straight. A fog is creeping through his brain. He returns to the kitchen, takes a bowl from the cupboard, and then nearly drops it when he hears rapping on the front door.

Hurriedly, Mike pulls open the kitchen drawer and takes out the small knife with the extra-sharp blade. He conceals it in the palm of his hand, sidles around the room, and positions himself to the right of the door, where it hinges.

'Let me in, Mike!' Ricky yells.

Mike lets out his breath and opens the door. 'Where the hell did you get to?' he says, glowering.

Ricky has purple rings under bloodshot eyes and a grey pallor. His hair sticks up on end. 'Out, walking up and down the road for three hours. Backwards and forwards, backwards and forwards, trying to get my brain to work!' Ricky is too tired to notice Mike pocketing the small knife.

'You left me with your fucking children!' Mike sighs. 'Have you heard the news?'

Ignoring the wail of his screaming daughter, Ricky collapses on to the sagging sofa, where Mike has neatly folded his bedclothes. Mike clenches his fists. He wishes Ricky would shift along, get his filthy arse off his clean sheet and blanket.

'What news?' Ricky can barely speak.

'Your father-in-law has gone missing. On the run, they said. He's a wanted man, apparently.'

Mike doesn't get the reaction he expects. Ricky's face is impassive, literally no emotion. And it's as if Ricky can't hear the horrible ear-splitting screeching of his infants. Mike hums under his breath to try to block it out. When it becomes apparent that Ricky isn't going to move, Mike kneels down in front of Ricky.

'Hey, man. I'm sorry about Donna, I really am. She was a great bird. But why aren't you reacting to the news that your father-in-law is on the run? I thought you hated him.'

'I do.' His words are muffled. 'But he didn't kill my Donna or Leanne.' The words catch in the back of his throat.

Mike rocks back on his black trainers. They squeak. He narrows his eyes. 'If Kevin didn't do it, who did?'

Ricky sniffs and doesn't say anything.

Mike stands up and faces away from Ricky. 'Don't tell me you did it.' His voice is low and soft and incredulous. 'Did you do it for the money?'

'What money?' Ricky says, sniffing.

‘The lottery money.’

Ricky jumps up from his chair, knocking it over. ‘Don’t be so fucking stupid!’ he screams. ‘I loved those women, and I don’t give a fuck about the money!’

‘Whoa!’ Mike holds his hands up in mock retreat. ‘Didn’t mean to offend, mate.’

Ricky is still for a moment. ‘Anyway, the money is Kevin’s. Bastard Kevin’s.’

‘I thought Donna said the money was…’ Mike’s words peter out.

Ricky narrows his eyes. ‘Donna said what?’

‘Nothing, mate. Nothing. Must have got it wrong. Look, have a seat and I’ll make you a cuppa. Tell me where you were this morning.’

Mike puts the kettle on.

‘I went back to retrieve this.’ He pulls a phone out of his back pocket. Ricky holds it up in the air as he strides towards Mike. ‘Do you recognise it?’ Ricky seems to have drawn strength from the phone. His eyes are flashing, his pupils pinpricks.

Mike instinctively puts his hand into his back pocket, fingers curling around the handle of the knife. ‘No,’ he says, frowning.

‘It’s Donna’s phone. My *wife*’s phone!’ Ricky shouts the word *wife*. ‘And do you know what I found on it?’

Mike shakes his head, but he senses where this conversation is going, and his fingers tighten around the knife.

‘Some bastard called Oedipus was threatening her. He said he was going to tell me about the affair she was having. An affair with you! You bastard! You were shagging my wife!’ He swings his hands forwards and grabs Mike by the neck. Mike drops the knife as he brings his hands up in an attempt to release Ricky’s clutch from around his neck.

‘No, you’ve got that all wrong!’ Mike’s voice is strangulated as he tries to breathe, to wriggle out of Ricky’s clutches. His height works in his favour, and he brings his knee up to Ricky's balls, jabbing him as hard as he can. Ricky collapses backwards with a cry, and Mike slides to the floor, rubbing his hands up and down his neck, trying to get his breathing back under control. But Ricky has seen the knife and he makes a grab for it.

'You've got it all wrong,' Mike says, panting. 'I'd never have an affair with Donna.'

Ricky crawls towards him, the knife held out in front of him. The light flickers off the edge of the blade. 'You don't think my wife was beautiful enough? You don't fancy her?'

Ricky creeps closer. Mike shuffles backwards, but there's nowhere for him to go.

'No. Yes. Of course I fancied her. She's lovely, your wife. But I wouldn't. I couldn't.'

'Not man enough?' Ricky sneers.

'I'd never do that with my sister!' Mike says, whimpering.

Ricky stops still, the blade just a couple of inches from Mike's throat. 'What did you say?'

'I'd never do that to my sister,' Mike whispers again.

Ricky sits back on his haunches and lets his fist holding the knife fall back down to his side. 'Sister? What are you talking about! Donna's an only child.'

Sensing the danger is over for now, Mike closes his eyes. 'No, she's not. I'm her bastard brother. The one Leanne tried to get rid of.'

'What?' Ricky gasps. 'Does Donna know?' It's as if Ricky has forgotten Donna is dead.

Mike shakes his head and keeps his expression neutral. 'I wouldn't hurt Donna. She was my sister.'

Both men are panting, eyeing each other like stalking cats, deaf to the children's wails.

'So who the fuck is Oedipus, then?' Ricky asks, almost to himself.

Mike shrugs his shoulders.

'Because it's Oedipus who killed her.'

'Yeah,' Mike agrees. The fog has lifted from his brain and his mind is razor sharp and spinning rapidly. He stands up, rubbing his sore neck. Ricky is still on the floor, clutching his balls.

'Sorry I went for you,' Ricky says.

Mike stares at Ricky, an unnerving blankness to his gaze. Ricky gets up and edges around Mike, retreating to the bedroom. Realising the door is locked, he turns the key and goes inside. As if he's an automaton, he changes Skye's nappy, takes Benjie to the bathroom and cleans him up.

When Ricky leads Benjie into the living room to give him breakfast, Mike has gone.

Actions speak louder than words, Ricky thinks as he realises Mike has done a runner. It's like he has been speared in the stomach. How could Donna not have told him that Mike was her brother? And is he really her brother, or was that just a lie to conceal their affair? Mike was meant to be his friend. Some friend.

And Donna – his lovely, innocent little Donna. He knows she found motherhood tough, and Leanne's death devastated her. But why didn't she confide in him? That photograph speaks volumes. Whether Mike was her brother or her lover, she was seeking solace in another man's arms.

Having fed the children, Ricky sits on the sofa and buries his face in his hands. Even if she had cheated, she didn't deserve to die like that. And how is he going to cope as a single parent? The children need their mother.

Wiping his nose with the back of his hand, he takes Donna's phone out of his pocket and looks through the messages. There are no texts from Mike; he's not even listed in her contacts. He reads through the messages from Oedipus again and tries to think who the hell it could be.

That psychologist. Philippa Durrant. He didn't like her. Just because she is a professional doesn't mean she is above the likes of him and Donna. He still can't work out why her photo was on Leanne's and Donna's bodies. Perhaps she's Oedipus. Perhaps she's been playing games. What if she commissioned the killer? Because he can't imagine a cow like her getting her own fingers bloodied.

'Dada, can we go out? Go to the park?' Benjie is hyperactive, jumping up and down.

Doesn't he realise his mother is dead? Ricky sighs. If he can wear them out, perhaps he'll get a bit of peace and quiet later on.

'Come on then,' he says.

Benjie goes and finds his coat and, for the first time in his life, dresses himself. But Ricky doesn't even notice. He's too focused on putting Skye back into the car seat. When he's shoved a blanket around her, he grabs Benjie's hand. They leave the flat, Ricky slamming the door behind them.

40

Pippa

Despite my fury with him for questioning my report on Kevin, I can't stop the smile edging at my lips when my caller display lights up with Joe's name. I wonder if he's calling to apologise.

'We've found Kevin. He's in hospital under police guard,' Joe says. 'It'll be on the six-o'clock news.'

'You didn't tell me he was missing in the first place,' I snap.

'Yes, well…' Joe blusters. I suppose Joe is telling me this so I feel safe. But I don't. I still think they've made a mistake.

'I think Ricky is innocent.'

Joe explodes. 'I've been telling you that all along! Kevin is the killer. We've got his DNA and fingerprints at both scenes. He has opportunity and motive. I wish you'd leave the investigating to the police. I know you mean well, but…'

We are both silent for a moment.

'Do you know about Oedipus?' I ask.

'What?'

'Donna was being threatened by someone called Oedipus.'

'How do you know this?' Joe asks.

'Kerry, Donna's best friend, told me.'

'Why the hell didn't she tell us? Yet another person withholding information.'

'She's scared, Joe. And she didn't want to unduly upset Ricky. She told me this in confidence, so I'd be grateful if you didn't call her in and read her her rights.'

He sighs. 'Understood. But we will need to speak to her again. How was this Oedipus threatening Donna?'

'Via text message. Did you not find Donna's phone?'

'Nope. We searched the house for it, but it's missing.'

'Can you get information from the phone without physically having the phone?'

'Only if it's switched on and even then with great difficulty. We need to find the phone.'

'Are we still meeting tomorrow evening?' I ask hesitantly.

'Sorry. Too much going on at the moment. And under the circumstances—'

'Yes, of course,' I butt in, trying to keep the disappointment out of my voice.

'Pippa, keep your doors and windows locked. We'll have a car keep an eye on your street.'

'Why?'

'We found Kevin, but he was unconscious. Punched and kicked and barely recognisable.'

'Like Donna and Leanne?' I say, gasping.

'No. Different MO. Looks like someone beat him up.'

'Do you think it's because he was recognised and someone was trying to avenge Leanne's and Donna's murders because they think Kevin is guilty?'

'Possibly,' Joe says. 'We're hoping he'll regain consciousness so we can interview him.'

* * *

Sleep is fitful and difficult. My dreams are vivid and involve chasing, but the detailed memories disappear like wisps of smoke when I awake, leaving behind a sense of unease and a taste of fear. The slightest creak wakens me, and even having Mungo sleeping in the bedroom doesn't help. When dawn arrives, it is a relief.

I take a couple of paracetamol and make myself a strong coffee. After taking Mungo for a short walk around the block, I put him in the car, and we drive off to Redhill to see George. It's early. Probably too early for visiting hours, but I will bluff my way in. I assume it should be easier now he is in his own room.

'I won't be long.' Mungo groans grumpily when he realises I'll be leaving him in the car again.

As I pass by the nurses' station, the spiky-haired nurse who was so kind to me previously glances up, an expression of confusion on her face.

'Mrs Durrant?' she calls, hurrying out to meet me.

I stop. 'Yes?' My heart hammers. Has something happened to George? Wouldn't they have rung me if he had deteriorated? As she smiles, relief runs through my veins and I take a gulp of disinfectant-smelling air.

'I'm surprised to see you here!' she says.

'Why? Is everything alright with George?'

'He was discharged yesterday afternoon. Didn't you know?'

'What?' I try to gather my confused thoughts. 'No. He didn't tell me.'

'His friend came to collect him. They were joking away.'

'What friend? What did he look like?'

'A young man similar age to George. Afraid I don't really recall much about him other than your son seemed happy to see him.'

'Brent,' I mutter to myself. I pivot around before remembering my manners and hastily thank the nurse for looking after my son. And then I rush out of the hospital, ignoring the tuts from people I barge past and the occasional double take as people recognise me but can't place me.

I'm breathless by the time I pull open the car door.

'We need to go,' I say to Mungo, who opens one eye and sighs.

I try calling George, but his phone goes straight to voicemail. I then try Brent. His phone rings out. He doesn't even have a voicemail facility on his phone. I call Rob.

‘Did you collect George from hospital?’

‘No,’ Rob replies, his tone quizzical. I suppose I knew the answer, as, however good Rob looks for his age, there is no way he could pass for a twenty-something young man.

In desperation I call Marie in Switzerland.

‘*Oui?*’ she answers immediately.

‘Marie, it’s George’s mum. Have you heard from him?’

‘Yes. He left the hospital yesterday. He said he will try to fly to Genève on the first flight he can get, hopefully this morning. I haven’t spoken to him today.’

‘Did he sound…?’ I can’t find the word and I don’t want to worry Marie. ‘It doesn’t matter,’ I say hurriedly. ‘Please call me as soon as you hear from him or if he arrives in Geneva.’

‘Of course, Mrs Durrant,’ Marie promises.

There is no reason for me to feel uptight. In fact, I should be happy that George is deemed well enough to be released from hospital. But I sense something isn’t right. Am I jealous that George asked someone other than me to get him from hospital? Yes. And I’m annoyed that he didn’t tell me because I’ve just wasted over two hours driving to and from Redhill. Of course.

But it’s Brent who worries me.

I think back over the years to that young, confused, angry teenager who somehow I managed to tame. I think back on those weeks he spent with us as a family and how at the age of twenty-one it seemed like a switch had flicked on inside his head, turning him into a responsible, level-headed adult. But can someone really change when one is fundamentally damaged through lack of love and stability? I would like to say yes, but at this point I am very unsure.

Brent obsessed over his birth mother for years, wondering who she was, why she rejected him. I know he followed every avenue he could to track her down. This business with Oedipus unnerves me. I have no proof whatsoever that Brent is Oedipus, or that Brent has anything to do with Leanne's and Donna's murders. In fact, it seems impossible to reconcile the young man I care about with a potential murderer. But I think back to what he told me. That his mother rejected him and then she died. Everything begins to slot into place.

'We've got to find Brent,' I mutter to Mungo.

I believe in the power of synchronicity or intuition or greater consciousness, whatever you wish to call it. It's not something I speak about, because for now such concepts sit more closely within the sphere of New Ageism than science, and I like to call myself a scientist. But this belief in a greater consciousness helped me through those days of hell when my beautiful daughter went missing. I screamed at a God I didn't believe in, but eventually as time has passed, I have found some sort of peace. Not with religion but within myself. But this peace is fragile, and right now I fear that it could be shattered all over again.

I wonder. Or have I been too trusting? Has Brent spent years cultivating that trust, waiting for the opportunity to do…? I mentally kick myself. I don't know what he has done, if anything, other than be a good friend to George and collect him from the hospital. For all I know, George might be getting on a flight to Geneva right now.

I try calling Brent again, and to my surprise he answers.

'Hi, Pippa, I was just about to return your call. How are you?' He sounds all cheery. Is he acting? I need to see him to be sure.

'I'm fine. Thanks. Is George with you?'

There's a momentary pause and then an upturn in his inflexion, indicating surprise. 'George? No. Should he be?'

'He was discharged from the hospital yesterday afternoon, and someone of your description collected him. I thought it might be you.'

'It's great that he was released. How's he doing?'

I notice every word now. Brent said *released* rather than *discharged.* Is that relevant? Is he thinking about detention in prison rather than being well enough to be let out of hospital?

'Um, I'm not sure. That's why I wanted to find out if he was with you.'

'Sorry, can't help. See you soon.'

He hangs up on me.

* * *

'Right, Mungo. We're going to Brent's house.'

I have Brent's address in my phone, and I plug it into Google Maps. I've never been to his flat. Before starting up the car, I send Joe a text message.

An outside possibility that I've found Oedipus. Brent Fowler. Going there now.

And then I chastise myself. This is Brent. He is like a son to me. Sort of. It's crazy to suspect Brent.

I park up outside the block of flats and leave Mungo in the car. The communal door is propped open with a brick, so I walk inside, up the single flight of stairs, and ring Brent's doorbell.

'Hello. Wasn't expecting you,' Brent says. The smile is forced and there are no creases at his eyes. He has dark rings under them and his face seems strained. 'Good to see you nevertheless,' he says huskily, leaning forwards as if to kiss me. I step back. I may be fond of Brent, but we have never embraced before. His face darkens.

'Are you okay? It sounds like you're going down with something,' I ask.

His laugh is hollow. 'No. Just tired.'

'Can I come in?'

I think I detect a hint of fear but worry I am not being objective. He stands to one side, and I walk straight into a barely furnished living room.

‘Tea?’ he asks.

‘Yes, thank you.’

With my hands behind me, I grip on to the top of the battered green sofa, take a deep breath and face him.

‘Brent, do you know the story of Oedipus?’

I’m ready for him this time and I see the flash of fear. It happens in a millisecond, his eyebrows shifting upwards and to the centre, the top of his eyelids moving up and the bottom of his eyes flattening out. The corners of his lips stretch out to the side, flattening his lips, and his hands flutter across his stomach before he controls them and lets them drop down to his sides.

‘No. Should I? Something to do with some bloke from the olden days screwing his mother? Why do you ask?’

It only takes that sentence for me to know.

But fear is contagious, and I can tell from the fleeting smirk that he knows I know. And right now I have no backup plan.

41

Pippa

I decide my best course of action is to pretend everything is normal.

Brent hands me tea in a chipped brown mug. I hold it with both hands in an attempt to control my shaking and sit down on the sofa. But my hands are quivering too much, so I put the mug on the table.

'Silly me, I must have got you confused with another of George's friends. I just couldn't think who might have collected him, but what do I know? I'm only his mother!' I'm blabbering, and my laugh sounds hollow.

'George doesn't know how lucky he is,' Brent says coldly, taking a seat on one of the wooden chairs.

'What do you mean by that?' I put my therapist's hat on and try to concentrate.

'He's got a mother, but he takes her for granted, doesn't he, Pippa? He pisses off to another country and doesn't give a toss as to what happens to you. But I do. I care very much.' Brent is practically off his chair, leaning so far towards me. He reaches for my hands, and I have no choice but to allow him to take them.

'I love you, Pippa. You'll be my mum, won't you?' He lets my hands drop and stands up, towering over me. 'We're going to be rich! I've found us a house, you and me. You'll live in one wing and I'll be in the other. I'll take care of you. You'd like that, wouldn't you?' He bends into his knees. His stare is cold and unblinking.

'Brent, have you got something to tell me?'

He stands up again, his hands on his hips. 'No.'

'Sit down, please.'

To my relief he does as he's told.

‘What was your birth mother’s name?’

He laughs. It is more like a cackle, and it sends tremors through my bones.

‘Oh, Pippa. Oh, Mum. Let’s not play games, shall we?’

‘Games?’

‘Now, let’s talk about the future. Everything is working out perfectly.’

‘Who was your birth mother?’

‘That is irrelevant. All I care about is you! You’re my mum now.’

‘Was it Leanne Smith? Was Leanne your birth mother?’

His fists tighten and he bares his teeth. Terror clenches my stomach and I can feel adrenaline pumping up my spine, through my veins.

‘Fuck Leanne Smith!’ he yells. He takes a step towards me – I think he is going to pounce on me – but then he stops and his face creases into a snarl.

‘Do you really want to know? Really?’ He narrows his eyes.

No, I don’t want to know, or do I? I can barely breathe.

‘She was such a disappointment. Cheap-looking, ordinary. Didn’t want to know me.’

‘Did you kill her, Brent?’ I speak so quietly I wonder if he hears me. There is a long silence. I think of my life, my children, a future that will never be mine.

‘Oh, Pippa. Mum. I would never do anything to harm you. I’m not a bad person, and murder is the worst of the worst. But Leanne. She was filthy, stonking rich. Did you know that? When she told me she only had one child and that was Donna, that hurt me. I told her, fair enough, don’t recognise me as your son, but give me some of that money. Who the hell needs one hundred and twenty million euros? You could run a small country with that amount. I didn’t even expect it there and then. Leave half to your daughter and half to me, I suggested. And you know what she did? She told me to go to hell! Tell me, Mum, what would you do if your birth mother refused to recognise you and refused to give you a penny of her obscene wealth?'

'And Donna?' I mumble.

'Ah, little Donna. So naive, so sweet. But you know what? She wasn't! She was a whore. Tried to come on to me! Can you imagine that? Disgusting, trying it on with her own brother.' Brent's lip curls and he shakes his head at the memory.

The doorbell rings. I have never been so grateful for a doorbell ringing.

'You stay right here!' Brent towers over me, his hands on either side of my neck, his breath in my face. I try not to recoil, not to show my fear.

I pray it is Joe Swain.

'Do you know where George is?' I ask Brent as he walks towards the door.

'George. My brother in blood.'

The breath catches in my throat as I ask again, 'Do you know where he is?'

'Might. Might not!' Brent has his back to me. 'You'd better be a good mum to me, and then I'll tell you what I've done to George.'

He swivels around to look at me. 'You be a good mum and keep schtum.' He places his finger across his lips and winks.

He then looks through the peephole and opens the door.

I am bitterly disappointed. I thought Joe Swain had arrived to rescue me, but instead it's Ricky carrying a sleeping infant in a navy car seat in one hand and holding the arm of a toddler in the other. I stand up. He walks to the other end of the corridor and then returns without the children.

'I'm so sorry, Ricky,' I say awkwardly.

'You're Oedipus, aren't you?' Ricky strides towards me, and jabs a finger in my chest as he sneers. I stumble backwards. This can't be happening. I shake my head vigorously and put my finger across my lips.

'Spit it out!' Ricky yells. I want to put my hands over my ears. 'What thug did you hire to kill my wife and her mother?'

'I didn't!' I shake my head again and glance towards Brent, but Ricky doesn't understand. He is too enraged to consider anything other than my culpability.

'And it wasn't Kevin. My father-in-law is a bastard, a greedy, selfish sod, but he's not a murderer.'

'How do you know?'

'I beat the crap out of him. Been wanting to do that for years. Blubbering he was, but he didn't kill them.' Ricky turns to Brent, who is leaning against the kitchen cupboard with his arms crossed and a smirk on his face. 'What's this woman doing here?'

'Got some things to tell you,' Brent says, pulling the other chair out for Ricky. 'Have a seat, bro.' He glances up at me. 'Don't look so worried, Mum!'

Brent sits down opposite Ricky.

'I've got something to tell you. You didn't give me the chance to tell you the whole story earlier. And it's great news! You see, the thing is I discovered that we're related, you and me, Ricky. Leanne was a right little tart, like her daughter. She was dating Kevin when she was a kid. Gave birth to me at sixteen.' He shakes his head and mutters *whore* under his breath. 'Didn't tell Kevin that she'd had a baby, just gave the baby up for adoption. A few years later she and Kev got married, had Donna, and she forgot all about me.'

'You?' Ricky spits.

'I'm your brother-in-law, mate! Cool, isn't it?' Brent smirks. 'What I was thinking was me and you split the dosh in half. What do you reckon?'

'What?' Ricky shakes his head and starts to get up.

'Now don't get antsy,' Brent says, leaning towards Ricky. 'We don't want another fight, do we? All you need to do is tell the solicitor I'm Leanne's other child and we're good to go.'

'But the money is Kevin's!' Ricky shouts.

Brent shakes his head and smirks. 'No, bro, it's not. I did a bit of homework. Under the Estates of Deceased Persons Act, a murderer can't inherit from the estate of someone whom he murdered. Who knew what you can find out online if only you know where to look? Leanne left the dosh to her children – that's me and Donna. As poor Donna is dead, that's only me now. But I'm happy to share it with you so the little ones can benefit. Won't be easy bringing them up as a single dad, so you'll need to pay for a nanny and all that.'

'Mike! You're fucking delusional!' Ricky is up out of his chair.

'Mike?' I ask. 'He's Brent. Why did you call him Mike?'

'One and the same, Mum! Didn't fancy a poofter name like Brent, so I've been Mike to everyone else for years now. I didn't tell you because of our special bond. I like it that you call me by a different name.'

'Who is Oedipus? Who was threatening my Donna?' Ricky's face is puce, his hair is on end, and his eyes are swollen and cherry red. He grabs the collar of my blouse. His breath is fetid.

'Calm, calm, bro!' Brent says.

'Oedipus is Brent,' I say quietly. 'Or Mike as you know him.'

Ricky lets me go and races towards Brent.

'What the…?' Ricky screams, swinging his fist towards Brent, but he's too slow. Brent pulls a knife out of his pocket and brandishes it in Ricky's face.

'Ricky, don't, please!' I scream. 'He's got George. We've got to let him go!'

'Daddy!' The little boy comes running into the room. 'Dada!'

'Get out, Benjie!' Ricky shouts.

But the little boy doesn't. He grabs his father's leg just as Brent slams his fist into Ricky's face. As Ricky concertinas to the floor, Brent seizes the little boy's arm.

‘No!’ I shout. ‘He’s just a child! Let him go!’

‘You’re such a caring mum, aren’t you?’ Brent leers towards me, still grasping the boy, whose high-pitched yells pierce my head. ‘Why don’t you care for me, Mum?’

And then the glint of silver from the knife comes towards me, and an arm curls around my neck. Tighter and tighter. I am choking and my scream becomes a hoarse yelp. The blade is inches from my face. My legs feel as if they are giving way.

Darkness envelops me.

42

Pippa

And then suddenly I am released. I am coughing, collapsing on the ground, the little boy staring at me, saucer eyes, his face white, shock from the horror of what is unfolding silencing him. I make a grab for the boy, pulling him into my arms, clutching him tightly to my breast, rocking him backwards and forwards. I put my hands over his ears to block out the grunting of Ricky and Brent, the sound of fists shattering bone.

'Stop!' I yell in vain as they crash into the plastic table. The mugs of tea fall on to the floor, shattering. The chairs are broken. The men slip and slide on the spilled drinks. Blood drips on to the carpet, but I can't work out whose it is.

'Get out, Benjie! Get out!' Ricky screams.

My legs aren't strong enough to carry me, let alone a child, so I crawl on hands and knees along the edge of the room, dragging the boy with my right hand.

'Run, Benjie. Run out of the room!' I whisper urgently to him.

'Dada!' he says.

'Please, Benjie. Go! I'm right behind you.'

And then he runs, his little legs pumping up and down, out of the room, into the corridor.

Police sirens. Thank God. They get louder and louder, and relief courses through me. I wonder if Ricky and Brent can hear them; they are so intent on killing each other.

I follow Benjie into a bedroom, where he cowers under the window, behind the bed. Unbelievably, there is a baby fast asleep in a car seat.

'It's going to be alright.' I hug Benjie again. 'The police are nearly here. Your daddy will be okay.'

There's a loud knock on the door.

'Stay here,' I tell Benjie. I run to the front door and hurl it open.

'Police! Police! Put your hands in the air!'

Two uniformed officers storm into the living room and pull Ricky and Brent apart. Joe Swain steps in behind them.

'Ricky Wiśniewski, I am arresting you on suspicion of murdering Donna Wiśniewski and for grievous bodily harm in the assault of Kevin Smith. You do not have to say anything. But it may harm your defence if you do not mention when questioned something which you later rely on in court. Anything you do say may be given in evidence.'

'No!' I scream as the two police officers handcuff Ricky. 'No! You've got the wrong—'

Brent staggers to his feet and throws his arms around me in such a tight bear hug, I feel as if I'm going to suffocate. 'No!' I try to say, but my voice is muffled.

'Don't breathe a word,' he whispers into my ear. 'Don't say a word, and George will be fine and you will be fine.'

'Are you alright?' Joe asks. I'm not sure if he's directing the question at me or Brent.

Brent releases me and turns to Joe. 'Thank God you're here,' Brent says breathlessly, wiping his bloody nose. His left eye is swelling up, and bruising is already starting to show. 'I thought the bastard was going to kill me.'

I look around the room for the knife but can't see it. I wonder where Brent has squirrelled it.

'It's Mike, isn't it?' Joe says. 'Ricky has been staying with you. Twice you have given Ricky an alibi; why have you been protecting him?'

Brent shrugs. It astounds me that he can be so calm, that he can cast off the fury and venom to be this much in control in front of the police.

We watch Ricky being led outside. From the bedroom Benjie yells, 'Dada, Dada!' I wait for Brent to look away, for any opportunity to appeal silently to Joe, but Brent doesn't let his gaze wander from my face.

'We've called for an ambulance. It should be here any moment. Brent, you'll need to get checked over. When you're done, we will take a statement.'

'Pippa is my therapist.' Brent smiles and places his hand on my arm. 'She's been caring for me since I was a teenager. She's the best.'

Why can't Joe tell that Brent is a liar and a murderer? Why can't he see the terror in my eyes? How can he have got it so wrong?

'Just going to get myself cleaned up,' Brent says. He leans over as if to give me a kiss on the cheek. '*Not a word, okay? And then Georgie Porgie will be okay*,' he whispers.

Calmly, he walks into the hall, and we hear a door gently close.

'The children. They're in the bedroom,' I say. 'I need to go to them.'

'Just a moment. Are you alright?' Joe puts a hand on my shoulder and peers at me.

I shake my head.

'What's—?'

'Shush,' I murmur. He frowns. I pull him towards me and whisper as quietly as I can, 'Brent, otherwise known as Mike. He's the murderer! It's not Ricky! Why did you think it was Ricky?'

Joe pulls away from me, his face creased with confusion. 'The hammer, which is believed to be the weapon used to kill Donna, was covered with Ricky's prints.'

'Sarge?' One of the policemen has returned to the living room. He's holding a phone. 'We believe this is Donna's missing phone. The man we have just arrested is swearing blue murder. Admits he beat up Kevin but denies murder. Says that—'

'Shush!' I yell. My head feels light; the room begins to spin.

On the edge of my consciousness I hear a door slam, a car start up and skid as it speeds away. I hear shouting, and then my world turns black.

* * *

When I come to, a woman dressed in a green uniform is leaning over me.

'George!' I murmur.

'You fainted, love. What's your name?'

'Philippa Durrant. Has anyone rescued George?' I sit up too quickly and feel nauseous. I swallow the bile, steady myself by leaning back on my hands, and glance around the wreck of the room.

Joe picks his way amongst the trail of debris and bends down next to me with creaking knees. 'Are you alright, Pippa?'

I nod. 'George. Have you found George?'

'Is he missing?'

'No, you don't know! Brent? Have you arrested him?'

Joe stands up slowly. 'I'm afraid he got away.'

'No!' I wail. 'He's the killer and he's got George. You need to find him now!' I'm screaming, crying, out of control. This cannot happen again.

'Madam, you need to stay calm,' the ambulancewoman says, taking my hand.

'Brent is a psychopath,' I whisper. 'And I never even realised.'

'Pippa, you solved this case. Without you we were likely to have convicted the wrong man, not once but twice. Now all we need to do is find Brent or Mike, or whatever he calls himself. You know him better than anyone else.'

'The children, where are they?'

'They are fine. They're in an ambulance, and Janet Curran, our FLO, is on her way over to care for them. They know her. But right now we need you to think. Where might Brent have gone?'

How on earth does Joe think I can brainstorm at a time like this? My mind is a confused blur. All I can think about is George, my beloved son. I have been here before. A lost child. Lightning doesn't strike twice, does it?

'Why did Brent put your photos on the dead bodies?' Joe urges.

I tell Joe how we took Brent on family holidays, how I was one, if not the only, constant in his life. How he has transferred his maternal desires on to me. How when his real mother, Leanne, rejected him, he still had me, his 'adopted' mother.

'It's not possible to put yourself into the mindset of a psychopath,' I say.

'He is jealous of George, I assume?'

I nod.

'Is there anywhere you went when he was a child that he may choose to escape to?'

'We went fishing on the River Test, but that's miles away, in Hampshire. I can't see how he would have taken George there. It has to be somewhere local.' But where, I simply don't know.

43

Pippa

'Your daughter. She went missing, didn't she?'

I squeeze my eyes shut. I cannot think about Flo, not now when all my energies need to be focused on George.

'I'm sorry to bring this up.' Joe's voice is heavy with compassion. 'Do you think Brent could have anything to do with her disappearance?'

I open my eyes and shake my head vigorously. 'No. Flo was on her gap year doing voluntary work in a township in South Africa. I didn't take Brent into our family until after her disappearance. I suppose I was looking to fill a hole. His friendship was with George.'

We are sitting in my car, away from the team of police who are combing through the disaster zone of Brent's flat looking for evidence, taking fingerprints. Confident that my blood pressure is back to normal and that I simply fainted from shock, the ambulance crew has left.

Mungo has his paws on the central console and I am stroking his head. My dog brings me a sense of calm.

'I can't believe I got it so wrong,' I keep on saying. I thought I knew Brent. I thought I had made a difference in his life. I thought I could read people.

'Stop feeling responsible for Brent and responsible for the fate of Leanne and Donna,' Joe says, removing my hand from Mungo's head and rubbing it gently between his smooth, warm palms. I wonder how he knows what I am thinking.

'You are as much a victim in this as the Smith family,' Joe says.

'I hate the word *victim*. It implies helplessness and apathy,' I mumble.

'There's my girl.' Joe grins.

Gently, I pull my hand away. Joe is right. I am not responsible for anyone's actions except my own. I must focus.

A phone rings. It takes a while for me to realise it's mine. Joe lifts up my handbag from the passenger footwell and hands it to me. By the time I fumble inside for the phone, it has stopped ringing. I have a missed call from Marie.

I call her back. 'Any news?' I ask breathlessly.

'Yes, Madame Durrant. George is in a taxi.'

'What? A taxi? Where?'

She sounds querulous. 'His plane landed, and now he is in a taxi from Cointrin to home.'

'Cointrin?'

'Geneva airport.'

'Are you sure he is in Switzerland, that he wasn't pretending?'

Marie laughs. '*Oui*, of course. I heard the flight announcements in the background, spoken in French. Why would George pretend? He will be here in ten minutes. We don't live so far from the airport.'

'Oh,' I say, biting my bottom lip.

'Is everything okay?' Marie asks.

'Yes. Fine. Could you ask George to call me when he arrives?'

'Of course. *À bientôt*, Madame Durrant.'

Joe is staring at me. I open and close my mouth, unable to form words.

'What is it?'

Mungo pushes his nose into my arm and it breaks my reverie.

'That was Marie. George's girlfriend. She says he's in Switzerland.'

'That's wonderful!' Joe smiles.

'I don't understand. Brent said he had George, that George was going to die.'

‘Perhaps he just said that to scare you.’

I shake my head in the hope it will dislodge the confusion. I speak my thoughts aloud.

‘So Brent collected George from the hospital and drove him to the airport, just like old times.’ It is hard to comprehend. ‘And then he went home. But I turned up and confronted him, and when he realised I knew he was Oedipus, and when it became clear I wasn’t going to fulfil his fantasy of becoming his mother, and when I exposed him as Leanne’s and Donna’s killer, his whole constructed reality crumbled and he became violent.’

‘Sounds about right. You are a very good detective, Pippa Durrant,’ Joe says, grinning.

‘It’s all my fault.’

‘No, Pippa. It is not. As I said before, you have solved this case. All we need to do is find Brent and lock him away for life.’

A wave of sadness washes through me.

‘I want to go home,’ I say. I need to go home so I can have a good cry and process my thoughts.

‘Brent is still on the run,’ Joe says, frowning.

‘It’s your job to find him. I’m going home.’

‘He could still come after you. He’s a murderer.’

‘Brent won’t hurt me,’ I say, fervently hoping I am correct.

‘I’m not happy about you going home alone.’

‘I’ll go to Rob’s, my brother’s, house.’

There’s a rap on the passenger-door window of my car. I jump. It’s a fresh-faced uniformed policeman with cheeks as rosy as apples.

‘Boss, can I have a word?’

Joe opens the door and hops out.

‘There’s been a sighting of the suspect’s van,’ I hear the young policeman say. Joe’s back is turned to the car. I reach over and pull the passenger door shut.

‘Sit down,’ I say urgently to Mungo as I start the car. Driving away as quickly as I can, I see Joe out of the corner of my eye gesticulating at me. With my left hand on the steering wheel, I use my right hand to tug the seat belt across me.

‘Lie down,’ I instruct Mungo. And then we’re off.

I need to go home. I need to think. Maybe I will go to Rob’s, but later.

* * *

I ignore my phone when it rings. Twice. It’s probably Joe chastising me for driving away. But he doesn’t understand. I crave solitude. As much as I like him, he has a job to do and so do I. I need to process what’s happened. I want to read through my file on Brent. I don’t know why I kept it, as I am rigorous about destroying records after seven years, burning the shredded paper at the bottom of the garden. I haven’t written up any notes on him since he was a teenager because I’ve been seeing him as a friend, not in a professional capacity. But I want to see if I missed something.

Emotionally and physically exhausted, I concentrate hard on driving carefully, slowly.

When I pull up outside home, I am surprised that it is still daylight. It feels like midnight.

Mungo hops out of the car and trots up the path behind me.

I turn the security key in the lock, but it isn’t locked. I always double-lock it. Did I forget in my hurry this morning? I pause, waiting for a reaction from Mungo. He will know if something is wrong, if someone is in the house who shouldn’t be. But Mungo stands next to me patiently, his tail swinging from side to side in his normal anticipation of going home and being fed tea.

I take a deep breath and walk into the hall, shutting the front door and attaching the security chain behind me. I follow Mungo into the kitchen. His tail starts wagging even faster, moving the air like a fan.

'Hello, Mungo!' He uses one hand to stroke Mungo's head and places the other in front of Mungo's nose, allowing him to lick his hand.

I stand stock-still, holding my breath. My photo albums are strewn across the kitchen table.

'Look! These are the sales particulars I wanted to show you.' He holds up a glossy brochure. The picture on the front is of a large, typical Sussex-period house – terracotta hung roof tiles, more hung tiles on the upper facade of the house, and red bricks on the lower facade. The windows have white-painted frames, a conservatory is attached to one side, and there are extensive lawns freshly mowed in straight lines. The logo of one of the South East's leading estate agents is printed on the top right-hand corner. The house must be worth a couple of million. He puts the brochure back on the table and beckons me over.

'I was looking through some of the photos of our holidays. I still think that first year, when George and me were fifteen, was the best. Do you remember when I caught that massive trout? I wanted us to take it home and eat it for supper, but the teacher made me put it back. George was telling me about the fish in Lake Geneva, where he lives. He says it's mainly perch. He caught a salmon once. You're allowed to catch up to one hundred perch a day. Can you imagine that? He said me and him can go fishing sometime, but not from October to January, when it's prohibited, or in May, when they're spawning. I think I'll go in July. I should have the money by then, so I'll be able to afford the flight. We might have moved into the new house too.'

'Brent,' I say softly as I pull out a chair from the table and sit down. 'Brent, how did you get in?'

'You left me the key, Mum. Under the blue flowerpot. I got it copied.'

I try to repress a shiver, furious with myself that I didn't get around to chasing up that locksmith.

'That was okay, wasn't it?' Brent leans towards me, an earnest look on his face. His left eye is so swollen it is almost shut. His cheeks are blossoming with brightly coloured bruises, and his lower lip is twice its normal size, crusted with congealed blood.

'Yes. It was okay,' I say softly. I pull some of the photo albums towards me and slowly turn the pages over, the memories flooding back of a time when we were a family of four – me, Trevor, George and Flo – and then even after Flo had gone, the one week in the year when Brent became our substitute child and we remained a family of four.

'That photo is my favourite,' Brent says, pointing to a picture of him and George, both lanky teenagers, grinning, standing on the edge of a river, rods in their hands, a bucket at their feet. I am standing to one side, my head thrown back, laughing. I have no recollection as to what was so funny.

'Yes, that's a great photo.'

'Can I have it, Mum?'

I slip the photo out from the plastic sleeve. With tears in my eyes, I hand it to Brent.

'Why did you leave my photo on Leanne and Donna's bodies?'

Brent is completely still, unblinking. I hold my breath.

And then he erupts.

'Because you rejected me! You…You've got this wonderful life, a son, a family and what have I got? Nothing!' He waves his arms around and then stands up and starts pacing around the kitchen. I grip the sides of my chair, wondering if this is the end of my life.

'All I wanted was a mother. You! My real mother! Not that bitch Leanne!' He jabs his index finger at me. 'That's not too much to ask, is it? I wanted you to feel some fear. To remember me! I want the world to know that I've got a mum too.'

I know I must stay calm. That I mustn't allow Brent to morph into Mike. That I mustn't let him know that I am terrified. This is not the time for therapy talk. If I am going to save my life, what I say now must come from my heart.

'I am so sorry that you felt I rejected you, Brent. I never meant for that to happen. You know, my life isn't as perfect as it might look from the outside. I've been sad too. But, Brent, I have always been there for you. I always will be, Brent.'

And just those short sentences and the repeated use of his name is enough for that glimpse of Mike to disappear and for gentle Brent to sit back down next to me.

'Thanks, Mum.'

We sit in silence for a few long moments.

'You know that Mike has done some very bad things and that the police are looking for him?'

He nods.

'You know that I'm going to have to call DS Joe Swain and tell him where Mike is?'

Brent's brow lowers, his nose wrinkles, and he shuts his eyes. I want to pull him to me, extract the pain from his soul and throw it away. But instead I reach for my phone and quickly type a text to Joe.

Mike is at my house. I'm fine. X

44

Pippa

This time there are no sirens, no flashing lights, no hollering. When I hear the car pull up outside, I leave Brent sitting at the kitchen table, fully immersed in happy memories. I open the front door and let in Joe and a uniformed officer. I speak quietly to Joe.

'Can your colleague stay in the hall? I think it's best if you're the only person Brent sees.'

'He's a violent man, Pippa!' Joe exclaims.

'Mike is, but Brent isn't. And right now Brent is here.'

Joe frowns, but I don't wait to give any further explanation. I turn around and he follows me.

Brent leans back in his chair and smiles as we approach the table. 'You want to see some photos of our holidays, Sergeant?'

Joe looks from me to Brent and back again, his face crinkled with puzzlement.

'Brent Fowler, I am arresting you on the suspicion of murdering Leanne Smith and Donna Wiśniewski, for grievous bodily harm in the assault of Ricky Wiśniewski, for causing serious injury to George Durrant by dangerous driving, and for breaking and entering the property of Philippa Durrant. You do not have to say anything. But it may harm your defence if you do not mention when questioned something which you later rely on in court. Anything you do say may be given in evidence.'

I hold my breath.

Brent sighs. 'It's *Mike* Fowler you're after.'

'Alright.' Joe speaks very slowly, as if he is talking to someone with learning difficulties. I dig my fingers into my thigh, praying that this won't trigger Brent switching to violent Mike, his alter ego.

'Mike Fowler, I am arresting you on suspicion—'

Brent stands up suddenly and interrupts Joe. My heart misses a beat. 'I got it. You don't need to repeat all that. Can I hug my mum first?'

I swallow a sob and swivel to face Brent, my arms outstretched.

'No!' Joe shouts. But Brent and I ignore him. He hugs me and I hug him back. He is shaking, and my neck is wet with his tears.

'I'm going now,' Brent whispers as he releases me. He turns around to face Joe, holding out his hands in front of him.

The policeman who has been standing in my kitchen doorway blinks rapidly whilst stepping forwards and clipping handcuffs around Brent's wrists.

'Bye, Mum.' He blows me a kiss and then meekly walks out in front of the police officer.

I stand stock-still, tears pouring down my face.

'Pippa, what is it?'

'Joe, I'd like you to go.'

'I thought we could have a drink, a meal perhaps, to celebrate.'

'No, Joe. I'm sorry. Please, can you leave me alone.'

I don't wait for an answer. I blow my nose, wipe my eyes, shut the photo albums and sweep them all into my arms. After putting the albums back in the bottom drawer of the wooden cabinet in the living room, I stride to the study, unlock my filing cabinet and extract Brent's file. I then walk upstairs, pull down the loft ladder and climb up to the loft. The light is dim and the attic space is small, filled with a couple of suitcases and my silver filing cabinet, full of my old client files waiting to be destroyed. The loft smells musty and is degrees warmer than downstairs. I hold the key in the palm of my hand, ready to open the filing cabinet. But I can't do it.

I place Brent's file on top of the silver cabinet, crouch down and carefully ease myself back on to the ladder. Slowly, I walk downstairs. I am going to have to report myself to the Health & Care Professions Council. I have made so many mistakes. I am going to need to examine myself again, work out why I got Brent's psychopathology so wrong, why I broke the boundaries I am normally so good at maintaining. I think of the promise I made eight years ago, that I would never work for the police again and wonder whether the time has come to permanently break that promise.

It doesn't surprise me that Joe has gone.

It does surprise me that there is a note on the kitchen table.

Please call me. I need a statement, and I've also got something I'd like to discuss with you. It's important. Jx

I wonder. Is this the start of something new? Is Joe interested in me or my work? I'm not sure. Either way, I will wait a day or two before calling him. A smile flickers on my lips in anticipation.

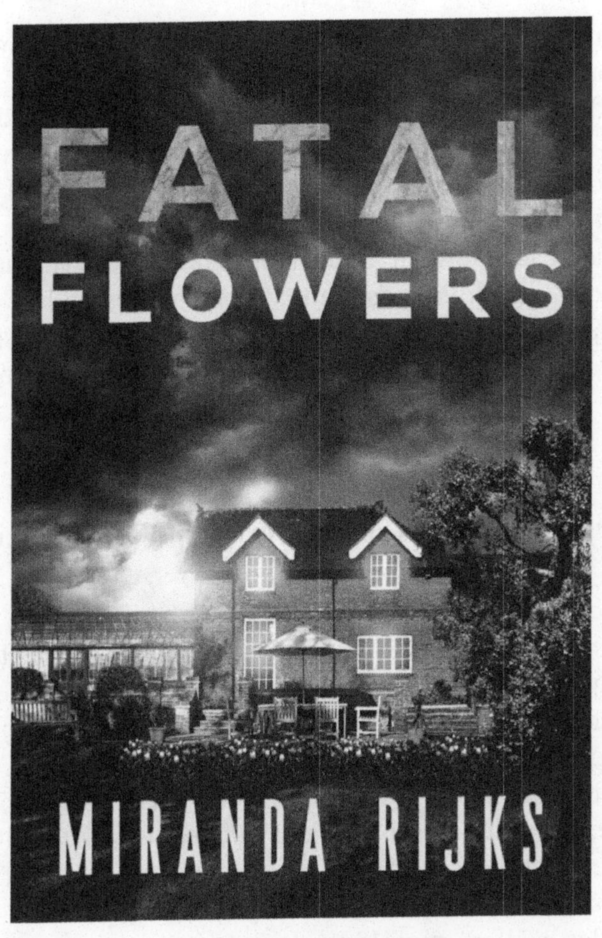

FATAL FLOWERS

BOOK 2 IN THE DR PIPPA DURRANT MYSTERY SERIES

Can Pippa unmask a killer before she becomes the next victim?

After a seemingly senseless murder at a garden center, the police turn to human lie detector, Pippa Durrant for help. Working alongside handsome detective Joe Swain, Pippa starts digging for the truth. But the Gower family, owners of the garden center, have deadly secrets -- secrets they want to keep buried.

After a second body is found, it's clear that the murderer is using flowers as a sinister calling card. And when Pippa receives a black rose, there's no mistaking who will be the next victim…

In a fast-paced investigation that takes her to Holland and back to England, Pippa soon realises that the gentle world of flowers is anything but. Using her unique skills in spotting lies and deceit, can she weed out the truth before it's too late?

GET IT NOW

Please enjoy this sneak preview of Fatal Flowers

PROLOGUE

I listen. There's the irregular thrumming of traffic from the adjacent road and my heavy breathing. Otherwise, there is silence. I kick the body. There's no resistance, just his stomach wobbling like a heap of revolting slime. For a moment, I consider moving him. But no. That would be more trouble than it's worth. I've switched off the lights and checked that there is no CCTV.

I'm alone and I'm safe.

I don't allow myself to think about tomorrow and the what-ifs. The man is dead, and he deserved to die. His eyes are open, staring up at the night sky like milky black beads wedged in his narrow face. Unseeing now.

I've done the world a favour.

The anger is still coursing through my veins. I pick up a terracotta pot and am about to hurl it to the ground, but no. If someone is walking along the road, they might hear the smashing of brittle clay on concrete. Instead, I give the body one last kick and stride back into the building. I take my anger out on the plants instead, swiping them off the benches, grinding my heels into their heads, spraying soil all over the floor. But I'm careful. Don't want any footprints left behind. I'm not stupid. Far from it. When I'm at the door, I remove the extra-large slip-on boots that cover my trainers. Two sizes larger than my normal shoes, they are. I place them in a plastic bag and peel off my gloves. My breathing is quieter now and my heart rate back to normal.

I let the light of my torch bounce around the building. Not too much, in case anyone sees it through the glass in the ceiling.

A garden centre is a veritable arsenal of instruments of death and torture. Spades, forks and knives, chemicals, wire. Even those deep fish tanks could work a treat if you're strong and agile enough. But in the end, I chose a simple piece of garden twine. Not the jute string that frays and snaps, but the extra-strong, green and shiny polypropylene twine. It's still in my hand. I wind it up and place it in the bag with the boots and gloves. Later, I'll burn the lot. But for now, I need to go home.

CHAPTER 1 - Sussex, England

'Where's Lily?'

Bella paces up and down the kitchen. It has all the mod cons, with a steamer oven and a Thermomix, those magical machines seen in the *Master Chef* kitchens, and a hot stone inbuilt into the black granite island. Everything sparkles, predominantly because Bella doesn't cook, but also because she has two cleaners, employed on alternate days. Bella wanted the best, and Gerry obliged. And, in return, Gerry travels the world, raking in the dosh importing plants and garden sundries, and bedding any girl who will have him.

Except not today. Gerry is at home, upstairs in his office.

'Sit down,' Annette says. 'You're making me nervous.'

'What am I going to tell the girls?' Bella ignores her mother and runs her manicured fingers through her newly dyed ash-blonde hair.

'Since when do teenage girls watch or listen to the news?' Ollie is seated next to Annette at the kitchen table. He picks at the side of his thumbnail. 'It's much more important that we keep our name out of the press.'

'Your name,' Bella says, her heels clip-clopping on the shiny marble floor. 'Thank God I married Gerry and took his name.'

Ollie thumps his forearms on the table. 'Right. This is what we're going to do. Mum, do a fire sale of the business—'

'What's a fire sale?' Bella says.

Ollie rolls his eyes. 'Sell the business at a low price just to get rid of it.' He turns his head towards Annette. 'As I was saying, sell the business pronto, or just shut the bloody place down. No one is going to want to shop there when they know a murder has taken place.'

'The voyeurs might,' Bella says.

Ollie ignores her. 'The real money, as I've been telling you for years, is in the site. I know at least two developers who would snap it up, apply for planning permission and build a load of nice executive homes. You'll make a few mil. Then you can jet off around the world or do whatever you want to do in your dotage. No hassle. Lots of fun.'

'There's a cruise I fancy. Gerry doesn't want to go, but I could take you, Mum—'

'Belt up, both of you!' Annette screams.

Bella and Ollie look up in alarm. Annette never loses her temper. The tic under her left eye that normally flickers like a gentle butterfly is violently hammering up and down.

'I have no intention of selling the garden centre, now or ever. It's your father's legacy, and it's thanks to him that you're both spoilt, rolling in money. Materialistic.'

Bella and Ollie start talking at the same time.

'That's not fair, Mum,' Ollie spits. 'I've earned a bloody fortune in the City.'

'And I married a wealthy man. The money in trust is used for the girls' schooling and the occasional holiday.'

Ollie and Bella scowl at each other. It's very rare for them to be in agreement, and they seem uncertain how to act in unity.

'The point is, I'm not going to sell, and you can't make me.' Annette enunciates each syllable slowly.

'If you refuse to sell, how are you going to manage this disaster? I've got a mate who runs a PR firm, and they do crisis management.'

Annette places her palms on the table and swivels her legs to the side. With some difficulty she heaves herself up. Bella hates it when her mum puts her large arthritic knuckles and soil-encrusted fingernails anywhere near the table, but she's learned not to say anything.

'I'm going home to take a tincture and spend some time in the potting shed. I don't want to be disturbed. If you get hold of Lily, tell her there's some cold chicken in the fridge.'

'I thought Lily was vegan,' Bella says.

'Last month,' Annette says. She looks every one of her seventy-three years.

Bella and Ollie watch their mother hobble out of the kitchen, both wondering whether the arthritis has stretched its tentacles over the whole of her body.

'Why the hell can't Lily and Stijn look after themselves? They should be making Mum supper, not the other way around. Poor Mum,' Ollie says when they hear her old Volvo spluttering to life. 'Can't be much fun finding a murdered man.' Ollie is good at empathising with his mother when she's not there.

'I've never seen a dead body. Have you?' Bella asks.

'Yes,' Ollie says without elaborating.

They both think of David, their father. He had a massive heart attack five years ago on a business trip to Holland. He returned home in a box, and the coffin was never opened. Annette's tinctures didn't do him any good.

Lily is a quivering wreck by the time she gets back to Annette's tumbledown farmhouse. The baby of the family, Lily has just turned thirty and still lives at home, even though she married Stijn eleven months ago. Bella used to call her 'the mistake'. Ollie called her 'the afterthought'. Annette had called her Dumpling until, at twenty-one, Lily screamed that she forbade her mother from calling her that ever again. David had called her 'my darling'. When David died, Lily wanted to die too.

She pours herself a brandy from David's stash, kept in a mahogany cupboard in the corner of the living room. After tipping the liquid down her throat in one go, she is still spluttering when she knocks on the door of Annette's potting shed.

'Potting shed' is a bit of a misnomer. It is an extravagant glasshouse built on bricks, held up with wrought-iron struts and electric louvred blinds that automatically open or close depending upon the heat and light, with a door painted oh-so-very-tastefully in Farrow & Ball's Cooking Apple Green. Annette calls it the 'potting shed' in memory of the semi-derelict construction that was its forefather. Everyone knew Bella and Gerry meant well when they packed her off to a spa for a long weekend. They wanted to emulate those television house and garden makeover programmes and give her the ultimate surprise. On Annette's return, she found this magnificent structure had sprouted out of the ground, replacing her very favourite place on earth. Lily had noticed her mother's expression of dismay, which she quickly replaced with a smile, and reached out to hold her hand. Lily knows her mother still misses the original version. It was all too much, happening just eight months after David died. Out with the old, in with the new.

The louvres of the shutters are closed, but Lily can see light escaping around the edges of the pale-green wood.

'Mum, can I come in?'

‘Just a moment, Lily,’ Annette says. Her voice sounds strangled. ‘I’m coming out.’

A few seconds later the lights go off and the door opens. Annette is wearing the same black tent-like dress with its enormous pocket at the waist that she’s been wearing all day. Her legs are encased in green tights, and her feet look large and ungainly in khaki rubber clogs. All three children agree that Annette has no dress sense. It wouldn’t matter if she had a model figure or was grossly obese; the garments she favours are so shapeless it’s irrelevant what is underneath. In fact, Annette is slender. The only parts of her that are oversized are those knuckles and the cascade of fly-away, silver-grey hair she piles on top of her head.

‘It’s awful, isn’t it?’

‘I can’t believe the bastard cut off all the heads of the houseplants. Those beautiful crimsons and pinks just scattered across the floor. The *Phragmipedium Schroderae*. It makes my heart bleed.’

Lily stares at her mother. Of course it was distressing that the plants were all beheaded, but a murder is far worse than the slashing of an orchid. In fact, to make a comparison is quite ridiculous.

‘Come on, love, let’s go and eat something.’ Annette puts her hand on the small of Lily’s slender back. Lily likes to think her mother has magical energy coursing through her, because otherwise how could she get all the plants to grow to be so strong and healthy?

Annette’s kitchen is nothing like Bella’s. The wooden cupboard doors are stained with ancient sticky finger marks, and the surfaces are ringed with water marks from cups of tea. The oven is from the 1950s, and Annette describes her fridge as modern because she’s only had it fifteen years or so. She doesn’t have a dishwasher, so every evening it’s Lily and Stijn who have to do the washing-up.

Annette takes some chicken leftovers out of the fridge, whilst Lily puts two baked potatoes in the microwave, an addition that Lily provided when she moved back home.

'I don't want one,' Annette says, pointing at the microwave.

'You need to eat,' Lily says.

'Not hungry, love.'

They both watch the turntable in the microwave go around and around.

'It was awful, wasn't it, Mum?' Lily says, wiping strands of auburn hair off her forehead.

Annette nods.

'The thing is, I'm sure I recognised him from somewhere. He had a narrow face, almost as if someone's put it between two books and squeezed together. I've definitely seen him before, just can't place where.'

Annette shivers. 'I'd rather not talk about it.'

'Other than the fact he was motionless and his skin was grey, you'd never have known he had been strangled. His shirt had a high collar. I didn't even notice the ligature marks. Did you?'

'Lily, change the subject.'

'Oh, Mum, I can't. We need to talk about it. Do you think we'll have any customers?'

Annette sits at the kitchen table and buries her face in her hands. 'People love scandal. I don't suppose it'll make much difference.'

'What are you proposing? Spot the ghost in amongst the terracotta pots?'

'Don't be facile, Lily.' Annette picks up her glass of green-brown mush. She takes a small sip. 'When can we reopen?'

'The day after tomorrow, assuming they finish their forensic examinations as expected.'

Annette pales.

'What is it, Mum? You're normally so brave and practical. Has this got to you?'

'Something like that,' she mutters as she stands up. 'I'm going to bed.'

'But it's only six-thirty!'

'And I'm not as young as I used to be.'

Lily frowns at her mother's retreating back. She can't recall the last time Annette went to bed before midnight. She took to her bed for fifteen long days after David died, but then she snapped right out of it and was back to their normal mum.

Lily sends Ollie a text message.

Mum's acting weird. Lx

What do you expect? Someone was murdered at her beloved business.

It's more than that. Lx

Ollie doesn't reply.

FREE SHORT STORY OFFER

Sign up to the Inkubator newsletter (Miranda's publisher) to receive an exclusive FREE short story, *Fatal Fury*, featuring Pippa's last case as a forensic psychologist — a murder so harrowing she decided to give up police work and go into private practice. You'll also get news of our other great mystery and suspense books and hear about special offers.

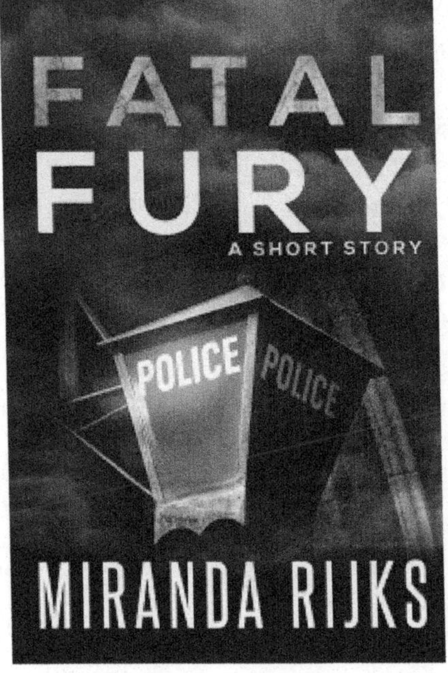

Sign up here

From Miranda

Dear Reader,
Thank you very much for reading *Fatal Fortune*. My thriller books are set in sunny Sussex, England, where I live with my husband, our daughter and our black Labrador.
I am so lucky to have phenomenal support from my family. My husband is the first reader of my books – and he does the cooking! Huge thanks to Becca McCauley and Adriana Galimberti-Rennie for answering my questions. All mistakes are mine alone. And thank you to Emily Tamayo Maher for her support during the last couple of years, and to Brian Lynch and Garret Ryan of Inkubator Books who continue to work their magic on my novels.
If you could spend a moment writing an honest review, no matter how short, I would be extremely grateful. They really do help other people discover my books.

Leave a Review

With warmest wishes,
Miranda

www.mirandarijks.com

Also By Miranda Rijks

FATAL FORTUNE

(Book 1 in the Dr Pippa Durrant Mystery Series)

FATAL FLOWERS

(Book 2 in the Dr Pippa Durrant Mystery Series)

FATAL FINALE

(Book 3 in the Dr Pippa Durrant Mystery Series)

Published by Inkubator Books
www.inkubatorbooks.com

FATAL FORTUNE is a work of fiction. People, places, events, and situations are the product of the author's imagination. Any resemblance to actual persons, living or dead is entirely coincidental.

Made in the USA
Coppell, TX
08 December 2022